The Witnessing of Matlyn Wren

JENNIFER LYNN JANUARY

The Witnessing of Matlyn Wren
Copyright © 2015 by Jennifer Lynn January

Dedication

When I was a kid, like every kid, I changed my mind every other week about what I wanted to be. An astronaut, a marine biologist, swimming with the sharks in the deep blue sea, a firefighter just like the great guys my mom hung out with. I wanted to be a lawyer (that one hung on the longest). Be it a circus clown or a brain surgeon, my mother's answer remained the same: "If that's what you want."

I never doubted I could do anything I wanted, even when the people around me did.

Well, I'm all grown up now, Mom, and I know what I want to be ...

Prologue

This Story began the day Fern Morales-Serrano, a horrid woman with a dark, twisted soul, passed away. Her Story was done. History. And only hours after her passing, a new one would begin some two thousand miles from Lima, Montana.

The mark on his arm, the tattoo that branded him for what he was, pulsed in a steady rhythm—a pulse he'd followed for weeks. Like a beacon, the beat pulled and tugged him forward until he stood where he was. New Orleans, Louisiana. His head snapped up, and his eyes scanned the early-morning crowd. Across the street a slender woman walked quickly down the damp sidewalk. Her hair was burnt apricot, cut in a long, choppy bob. She weaved between business suits and dodged tourists with a tray of coffee in one hand and a brown bag clutched in the other. The glasses perched on her head bounced with each step of her cherry red Docs.

His deep gray eyes zeroed in on the girl, and a painful throb bloomed beneath his skin, running bone deep. She hooked a sharp right and took off down an alley, her boots kicking up spray as she marched through the puddles littering the alleyway. As she disappeared behind a building, the tattoo's trembling rhythm receded.

He'd found his Story, and as he stood staring down the alleyway, he felt the first words incise into his right shoulder. He was there to Witness her story from wax to wane. And that story was to start here, on the corner of Toulouse and Royal.

He pushed up his sleeve and watched as darker than black print appeared. Two words started off this Story. Much like '*the end*' brings a story to a close, these two words would open it:

Matlyn Wren

One

❧

Humid. The rain broke the heat bubble that had surrounded the city and left everything damp and sultry. Moisture clung to her body and weighed down her hair, but she smiled and breathed in the smell of rain and wet asphalt. She looked at the heavy door before her and then down to her full hands. Her booted foot shot out, and she kicked at the gray, steel door.

"Open up, whore, or I'll dump the coffee!" Matlyn hollered her watery threat with a bright smile.

The door slowly swung open, revealing a busty, curvaceous platinum blonde with bright red lips that quirked in a smug grin. She held the door open with her foot, standing off to the side, and made a grand gesture with her hand.

"We both know you're full of steaming shit, Little Bird," the curvy blonde said, snagging a cup from the tray as Matlyn waltzed past her. "You need this juice just as much as I do."

Matlyn just chuckled, walked to the front of the shop, and tossed the brown bag full of doughnuts from Blue Dot Donuts on the reception desk. She pulled a coin from her pocket and held it up. "Ready, Miss Adeline?"

Adeline nodded and eyed the coin pinched between Matlyn's fingers. She hated that coin, or rather the task associated with it: the fucking supply run.

Every Friday they flipped a coin. Loser had the misfortune of dealing with the local supplier—and pervert—Alan Wingerbe. Alan thought he was the bee's knees. Sadly, he was alone in that belief. He was ruthless in his pursuit of *tail* (his word, not theirs). Spending even the briefest amount of time with him left the girls feeling dirty and *skeezed over* (Adeline's words).

Matlyn flipped the coin and it toppled head over tail before landing in her palm. She opened her fist and together they peered at the dull silver coin.

"Heads. You're it, Little Bird," Adeline said, patting her friend on the shoulder, looking far more pleased than she should. "For the best really. I swear if that skeevie bastard smacks his lips at me one more time, we're gonna need a new supplier, and I'mma need an alibi." The lazy, whiskey soaked drawl of Adeline's voice gave her away as a southern Louisiana belle. Her e's and r's often dropped away or rolled into an ah sound. Matlyn's accent, by comparison, was soft with just the tiniest hint of smoke and wine to it, barely noticeable.

Matlyn and Adeline went about the opening routine: cleaning work stations, topping up the artist supplies, and going over the appointments scheduled for the day.

Parabola Tattoos and Body Modification was all Matlyn had ever wanted. She'd gone to community college for business during the day, apprenticed with a local tattoo parlor in the afternoons, and busted her ass at a hole-in-the-wall pub every night and weekend for years. She tucked away every spare dollar and saved every tip until the day came that she could afford a shop of her own.

Parabola had been open and thriving in New Orleans for four years, and Adeline—Addy—had been a part of it from the get-go.

"How'd the date with Dr. Smiley go?" Addy asked, dropping the tubes and needles into the bleach solution.

"Greg?" Matlyn spun in her chair to face her friend. "Meh." She shrugged and twirled a pen between her fingers. "He talked about teeth a lot. Molars, crowns, and the highlight of the dinner … abscesses."

Addy snorted, dropping the last of the tubes in the container and pulling the gloves from her hands.

"Pasta and abscesses. Charmin'. So I take it the dry spell continues?"

Matlyn rolled her eyes. "Longest streak ever!" Tossing the pen down on the desk, she spun again, wheeling around in circles, and said in a sing song voice, "Oh, but the beautiful boy that waited on our taa-ble." She sighed dramatically and fanned herself. "Hotter than two goats in a pepper patch."

"Oo?" That piqued Addy's interest.

"Hmm." Matlyn hummed. "Poor Greg. Caught me in

a hot little daydream. Mouth full of Cajun shrimp and my head a million miles away."

Addy rolled her chair closer, her brows raised in a curious look. "Hot?"

"Pinned against a wall, lip-biting kinda hot. Then Greg went and popped my steamy little bubble by opening his pretty mouth again. Did you know that dentists have one of the highest suicide rates in the US?"

"Everyone knows that, Mat."

"Well I didn't. An' who in the happy fuck says shit like that on a *date*?"

Addy's upper lip curled, and she shook her head.

"Yea, that's where the date ended."

"On such a sweet note," the platinum-blond said in a flat voice, her eyes crossing and her mouth gaping. "Next one's my pick, Matty girl." She grabbed a doughnut and bit into it, giving Matlyn a sharp look.

"Right, so long as you let me introduce you to Pacey."

Mouthful of doughy goodness, she mumbled, "No point." The busty blond dusted the sugar off her chest and stood, taking a bottle of Windex and a cloth with her, determined to avoid the topic, even if it meant doing the fucking windows.

"Come on—"

"Men want skinny bitches like you. They can't handle the curve, darlin'." Her hand grazed her side, skipped over her rounded hip, and then smacked her ass, looking over her shoulder at the redhead shoving a whole doughnut in her mouth at once. She always tried to keep her excuses and gripes light, but the notes always dropped a little too sour.

"Pacey's not like that. He's not like most men."

"They're all the same, Little Bird. Testosterone fueled and media brainwashed."

Matlyn heaved a sigh. "He's sweet, and funny, and damn hot, and I think—"

"Stop thinkin', doll."

"Like arguing with a fence post," Matlyn grumbled. She walked up behind Addy and placed her hands on Addy's hips. "You're sexy as hell."

"I'm fat." She sprayed the window in front of her and stared straight ahead, not really seeing the movement out on the street, or the man standing under the lamp post watching the shop.

The redhead pressed her body against Addy's beautiful form. "You're afraid," she whispered.

Six years ago Addy's world had been twixt and twined with that of one Kurtis Freeman, a man so far above his raisin' it was hard to see the attraction. A snob through and through. Kurtis was six years her senior, and Addy was the quintessential eye candy, trim with curves in all the right places. Adeline was a trophy, something to show off to his high-society friends. Bright and shiny for the outside world, but behind closed doors things were dim, tarnished, and sometimes downright bloody.

The day Adeline Sonnier left Kurtis Freeman, she swore no man would ever get that close again. She'd never allow another to build her up so high only to break her down like that. Addy gained thirty pounds that year. She built a wall around her, packed on flesh like armour.

"Wear my shoes, pumpkin," the plump woman said in a sad voice. She dropped her tattooed arms to her sides.

Matlyn had no idea what it felt like, sweet and loving as she was, she'd never lived through what Addy had.

"Take 'em off! Buy new shoes." She squeezed Addy's hips and rested her chin on her friend's shoulder.

"Am I interrupting an intimate moment, ladies? Mind if I watch? I promise I'll be quiet as a June bug."

Matlyn and Addy turned slowly.

Scott stood, arms crossed over his lean, sculpted chest, swirls of color peeking out around the sleeves of his tight black shirt. His blue-dyed and shaggy hair was standing in every direction. Black, blue, and gray smoke crawled up the back of his neck and licked at his chrome pierced ears. His sky blue eyes twinkled with mischief and maybe a little too much hope.

Addy wrapped her arms around Matlyn and pulled her close.

"Ladies, don't tease." Scott's grin grew into something much more indecent.

"Maybe we call Rumor, see if she wants to join in," Matlyn suggested in a coy voice.

"Wifey is *always* down. You know that." And indeed she would have been. Scott walked to his station, flipped open his laptop, and scanned his appointments for the day.

* * *

An hour later, Matlyn flipped the switch on the neon "Open" sign and unlocked the door.

"So Wilson'll be in at noon for that back piece he's got going. Campbell's got two smaller tats, so she'll be on walk-ins, and my lucky ass lost the coin toss this morning, so I'm on supplies." Matlyn grabbed the inventory list off the desk and shoved it in her pocket along with her phone. "If the shit hits the fan, call. Otherwise, kiddies, I'll be back in about two hours. Wish me luck!"

* * *

Across the street the Omen stood, quiet and still; his smoky gray eyes fixed on the slim redhead that slipped out the front door of *Parabola Tattoos* and snaked down the street with ease. He walked two blocks, parallel to Matlyn, watching her as she twirled a key ring around her index finger. The girl rounded the driver's side of a lime green 1968 Camaro and slid into the seat like warm butter into a frying pan.

This was her safe spot, her favorite spot, and it showed in the way her body molded to the sticky, warm leather interior, in the way her fingers curled around the wheel, and in the way her face relaxed and an easy smile melted across her lips.

"Nice wheels," the Omen said to no one at all, nodding his approval. "Terrible fuckin' color though." Once the engine of the green car purred to life, he spun on his heels and made a quick move for his own vehicle, a 1957 Chevy pickup truck in a perfectly respectable gunmetal gray color.

The curious Omen tailed her for about thirty-five minutes before parking her happy place in the parking lot of *Wingerbe Body Modification Supplies*. The name *Wingerbe* took up most of the overhead sign; the rest was pretty much fine print.

The man dropped his head and rolled his eyes. "The human ego, ever the fucking same."

He cut the engine and watched as Matlyn took a deep

breath and pushed the door open. The corner of his mouth twitched into a smirk at the girl's reluctance.

His arm burned and his nerves jerked as new words wrote themselves into his skin. He sighed and rubbed his arm, used to but never comfortable with the Witnessing.

* * *

Alan stood, cocksure and smiling, behind his sales counter. The closer she stepped, the larger his grin grew. His dusty brown hair was slicked back, and his *come an' get it* look unnerved Matlyn.

"Cupcake, what can I do ya for?" The sleaze ball's grin went supernova, and she had to fight an eye roll.

Matlyn stitched on her pleasant smile and said, "Hey, Alan." She fished the list out of her back pocket and slid it across the counter. Tapping it once with her index finger, she looked up to Alan, who was—predictably—staring at her chest. Her Miss Nice smile slipped. "It's not *cupcake*, it's Matlyn. But you can call me Miss Wren."

She loathed his pet names: cupcake, sweets, sugar plum. All of it screamed chauvinistic pig. He clucked as if she'd said something cute and charming, looking over the list once, Matlyn twice. "Give me ten minutes or so to get this together."

Nodding, the annoyed ink-slinger leaned into the countertop, admiring a Dragonfly tattoo machine in "crazy lime," a color not far from the shade of the Camaro sitting in the parking lot.

Less than ten minutes passed when Alan re-emerged from the back, a brown cardboard box in his arms. He placed it on the glass counter and then bent over it, moving closer to Matlyn.

"So, uh … we should go grab a coffee, ya think?" His thumb swept across his lips and his tongue followed in a move that was surely meant to be seductive but fell dead flat.

Slapping a credit card down on the glass countertop, she reached out and pulled the box to her chest. "Just ring it up, Alan." Her seafoam eyes begged him not to fuck with her.

The shifty store owner barked out an annoyed grunt, then went about his job, plucking the card off the counter and swiping it. Matlyn ignored him and busied herself with her phone.

Mat: On my way back.

Add: Did ya feed him his balls?

Mat: Nah, feeling generous today. But I could eat. Tell me my lunch is waiting for me.

Alan handed her the receipt to sign, and with a saccharine grin, she penned her name, clutched the box close, and made for the door.

Add: Lunch is waiting … and your sister's in the back room blowing Wilson.

Two

❧

A small, cherubic looking woman with long, strawberry blonde hair sat behind Matlyn's desk, legs crossed and foot bouncing as she hummed a peppy tune. Her heavily-lined eyes meticulously scanned columns of numbers: cost versus profit, overhead, expenses ... numbers, numbers, numbers. Her coral sweater and pinstriped, charcoal skirt hid the cherry blossoms creeping up her left side; a delicate pink blossom caressed the underside of her breast.

"Everyone knows," Matlyn whispered from the doorway, startling the petite woman. She walked forward, eyeing the girl, placed the box of supplies on the desk, and took a seat across from her sister.

"I'm sure I don't know what you're talking about."

"Wanna bet?" Matlyn reached across the desk, opened the top drawer, and groped around until her fingers found what they were looking for: a bag of cherry licorice. The eldest Wren plopped back down in the chair and pulled a stick from the bag, pointing it at her sister like a weapon. "I don't understand why you're playing hide-and-go-fuck with Wilson, Parrish."

Parrish shook her perfectly curled hair, her cheeks pinking up a little. "Nope. No, there's been no fucking."

"Fellatio only, then?"

"Heavy petting, mostly. And his digits may have slipped once … err … four times." Parrish's face bloomed red as a tomato, giving highlight to the smattering of freckles across her nose and cheeks.

Matlyn snorted. "So why you sneakin' around, then? You like him, right?"

"It's just th—"

"No, Pare. Yes or no: do you like him?"

The strawberry-blond slumped a little further into her chair, her eyes refusing to meet Matlyn's. "Yes."

"Do you want him?"

"Yes," she said in a whisper.

"Then whatever bull-hucky excuse you're about to feed me, whatever *but* you're about to spew … stop. Wilson is smart, talented, sexy as fuck, well off. You're twenty-seven, not seventeen, so don't make this about the numbers. Eleven years is peanuts, baby girl. Fucking peanuts, and no reason not to go for it." Matlyn was used to this—the laundry list of reasons why not to get involved with someone. She also knew why Parrish did it, why she looked for excuses to push people away.

* * *

April 7, 1999, 11:23 p.m. ~ New Orleans

A dark-skinned, dark-haired Omen stood at the end of the Crescent City Connection bridge, invisible to passersby, the rain coming down in thick sheets. Her clothes clung to her soaked body, her makeup ran down her face, mixing with the rain and her tears.

The Witnessing was near its end; she could feel it. Words were quickly searing into her skin, making her back ache and burn.

Lightning streaked across the night sky, and bright blooms of white, blue, and pink lit the dark street for a quick moment.

Tires screeched.

The clap of thunder overhead swallowed the sound of glass shattering and metal crunching.

A final breath was exhaled, and with it the last words of the Story were branded into the Omen's skin. Their history had been Witnessed and told. She turned away from the wreckage and disappeared into the storm, following the pulse and pull of another Story waiting for its ending.

* * *

"So that's that, Parrish Lee! You're gonna claim Wilson as your own. End of fucking story."

"And say what, Little Bird?"

The nickname, Little Bird, was born years ago, and Matlyn responded to it as readily as her given name. Cohen, an ex-boyfriend, had assigned it to the ginger-haired woman and it stuck. It wasn't terribly creative, mind you. Her surname and the root of the nickname, was in fact a rather small bird. Only eleven months sat between the Wren sisters, but coming from her younger—and nearly a foot shorter—sister the name seemed almost absurd.

"Oh, I don't know, maybe, 'I like you, and I'm pretty sure you like me.' 'Cause, ya know, you put your dick in my mouth and all. So let's make it official.' Something like that might work." Matlyn bit a piece of licorice and quirked an eyebrow.

With her hand to her head and mock shock spray-painted on her pretty, pale face, Parrish said, "Such a foul fucking thing. Don't ever change." They chuckled and the tattooist chewed on her cherry candy. "So that's it?"

"Uh-huh," the licorice-breathed girl hummed, bobbing her head.

And with that, the conversation was closed. Parrish went back to the books and Matlyn neatly put away the supplies she'd purchased.

* * *

A woman with soft brown hair, a neat floral dress, and light blue patent heels sat at a café two doors down. She sipped her pricey mocha and grinned as the Witnessing began and a familiar, comforting warmth spread down her back. The Light Omen smiled and looked up to the cloudy, darkening sky. Clouds began to roll above as an easy bliss settled inside the woman. A name surfaced in a fine, lovely script on her right wrist. Turning her hand to read the name, she sighed as the first drops reached her bare shoulders.

* * *

Across town, in a small, dingy hotel room, Baker sat on a

brown—might have been gray at one point—ottoman, the TV throwing a green-blue glow around the room. Long shadows stretched along the walls, flickering and dancing in the TV's glow. The bed was rumpled and two pancake-thin pillows lay stacked, one upon the other, his shirt unceremoniously chucked just inside the door of the not-so-cozy hotel room.

Following the dull pulse burrowed under his skin, Baker arrived in New Orleans a little more than two weeks ago. Sometimes it took months to find his Story, others only days. In the time since he'd arrived, he managed to secure a job at a pub around the corner. Unfortunately, Omens were not well compensated for their *services*. The constant moving left no room for any sort of life or career. He'd been around the world and back again in his hundred plus years. It'd been nearly a century since Baker had a home of his own or a lover in his bed for more than a quick blink. Dark Omens lived lonely lives. Part of the punishment, he presumed.

His started at the pub in an hour, and he was more than happy to be leaving the confines of the tiny, old shoe-smelling room. In a past life he wouldn't be caught dead in a place like this, and the years hadn't curbed his bitterness one bit.

The grumpy Omen rose from his seat and pulled a black button-down off a hanger. He shrugged into it and rolled the sleeves up to his forearms, leaving plenty of material to conceal the Story silently unfolding on his bare arms. Grabbing his keys, Baker made for the door and out into the night, disappearing into the shadows of the streets below.

* * *

Lucy's Retired Surfer Bar was in full swing. The heat of the night air seeped into the bar, stealing the crisp coolness the air conditioner tried exhaustively to maintain. Bodies moved between the restaurant and the open patio outside. Drinks with small toy sharks bobbing in bloody-looking liquor seemed to be a crowd favorite. Music, quiet enough for conversation but loud enough to head bob or for an ass shake from time to time, piped through the bar.

"That would have been a lot less awkward—maybe even romantic—if she'da left out that bit about his junk," Campbell said, her nose wrinkling.

The youngest artist at *Parabola* was, oddly, the most prudish. She never swore, never drank; though newly twenty-one, you'd think she'd be swimming in it, beer goggles firmly in place. Any mention of a reproductive organ had her mocha-colored face puckered in a comical grimace. Given the company she kept, her face looked like that a lot of the time.

"Well, I for one am damn proud of our little closet freak. Took balls to say that to his face," Addy said with a smirk, taking a little too much enjoyment in the way Campbell's brown eyes narrowed at her.

"My little sister's growin' up." Matlyn put her hand over her heart and wiped a nonexistent tear from her eye.

"Little sister's likely in the back seat of Wilson's car with her panties around her ankles." Scott winked and raised his beer in salute, his wife, Rumor, tucked close to his side.

Campbell rolled her chocolate eyes, and Matlyn chuckled.

Matlyn's phone vibrated on the table in front of her. Taking it in her hand, she glanced down at the screen.

PacMan: Is it safe?

Mat: Four drinks in. She's feeling friendly.

The sneaky redhead put her phone face down on the table and looked up at her unsuspecting friend, giving her a wink and mouthing "*I love you.*" Addy's brow furrowed for a quick second and then her scarlet lips picked up in a tipsy smile. Three minutes later, that smile went sideways.

"Pacey Hudson Ledet the second," he said, extending his hand to a stunned and steaming platinum-blond.

"Adeline Sonnier," she said, smiling sweetly at Pacey, but throwing daggers at her redheaded pal. She held out her hand and gave him a dainty shake.

"Don't worry, Pace, that stick up her ass isn't permanent. Enough lube and it should slide right out." Matlyn wagged her eyebrows and waved a curly-haired waitress over. "Speaking of which, ya'll want another?" She looked around the table. "Three beers, refill that Coke there, and can I getta gin and tonic for the sexy blonde over here?"

"Course, darlin'." The waitress smiled as she cleared the empties. Her teeth were as crooked as her nose, the effect oddly charming.

The curvy southern belle leaned sideways, her face bobbing close to Matlyn's ear. "Gettin' me drunk won't make the ass beatin' I'mma give you any less painful, Little Bird." The gin saturated her accent and endings dropped from words left and right. Matlyn only smiled widely.

As the night went on, the thick-accented gentleman inched closer to Addy, and maybe it was the booze, but she didn't seem to mind. Pacey's kindness made her comfortable.

His easy smiles made her naturally friendly disposition shine through, almost enough to overshadow the insecurities she harbored. Though the tipsy girl giggled at his jokes and seemed to enjoy the conversation, her back remained tense and straight, and sometimes he'd catch a quick flicker of something in her eyes.

* * *

"Hold on to this asshat while I flag him a cab, will ya, Zack?" Baker handed off an obviously drunken cowboy to his co-worker and stepped out onto the dark street in front of Lucy's. He hailed a cab and wrenched open the door.

Zack passed off the sloshed man, shaking his head at the incoherent ranting coming from his whiskey-soaked mouth. Baker roughly folded him into the back of the cab, wished the driver luck, and shut the door. Turning abruptly, he collided with a slender girl.

"Oh shit, I'm sorry," Matlyn said, looking up into deep pools of smoky gray.

Three

❧

_____

The moment the front door closed behind her, the drunken tattooist began pulling off her clothes and dropping them like breadcrumbs behind her. She stood in her bathroom wearing only Coca-Cola red boy shorts and a sheer black bra. She cupped her breasts, hefted them, and then let them drop. "Meh," she said with a shrug. "Parrish got the tits. But this ass..." she smacked her behind "...thank you, Momma!"

The quiet laugh died in her throat. "Momma," she whispered. For a moment Matlyn was quiet, and then a sloppy smile stretched her lips. "You'd be proud, Mom. Well, maybe not so much of the delivery." She waved her hand in front of her own lady bits and giggled, remembering the way her sister had declared herself to Wilson earlier in the night. "But, yeah, Parrish told a boy she loved him. Not liked, _loved_. Skipped right past like. Quite a big thing for her, though I suspect the three tequilas she poured down her throat had something to do with it." She nodded her head, agreeing with her own speculation.

With both hands gripping the sink, her body swayed just a little as the beer she'd drank buzzed through her blood. Matlyn looked up, meeting her own reflection. "I miss love," she admitted to the blurry-eyed girl in the mirror.

It'd been seven months since Kory-Rae. Kory was an audacious blonde with a dirty mouth and curves that could make grown men cry. She drew the attention of everyone in the room without so much as a word. Matlyn fell into her easily—fell for her desire and the way she wanted and wanted and wanted. Kory wanted every part of Matlyn, wanted to own her. And though the idea of being desired that much was appealing, and initially intoxicating, it wasn't what she needed.

Matlyn had always been a one man, one woman kind of girl—as in one man *and* one woman. Something Cohen had not only accepted but loved about her. Kory-Rae simply tolerated it … until she didn't. Kory handed her an ultimatum: me and *only* me, or nothing at all. Though it broke her heart, Matlyn went with door number two, knowing full well that wasn't who she was, or ever would be.

Monogamy wasn't in her catalog. She craved both the soft skin and delicate touch of a woman, and the hard planes and rough fingertips of a man. She'd tried more times than she could count to be with that *one* person, but the need, the crave for the other always crept back in, forcing her to make choices about who she was and how she was going to live her life.

Her relationship with Cohen many moons ago hadn't ended quite so dramatically. His job moved him out of state, and Matlyn hadn't been willing to follow. The two remained friends, chatting on-line from time to time. No hearts were broken, but after Kory-Rae she'd come to the decision that trying to be something she wasn't, wasn't worth the ache. From that point on, she was determined to be with people that fully accepted her and understood that they could only have all of her if they were willing to give over half of her.

Matlyn pulled herself away from her thoughts and corralled all images of Kory back into the past. Closing her eyes for a moment, she saw gray eyes, unruly black hair, and a crooked smile she'd bumped into earlier that night.

* * *

"Oh shit, sorry." Matlyn's eyes had met a handsome, if slightly brooding face.

He stood stock-still for a moment, lips parted. "No, no. Fault's all mine." He tipped his head to her.

She turned away, then back again. "You work here? At Lucy's?"

"Yeah, on the occasion. You drink here?" The man's voice held a note of an accent. Irish maybe, Matlyn thought.

"On the occasion." The intoxicated girl smiled up at the raven-haired bouncer-guy, hoping the booze hadn't fucked with her face yet. It was one thing to down a few and slur every third word, but when you looked *slurred, it was time to put the bottle down.*

He cracked a smile and chuckled.

Yup, facial slur. Fuck, Matlyn thought, looking down at her red Docs. Campbell just stood there, watching and waiting with her keys in her hand.

"You need a cab?" he asked, pointing out to the busy street.

"Nope. DD." She jabbed a finger at Campbell.

He nodded and shoved his hands in his pockets. "Have a good night, then." And with that, the pretty Irishman and the doorman disappeared into the crowded bar.

"Fucking crap!" Matlyn marched toward Campbell's car, Campbell giggling behind her. "On the occasion," she mocked herself. "Fucking tool!"

"Smooth you were not, Matlyn." Campbell had aimed the key fob at her car and the lights blinked.

"I really wasn't. What the happy fuck was that?"

"A missed opportunity."

* * *

Remembering the cocky grin, the open button exposing his neck, the curve of his lips, and his slate eyes, Matlyn slipped her fingers beneath her panties, one hand still gripping the sink.

Her fingers worked quickly, months of frustration fueling them. She came with a loud moan, leaning over the sink, her legs shaking and her face flushed.

"Yeah ... hot," she mumbled in a throaty voice. "He was most certainly *hot*."

* * *

Shutting the door with his foot, Baker unbuttoned his shirt as he walked. Passing by the maybe-gray ottoman, the Dark Omen grabbed the remote sitting on the arm and turned on the TV.

The bathroom light flickered above the mirror, washing the small room in a dingy yellow light. Baker shrugged out of his shirt and let it fall to the floor, pooling like black ink on the cracked, white tile. He turned on the shower and stripped off the last of his clothing, leaving it in a messy heap. Baker stepped under the hot but weak spray and let his eyes slip shut. Exhaling, he felt the smoke and the smell of the bar trickle down his body. His muscles bunched and relaxed under the meager stream of water. His arm burned and his mind pulled up the image of the lean girl with the cinnamon red hair. Her half-slurred, husky voice echoed in his ears, and he smiled.

The way the girl chewed on her lip, blushed, and kind of batted her eyelashes, which he was sure was completely unconsciously, made him chuckle.

And just as quick as his smile had spread, it vanished with the knowledge of what was to come.

* * *

September 1907, 10:27p.m. ~ Oregon

A loud rumble tore through the city, shaking the ground beneath its citizens, but only one fell while another dissolved into the shadows, counting on the chaos of the scene to be his cover.

The body of Sheriff Harvey Kimble Brown, a well-loved and respected pillar of the community was the sole victim of the bombing, the sole target.

They brought in dogs and private investigators from out of state, but not a single lead was ever stumbled upon. The case was never closed, and no one was held accountable for the bombing or death of the beloved sheriff.

Samuel knew they'd never close that book. No one

would ever come for him. He'd learned all he knew from his father, Finn Heeney. And he was good at what he did.

"Don't give 'em reason ta suspect ya, boy. Act shady, and they'll think yer shady," he would tell a young Samuel. "An' cover yer tracks. Don't ever lead 'em home."

He'd breezed into the county on charm and a well-made suit, under a false name, Baker O'Dolan, supposedly looking to move his young wife to a sweet little city like theirs. The only bit of truth in all of that was the name. Baker had been his middle name and O'Dolan his mother's maiden name.

He spoke to the right people, asked the right questions. And no one would ever know about the back alley dealings their shiny sheriff conducted in the dark of night.

When Samuel returned to Chicago later that week, his handsome father offered him congratulations and one of the few looks of pride he would ever bestow on his only son.

The first came the day he put a gun in the hands of his eleven-year-old son and taught him how to shoot.

* * *

March 11, 2015, 7:30 p.m. ~ Lucy's Retired Surfer Bar

The nights flipped by quickly, like pages in a book, pages without any real event or consequence. Boring. More than a hundred years of wandering in an ever-evolving world could suck the joy and pleasure out of the human experience in a way the Omen never considered.

Everyone wanted to be young and beautiful and live forever, but forever was torture. Technology changed and advanced in mind-blowing ways every day, but people, they remained the same. What they wore and how they spoke morphed throughout the years, but the brass roots of human behavior had never really strayed, and that made the prospect of *forever* utterly boring.

Baker's world was nothing but death and tedium.

Until *she* batted her big green, kind of bloodshot eyes at him. Then Baker's world became death, tedium, and a minor but growing obsession. She was a bug bite he couldn't help but scratch.

Every night at the bar, Baker searched the faces in the crowd looking for the drunk-flushed, beautiful face of Matlyn Wren, his Story. She hadn't returned to Lucy's that week, and stalking—sorry, *Witnessing*—her outside her tattoo parlor every day, wasn't enough. He would watch from across the road, sitting under a street lamp, as the pretty little shop owner greeted customers and bustled around with a kind of contented look about her. Words would painfully scroll across his skin, adding to her tale, bringing it closer to the end.

He was there to Witness, to gather her story and watch it unfold, but never to intervene, and as a personal rule: never get involved or give a shit in any way. Emotions built attachments, something the Dark Omen could not afford.

Pulling his head out of his ass and tucking his increasingly crappy mood away, he shook his head and shifted his attention to the crowded bar.

"Lost in a good dream?" a portly but kind faced man said, taking a seat in front of Baker. He propped his elbows on the bar top and wiggled his blue button-down-clad gut close to the bar's edge, leaning toward Baker.

"Something like that," he answered.

Laying a bill down on the bar, he said, "Whiskey sour. What's her name?"

Baker chuckled and shook his head. "Matlyn. Makes a beautiful lush." He remembered the way she swayed on the sidewalk and the glazed look in her eyes. Booze and a warm Louisiana night made her face as pink as a rose petal.

"Matlyn," the man repeated, "beautiful name."

Baker passed him a glass and watched the man bring it to his lips and tip it back. He pushed the image of her into a dusty corner of his mind again and again, determined to keep his distance.

* * *

"Skinny jeans ... best fucking thing ever," Baker said as his hands cupped the rounded curve of a pert ass.

An airy giggle bubbled out of the mouth of the bleach blonde he had pressed up against the cold metal of his Chevy.

Kymmy, she'd introduced herself as, spelling her name slow and clear. K-Y-M-M-Y. She'd swished and swooped her pinky finger in the air, making a Y shape. Something Baker found ridiculous.

Kymmy was vapid, under intelligent, with dark roots, glazed-over dull blue eyes, and an impressive C-cup. Her lips tasted like strawberry and the way her leg slid against his left little question as to just how far she was willing to go tonight.

Baker blindly reached for the truck's door, pulled it open, and stepped back. He gestured for her to climb in and then jumped in behind her.

It took her all of about four seconds to straddle him.

The orange sequined top came off first, and the ink-haired Omen took a moment to thank the sweet Lord above for the careful work he'd put into her, particularly her chest. Her tits were perfectly round and her light pink nipples reacted beautifully to his mouth and his hands.

"Christ, I take it back," Baker panted, pulling at the jeans that clung to her like a second fucking skin.

She giggled a kinda sexy, kinda annoying giggle and finally wiggled free. With the jeans set aside, Kymmy went to work on his pants.

Baker let out a soft moan as she slid her hand over his length, and again when she rolled the condom down his shaft.

She bounced on him, whining and moaning loudly. She fucked like someone without a thought of the morning after. She rode him hard, like the consequence-free tourist she was. The thrill of a one-night stand in a strange city with a strange man had her screaming like a porn star.

That's … not attractive, Baker thought, wishing she'd shut her fucking loud mouth and come already.

She came in dramatic fashion, seat gripped in one hand, head thrown back, chest heaving, and a string of "fucks" flew from her pink, plump lips. But it was all wrong. The shape of her body, the airy quality of her voice, even the faux blond hair, was wrong.

He loathed his body for wanting anything other than the pretty girl seated on his lap. Nothing amplified loneliness like a quick fling in the front seat of a pickup truck. He poured his frustration into her, thrusting up in quick hard movements, gripping her hips with bruising force. He came with an angry grunt.

As he grabbed for his shirt, the tourist reached out and caressed the inky words on his shoulder and arm; she tilted her head curiously.

"I … Are they moving?" She looked up at the man in amazement and let her finger trace the loops and dives of the words. "The words … I could swear …"

"Rye and Coke," Baker answered in a flat voice. "You're drunk." He handed her the sequined top and refastened his jeans.

She gave the elegant lettering a long look and shook her head. "Who's Matlyn Wren?"[1]

Four

❖

___

Baker paced the street outside the tiny bistro for nearly a half hour. The street around was all hustle and bustle, and drunken tourists with green painted-on clovers and "Kiss Me, I'm Irish," T-shirts stumbled this way and that.

Matlyn had ducked inside the building about forty minutes ago, and Baker had been hoping to "run into" her on the street outside, so he pivoted on his heels and walked down the block some and up again. Dodging a young woman and her well-past tipsy friend, Baker moved quickly to the left and before he could step away, the bistro door swung wide and clipped the side of his face.

"Bugger!" he croaked, grabbing for the door and

holding it still so it didn't have the opportunity to accost him a second time.

"Oh, that didn't sound good." A copperhead with round, dark-rimmed glasses peeked around the swinging door. Two people followed close on her heels. A curvy blonde and another woman undeniably related to the redhead that stood before him. Peering down at Matlyn Wren, the Irishman smiled and stepped back, opening the door a little wider and motioning for her to come on through. "Nah, my fault. I should have listened to my mother. 'Your feet aren't so important that ya can't keep yer eyes up, Baker'," he said, impersonating his mother in a rather unflattering way.

The smell of beer surrounded them, and the green four-leafed clover painted on her left cheek bounced as she laughed. She threw her gaze to the cherry Docs on her feet for a brief moment and then said, "You're, um ... I know you?" Green eyes shifted left then right.

Baker scratched at the dark scruff on his face and met her gaze. "Yeah. The bartender. Lucy's."

"Right. I was drunk, you were there."

"Right," Baker answered, feeling like a baboon.

"Here you are now ..." the other redhead pointed out "... and she's three green beers outsida sober. You guys are oh-for-two. Can we get movin', Mat?" She tapped her foot.

The tiny, tattooed beauty laughed again and tucked a loose copper chunk behind her pierced ear, offered him a soft smile, and bid him a good and safe night and went about hers.

It was nothing. Almost nothing, but it was enough to know what her laugh sounded like. It stepped over lines the Omen drew decades ago, and though there was a certain amount of satisfaction, he knew that laugh would haunt him in ways he wasn't prepared for. Baker trudged back the way he came, doing his best to ignore the flash of pain that suddenly rocked his body.

New words were being written. They seared and stung, and Baker pitched his focus to his breathing.

In. Out.

Left foot forward. Then right.

* * *

March 20, 2015, 2:04 p.m. ~ Beckham's Bookshop

Two tables over, Ingrid watched Parrish Wren pick up random books, flipping them in her hands. She smiled at the way the young woman read the jacket covers, silently mouthing the words, and chuckled when her nose wrinkled and the book was set aside.

The easy, warm, and intoxicating feeling of new words being written upon Ingrid's olive skin fell over her, and she sighed deeply, loving the quick but gentle rush it offered the Light Omen. Eighty-six years of Witnessing and she still pulled pleasure from the process.

"Find anything good?" Strong arms wrapped around Parrish's compact frame. The man was lean, tan, and towered over the Wren girl. The crow's feet that sat at the corners of his eyes, not at all hidden by his dark frames, made it evident that his handsome face had seen a lot of smiles in his lifetime. His dark brown hair was curly and just beginning to gray, creating a subtle salt and pepper effect.

"This…" she picked up a book with beautiful but blurry cover art "…is some depressing shit, Wilson. Why in the holy hell would anyone want to read a book like this, huh?" She dropped the book back down on the table and picked up another. "And *this* fluffy bullshit. Blah. 'Cause life is all sunshine and fuckin' kittens. Right."

The Light Omen two tables over chuckled softly to herself.

"So books aren't your thing," Wilson said.

"They bore me. Too much work reading all those words." Petite shoulders shrugged. "What about you?"

The older man tipped his head, gesturing to the small tote full of books.

Parrish looked down and then turned in his arms. "Nerd." She scooped the first three books off the top of the pile. Historical drama, art, and naked people. "Really, dude, a book full of T an' A?" She cocked her head.

"Look at this, Parrish." Wilson flipped the book in question open. "The lighting … look at these black and whites," he gushed.

Ingrid stopped and turned fully toward the couple and glanced at the book, recognizing the work. She looked on as Parrish scanned the photos, taking it in. Bodies of every shape, age, and skin tone sat in various poses. Parrish's finger traced the curve of a hip, and she tilted her head.

"Wilson, these are beautiful." She closed the book and placed all three back in his tote.

"Wonderful skill he has for capturing the body in its best light." The Omen stepped forward, looking toward the book.

"Great eye," Wilson agreed.

"I met him once at a gallery show. He's a quiet man. Not *I'm-an-artist-weird-quiet*, just quiet. Ingrid Stokes," she announced, holding her hand out to Parrish first then Wilson. They introduced themselves politely.

"He hasn't done a gallery show in … like ten years," Wilson said, seemingly sizing the woman up. She couldn't be any more than thirty. Her eyes seemed so much older, though.

"Yes, that sounds about right," the Omen in the violet dress conceded. "Well, enjoy your books." She gave a cordial wave and made her way around them. Wilson tipped his brown plaid fedora at her as she passed by.

Ingrid practically buzzed from the exhilarating high. Words dashed quickly down her rib cage, the couple's names intertwined in an inky script that writhed in a hypnotic movement.

* * *

January 30, 1928, 5:42 a.m. ~ Kiwanda Cliffs, Oregon

It hadn't shocked Ingrid one bit when Death found her; she'd forced its hand after all. Tragedy seemed to be stitched to Ingrid's shadow and never far behind. At the age of seven she watched, helpless and terrified, as her baby sister, Bernice succumbed to scarlet fever. Only three years later, her lovely mother died giving birth to a baby that never took its first breath. Nine years passed in relative peace, and then Death saw fit to steal away the only thing she had left: her father.

Having no one, the orphaned woman turned to her family's neighbors and friends. They took her in, quickly marrying her off to their eldest son, Charles. And for a brief moment in her life, Ingrid believed she'd pulled free from the tragedy and the pain, not knowing that what she'd walked into was so much worse. Charles Stokes was a monster with an angel's face, and when he went off to war, she prayed he wouldn't return. The night her prayer went unanswered and he came home, Ingrid Stokes turned her back on her faith. When she learned that she was carrying his child, she fled, refusing to let a child grow in a house built on fear and pain.

Joseph Merrick Stokes was born January 17th, 1928, died January 25th. January 30th, Ingrid Ann Stokes, daughter of Henry and Abigail Browning, jumped to her end. When she dove off the cliff into the raging water below, she thought she would simply sink to the bottom and drown. She didn't count on the water being so … hard. The water felt like marble—solid and cold. And when her body could no longer fight, a strange sight unfolded in front of her. A man with dark hair, wearing a dark suit, appeared only feet from her. His clothes were perfectly unaffected by the frigid water that swirled and swooshed around them.

He held out his hand and said, "You've seen enough hurt, girl."

* * *

Tossing her keys on the table by the front door, Parrish looked up the staircase that led to both her and Matlyn's rooms. Thick baselines thumped off the walls and rattled down the hall, catching in the stairwell. She shook her head and plunked her purse down on the table, smiling.

"She's either painting or masturbating," she surmised, pointing up to the second floor as her boyfriend closed the door behind them.

"Maybe she's got company," Wilson offered with a shrug.

She kicked her kitten heels off and pranced down the carpeted hallway to the kitchen on her bare feet. "Nope. She would have texted."

Deliciously defined muscles lifted the bag of books to the countertop then stopped to pick up the tiny cat winding its way around his legs. She was black with orange blotches all over her, as if someone had flicked a paint brush at her. He brought her fuzzy face to his, smiling when she reached out her puffy little paw and touched his cheek. She let out a sort of pitiful meow and dropped her paw.

"What's up, Syn?" he asked, blowing in her face and laughing at the way she shook her head.

Syndal was the eldest Wren's cat. She never took much interest, like most cats, in people—except Wilson. And, oddly, the mailman. Every afternoon, like clockwork, Syn would perch her body on the window nearest the mailbox and meow like the annoying little fucker Parrish thought she was.

"She probably wants into Mat's room." Parrish opened the fridge and grabbed two beers, one for her and the other for the lovely gentleman standing at her side. She traded Wilson a bottle for the cat. "Come on, ya poor pussy, let's get ya back to Mama."

When she reached the top of the stairs, she hooked a right—Wilson went left— and knocked the bottle's bottom against the door in front of her. Syndal squirmed in her arms, and Parrish huffed. The music quieted and the door opened. A cloud of grayish smoke wafted through the open space and her sister stood, wearing an old white racerback covered in paint and equally smeared gray shorts.

"Glad it was option one," Parrish mumbled to herself.

"Cat." She thrust the furry thing forward, and Syn leaped to the ground and made a quick dart down the stairs.

Matlyn laughed and stretched out her hand, offering her sister a drag off the joint she'd been enjoying.

"Yup, fuck you too, Syn!" the strawberry-blonde called after the cat. "And don't mind if I do." She inhaled deeply and coughed, like always, and handed it back to Matlyn.

"Wilson here?"

"Yeah, hidin' just in case it was option two."

"What?" Matlyn's nose scrunched, canting her head.

"The loud music," she pointed out, waving her hand around at nothing. "You were either painting—"

"Or getting off," the paint-covered sister finished. "Sadly, just painting. Wanna have a look?" She stepped aside and let Parrish into the room.

A large canvas lay on the floor and dark colors dominated the scene. A man in a dark suit, seemingly stretched just slightly beyond the normal portions, stood dead center. Everything that surrounded him was blurry, as if the world around him were out of focus.

"Can't even draw stickmen." Parrish shook her head, awed by her sister's talent. She took another long hit, pulling it deep into her lungs when Matlyn handed it back to her. She kissed her sister's face and left the room, leaving the joint behind. "Turn the music back on," she called over her shoulder.

In her room, she found Wilson lounging on her bed, shirt off, the TV remote in his hand, and his sex-hat—Parrish's term for his brown fedora—on the bedside table. The feisty, copper-blonde kicked the door shut and walked out of her red peddle-pushers, leaving her in a white eyelet tank top and black lace underwear. Knees bent with her back against the headboard, she sat. She twisted the lid off the beer, tossed it to the side of the bed, and let the cold amber liquid slide down her throat. She knew she was being watched. She could always feel his eyes on her; roaming her skin, searching her face. She peeked out of the corner of her eyes, and sure enough, the man was staring at her. She smiled around the bottle.

"You might be the sexiest thing I've ever seen, Miss Parrish," Wilson professed, his voice dripping slow like warm honey.

She put the bottle down and stretched her legs out in front of her. Looking nowhere but the TV, she dared, "Prove it."

The corner of Wilson's mouth hitched and he took the cold bottle in his hand and skimmed it up her bare thigh. Goose bumps sprouted and she shivered. Slowly, he tipped the bottle, the mouth of it hovering inches from her lace underwear. As the cold drink trickled down and pooled between her closed thighs, she let out a hushed curse that sounded a lot like begging.

Reaching back, he placed the bottle on the nightstand and returned his attention to the sticky-sweet girl. His head dipped down to her thighs and his tongue poked out to lick the beer. She moaned and squirmed a little, and she couldn't have held back the sounds if she tried. He pushed her legs open and tucked his head between them, taking a long lap at the booze-soaked lace. Her hips bucked as he flattened a hand against the lower part of her stomach.

Delicate hands gripped his chocolate and sugar dusted locks and a near-silent "*yes*" fell from her lips. He stayed there, face to her swelling clit, until she shook. He stood quickly and stripped off his jeans and boxer briefs, leaving them pooled on the floor. He climbed back on the bed, hovering over Parrish. He pushed an arm under her soft frame and pulled her further down the bed. Without a word, he moved her panties to the side and pushed inside her. They groaned at the feel of warmth and fullness, and wet, sticky heat.

His fingers tickled the petals that covered her rib cage, and she smiled. Grabbing her knee, he pushed it toward her chest and drove deeper into her, loving the way her body welcomed him and pulled him in. He braced his hand on the headboard and moved slow, each thrust rocking her body.

Parrish's warm hands rested in the center of his chest and after a moment gave a gentle push. "As good as this feels, my knickers are ridin' up my ass," she said with some amusement.

Wilson chuckled and rolled off her, grunting at the feel as he slid out.

She dug her thumbs into the waistband, peeled the offending panties from her body, and unceremoniously hurled them clear across the room. Without missing a beat, she grabbed his cock and straddled him, lowering herself onto him in one quick, almost violent movement.

"Fuck," she cried. Stilling herself for just another moment, she pulled the white top off and let it drop to the bed beside her.

She rode him hard and wasn't quiet about it. Now that she had him, really had him, she'd never again hide how she felt.

* * *

"There's something in every fucking painting," Parrish said just as absently as she ran her fingers from Wilson's navel to torso.

"Hmm?" Wilson tipped his head down to look at the petite, red-haired woman.

"Matlyn's paintings. All of them have something of my parents in them." She lifted her head up and looked Wilson in the eye. "The one she's working now … the bridge is in the background." Parrish didn't need to explain the significance of the bridge, she'd shared that story with him before.

"It's how she deals, how she works it out, Pare. You push people away, keep them from seeing you. Matlyn paints what she remembers."

"I don't push—"

"You *do*, and that's okay. It's how *you* deal."

Her face fell and she let out a deep, thoughtful sigh. "I don't mean to," she whispered against his naked chest.

"I know, kitten. I put up with your shit 'cause the head is *amazing*!"

She swatted at him and rolled to her side, a light, happy grin pulling at her lips. "Good night, Wilson." She popped her butt out and let him tuck himself to her.

"That's Major W.D. Kenning to you, ma'am," he said, exaggerating his lazy accent and fingering the dog tags resting on his chest.

Her body gave a slight tremble, and not the good kind. "Oh God, that's skeevie. I'm not calling you Major. Don't ever say that again."

* * *

Down the hall the music stopped and Matlyn pulled off her paint-covered clothes. Peeking down the darkened hallway, she risked the naked jaunt across the hall to her own room. She washed her hands, scrubbing the drying paint away, washed her face, and brushed her teeth. As she lay in bed, she pictured the Crescent City Connection Bridge, rain falling, and a man in black moving between the heavy raindrops.

Five

❧

_____

April 11, 2015, 6:36 p.m. ~ Lucy's Retired Surfer Bar

"A repeat offender," the bouncer said, holding the door for Matlyn.

Her eyes went up, up, up and met the gaze of a dark-skinned man. "What?" she questioned, seeing the amusement in his pitch-dark eyes and couldn't help but smile at him.

"I've seen you here before." He watched a couple leave hand in hand, the girl tipsy on her way-too-high heels.

"Oh … yeah." Matlyn nodded. Surreptitiously, she hoped the doorman's fuck-hot co-worker was here, but she didn't hang her hopes on that. She hadn't seen him since St. Patrick's Day when she'd assaulted him with a door. Her eyes searched the bar while some kick-ass '90's song she couldn't remember the name of piped through the sound system. She tousled her hair and it fell the way it always had, straight and messy. She saw Pacey wave her over to the booth he shared with Addy, Scott, and Rumor. Pacey stood out like a swollen thumb, his thick muscles, tanned, unmarked skin, and curly brown hair at odds with his company.

After five visits to the shop, six lengthy conversations that consisted mostly of him begging, and one bouquet of crazy daisies, Addy finally agreed to a date with the proper-looking man. The one condition was that it be in a group; Pacey happily agreed to those terms.

Matlyn kissed her friend's super-blonde curls as she squished into the booth next to Rumor, who gave her bare leg a quick squeeze. She didn't often wear skirts, but when she did they were leather. Led Zeppelin T-shirt, pink and blue plaid button-down, cherry Docs, and her favorite mini skirt, Matlyn felt good in her skin tonight. Color peeked out anywhere her pale skin was exposed.

Rumor eyed her, her teeth scraping across her bottom lip. "Drink?" she asked, swirling her own glass.

"Yes," Matlyn answered, waving the waitress over. A nice glowy buzz was her aim for the night, not stupid drunk, so she stuck with beer. She could only tolerate so many of those before her taste buds reminded her that she wasn't a frat boy.

With little more than a nod in her direction, Scott continued his story. "Shoulda seen Campbell's pretty little face," he said with a snicker. "Dude pulled down his pants, and that was it. Campbell was fuckin' outta there. Her eyes were all big and shell-shocked. Poor thing might never recover."

"So Campbell's twenty-one?" Pacey asked the table.

Heads nodded and a bubbly "*yup*" popped out of Addy.

"And she doesn't drink, doesn't smoke, doesn't swear … and is likely a virgin?" he surmised. More head nods. "At *twenty-one?*" He sounded utterly incredulous.

"She's likely at home worryin' over the consequence that shit had on her soul," Matlyn joked. "But in fairness that guy's prick was hideous." She snorted and picked up her drink.

"Who booked that fuckin' appointment anyway?" Rumor demanded. Scott raised his hand timidly, and the miffed girl turned to stare down her husband. "Tell me you didn't know what he wanted? *Where* he wanted that tattoo?"

"He might've mentioned it." Mock guilt and way too much amusement lit his face.

Smacking his upper arm hard, Rumor barked, "You mighta traumatized that poor girl for life. You call her right now, Scott Ellis, and say you're sorry!"

"Oh shit, son. You got middle named," Pacey said and chuckled, slapping the table top with one large mitt, the other squeezing Addy's knee.

"She'll be fine." Scott didn't sound as sure as he was putting off.

"Scott, I'll call your mama." The threat rolled off Rumor's tongue and landed heavy on Scott's balls.

He sagged a little in his seat and placed his drink back down on the table. "You wouldn't." His challenge was weak and everyone knew it.

She dipped her head, looking for all the world like the smuggest bitch in town.

He spared another second of contemplation then reached into his pocket for his phone, cursing his beautiful wife. The table burst out in laughter, and Rumor sat back, pleased with herself.

Matlyn smiled at the easy posture Addy had settled into. She looked genuinely happy to be sitting next to Pacey, and more importantly, comfortable. Again, her seafoam eyes scanned the bar, looking for gunmetal eyes and a dark head of hair. Behind the bar stood a man in head to toe black. She couldn't see his face, but knew damned well it was him.

* * *

Baker mixed this with that and held the resulting martini out to a woman, nodding as she thanked and paid him, dismissing the way her wanton eyes climbed his body. He wanted nothing to do with her, or the brunette she offered as part of the deal. He rolled his eyes and turned away from her, leaving her gap-mouthed and huffing.

He knew she was here. He'd seen her walk through the door. It made him a little surly—equal parts pissed and excited. And the excited part just pissed him off more.

"Abita Amber," a saucy voice said, catching his attention.

Baker spun to address the customer. His fists clenched and his heart pumped hard. Standing at the bar was the girl with the aquamarine eyes and name tattooed on his shoulder. The girl with the cherry Docs and whiskey-soaked laugh.

"We need to stop meeting like this. With the booze and all. It's painting me in a very bad light." Matlyn chewed on the corner of her lower lip and watched the dark-haired man she'd bumped into twice now.

"Sure," Baker said curtly, everything about him tense.

Her brow furrowed a little, hearing his snappy tone.

"What's that look about?" she questioned. The silence he offered said it all. She drummed her fingers on the bar, her lips pursed in a thin line.

A beat later, Baker turned and his face was a tad softer, a contrite little smile playing on his lips. He handed her a beer and an apology. "Excuse my inner asshole. He gets out more often than I'd like."

Matlyn took the beer and gave him a polite nod. "Rough day?"

"Rough life, but that's not how this…" he motioned between them "…works. You're supposed to unload your worries on me. Part of the job description." The Omen placed his elbows on the bar top and leaned forward, ready to take on her woes.

The stunning girl put her beer down and stepped closer. "Matlyn." She introduced herself, pitching her hand out in a friendly gesture.

He took her delicate hand and shook it. "Baker."

"So you want my sad stories, huh?"

"Happy. I get enough tragedy," he replied, thinking about how true and unfortunate that was.

"Happy. Well … see those two right there?" She looked over her shoulder and pointed in the general direction of her table.

"The voluminous blonde knockout or the pretty little punk?"

"Knockout," Matlyn qualified. The bartender nodded. "They're on their first date. I set them up." She looked quite pleased with herself, smiling smugly.

"To beautiful beginnings, then."

"To beautiful beginnings." She smiled and tipped

the bottle back, taking a healthy swig. "So you're new," she blurted out.

Baker chuckled, bobbing his head.

"Sorry, just meant that I'd never seen you here before … before the last week … or three? Whatever." Sparkling green eyes rolled to the side as if she were trying to pull the correct information from some secret place in her brain. "Yeah, then," she finally murmured.

"Yeah, your face was a little more—"

"Drunk," she interrupted.

"I was going to say flushed."

"You're too kind, Baker." The sound of his name on her lips was sweet. He wondered what it would sound like screamed and half breathless. That thought brought a fleeting spark to his eyes.

"I'm not."

He was being honest with his words, but even he could hear the layers of deep hurt she couldn't understand; so much loaded into two little words. Matlyn shifted her weight and narrowed her gaze. She gave Baker a good long look.

"You're trying though. Have a good night, Baker," she said, letting her hand fall away from the bar as she slowly turned her back and walked away.

Baker smiled, looking down at the business card she'd left behind. Her cell phone number and name were written in clear, strong black ink on the back. The girl had balls. Most women were overconfident in their pursuit. They would lean in too close, find any reason at all to touch him, throw sexual innuendo around like confetti, and hand him room keys like they were handing over the keys to fucking Buckingham Palace. Matlyn was quiet about it, and he respected that.

* * *

"The cat was a spiteful purchase," Matlyn admitted, eyeing the remains of the beer in her hand. "Not really a fan of the grumpy little fucker, to be honest."

Everyone chuckled.

"Why'dya get her?" Addy asked, melting words together in a way that only liquor could.

"Parrish scratched my car, so I got somethin' that would scratch back."

They all gasped at the mention of the injury to Matlyn's green car, knowing good and well how she felt about that car.

"Oh, right. I remember now," Addy declared, not at all oblivious to the way Pacey had shuffled closer, his thigh touching hers. "Bitch did it on purpose. Something about Matlyn ruining her life, blah, blah, blah."

"She was drunk off her tiny ass and blamed me for her breakup with Matt. Mighta told her to suck an egg—or dick. Whatever. Then she keyed my car. So I bought a cat the next day. She hates cats. Neat how things find a way of working themselves out, huh?" Matlyn smiled and shrugged innocently, earning a round of laughter.

Rumor looked sideways at Matlyn, ran her fingertips up Matlyn's thigh, and left it tucked neatly between her legs, leaving no question as to what was running through her pretty little head. She'd been dropping wee hints all night, which, by and large went unnoticed by the rest of people at the table. Not that anyone would have cared. No one here would judge them.

Since her chat with Baker the bartender, Matlyn's head had been bobbing in and out of the gutter, a place her mind frequently roamed to lately, and she'd readily admit to feeling a little … frisky. She leaned to her side and whispered, "Alley," then got up and walked out the side door of the bar without looking to see if Rumor had followed.

Lucy's Bar sat on a corner lot, and the building next door created a narrow alleyway that backed onto the outdoor patio. The patio wasn't visible from the alley, but the Girod St. traffic was. It was dark and that offered just enough concealment for Matlyn to be comfortable.

Besides, she thought, *sex in alleyways is 'bout as common as Sundays around here.*

She leaned against the brick wall and watched as Rumor stepped into the night, followed by her husband.

Two for one, she thought, and a wave of heat flooded her veins.

* * *

Baker's eyes followed Matlyn out the side door and then grew wide when the very female, very beautiful punk stood to follow. His head swiveled and his eyes popped wider still when the man sitting next to her pushed his way out of the booth as well.

Well now, Baker thought, curiosity winning.

Gathering the trash from behind the bar and then the kitchen, he let Zack know he'd be right back, gesturing to the back door. Baker quickly hurled the two bags of garbage into a giant bin and stealthy crept around the side of the building to where he'd seen Matlyn and her friends go. He assumed they'd ducked out to spark up, but that wasn't the case.

Matlyn's shoulders were pressed to the wall, her hips set away from it. Her hands were anchored to the hips of the cute friend. The small amount of light that filtered in from Girod St. washed out the pink highlights in the brunette's hair. That friend had her tongue in Matlyn's mouth.

Baker's eyebrows shot up.

"Really?" he whispered to no one.

Standing opposite the girls stood a tall man with a mess of blue hair that Baker presumed was the husband of the woman now standing between Matlyn's legs. Like Matlyn, they were covered in ink. The woman much less, but it had still been visible from the bar.

He watched fingers disappear beneath Matlyn's black skirt, and a blast of jealousy hit him. Lust, sure that was reasonable, she was stunning, but jealously wasn't … acceptable. Just as he was about to turn and head back into the bar, Matlyn pushed away from the wall and spun, trapping the other girl against the brick. She reached her hand back, the man took it, and she pulled him close.

Jealously rolled into rage. Baker's jaw ticked and his hands balled into fists, but he stayed right where he was, watching.

The blue-haired man's hands moved around to cup Matlyn's breasts as her fingers undid the top button and unzipped his jeans. Matlyn's hand slipped beneath the fabric of the girl's jeans and it was clear, by the way the brunette's back arched, when she pushed inside.

The back of Matlyn's skirt shimmied up, her free hand slammed against the wall, bracing herself. The tattooed, blue-haired mess positioned himself behind her and pulled himself free of his dark jeans. Quickly, he rolled on a condom, stuffing the wrapper into his back pocket. The man had to bend his knees a little to get the angle just right, and then he slipped inside the redhead.

Baker heard the moans from where he stood. He hated wanting to be the one pulling those sounds from her, hated that the thought even entered his mind. The last ninety-nine years of his life as an Omen had been a punishment, but this by far was the cruelest thing he'd been subjected to yet, and he groaned in anger.

Matlyn's head jerked to the side and her eyes landed on him. For the quickest second, she looked nervous, and when that dissolved, a suggestive smirk graced her face, and she winked at him. He shouldn't have been able to see the tiny gesture, but the lights of a passing car lit the alleyway for the briefest second, and she fucking winked.

Six

April 13, 2015, 9 p.m. ~ New Orleans, Warehouse District

Baker flipped the card in his hand, studied Matlyn's handwriting, then slapped it down on his dresser and walked away with his hands clenched in tight, frustrated fists. With a quick tug, he pulled the black Beastie Boys T-shirt over his head and threw it to the floor. He stepped out of his jeans and turned on the hot water. He waited—not so patiently—for the water to warm up.

"Fucking pipes," he cursed, staring at the showerhead, as if his glare alone could correct the temperature. Side-eyeing the dresser where he left the card, his tongue ran over his teeth, and he hissed in irritation as he grew hard. Again.

Under the lukewarm spray, a slide show began behind

his tightly closed eyes: Matlyn with her head thrown back, laughing; Matlyn's soft smile as she stood at the bar and the wicked wink she offered him in the alley; her body pressed between two others—to one she offered pleasure, from the other she took it.

After he dried off, letting the damp towel crumple to the floor where he stood, he waltzed over to his dresser and pulled out a fresh pair of boxer briefs and yanked them on.

You're going to regret this, the Omen thought, snatching the small business card off the dusty surface of the dresser. He rooted through the jeans he'd left on the bathroom floor and pulled out his cell phone. It was kind of an antiquated thing that flipped open. It was a reminder of Baker's solitary existence. It never rang and was rarely used but for the odd pizza delivery.

His eyes slid back and forth between the tiny card taunting him and the sad excuse for a phone. He growled at both then sucked in a deep breath and dialed her number.

It rang twice, three times, and on the fourth he was ready to snap the damn thing shut and do his best to avoid the beautiful Story he'd been sent to Witness.

Once, in 1944, he tried to refuse Witnessing the story of a seven-year-old boy. He walked away, fled the city as fast as he could. It didn't go well. The pain became utterly intolerable, and Baker had been forced to return and finish the Story handed to him. Never again did he turn his back on Witnessing.

"Hello?" A sexy, husky voice piped through the tiny speaker, shocking Baker.

He brought his face back to the phone. "Hello?" he said, unsure.

"Umm … hi?"

"Baker," he offered.

It was silent for a short moment and then, "Baker … hot, asshole bartender at Lucy's, *Baker*?"

"That'd be the one."

"Didn't think you'd call," the girl said, a hint of challenge in her voice.

"Why? Because I saw you get fucked in an alley." The Omen smiled to himself.

"Yeah. That."

Baker made an unimpressed sound and shrugged his shoulders. "Whatever does it for you. And apparently that's men … and women." The smirk on his face grew.

"Why are you calling, Baker?" She paused, but not long enough for him to answer. "After the eyeful you got the other night, either you think I'm an easy fuck, or you're intrigued."

He answered without hesitation. "Intrigued. By *you*, not your proclivities. People aren't as fuckin' odd as they think they are." His overlong existence taught him as much. Humans and their desires … it was all old hat.

"So … a drink, then?" Matlyn asked.

"Where?"

"There's a hole-in-the-wall. Redd's on Maple Street. I'm about ten minutes from there." He heard shuffling in the background, as if she were searching through a drawer. "You know it?"

"No, but I can find it." Moving the sweating bottle of beer, he opened the outdated phonebook that served as his coaster and quickly looked it up, mapping it out on the local trolley route.

"Right. See ya then."

The ink-slinger hung up and Baker pulled on a clean pair of jeans and a reasonably clean T-shirt that fit him like a well-worn, old glove. Sweating, he thought for a second he'd skip the second shirt because it was so damned steamy outside, but the writhing, blacker than pitch ink creeping down his arm made that a tad difficult. So, grudgingly, he tucked himself into a light gray and blue plaid button up.

Sliding his wallet and room key into his pocket, the Omen shut the door behind him.

* * *

"Where ya headin' off to?" Parrish asked, reaching into the dishwasher, lemon-scented steam rolling over her face.

"Nowhere if I can't find my fuckin' keys."

"Next to the fridge." The little Wren tipped her head to the hand-blown glass bowl on the countertop. "Lose your head if it weren't sewn on."

Matlyn reached into the bowl and plucked out her keys. "Swear they make a game out of hidin' on me." She spoke to the keys before shoving them in her pocket and turning back toward the front of the house.

"Not gonna tell me, huh?"

"Redd's for a beer, nosey bitch," she called over her shoulder, blowing her sister a kiss. She bent for a moment, rubbing Syndal's tiny head. "Be nice to Auntie Parrish. She's fixin' to stew your furry ass for that stunt you pulled yesterday." Secretly, she was a little giddy about the peep-toe Syndal had snacked on. *Retribution*, she thought, remembering the twelve-hundred dollar bill for her pouty, little sister's hissy fit.

The tattooed redhead slipped out of the air-conditioned

house and into damp heat. The night air was warm, almost too warm, and wrapped around her as she walked the ten minutes to Redd's bar. She pulled the door open and looked around.

OK, not a dive, per se. More a cozy, rustic hole.

Matlyn took a seat at a small booth facing the door and ordered a beer.

I'm having a drink with a bartender I met at a bar ... that watched me take part in a three-way ... in an alley. Par for a Saturday night.

Her mind wandered while she waited, and her brain began to sketch and draw on the blank canvas her mind created. Colors layered together, shapes took form, and soon enough the picture of an owl appeared. Not the cute, wide-eyed owls that were popping up all over the place, but a large, menacing bird of prey. She pictured it perched on a fallen tree, its eyes focused on something far away. The steadfast stare made her skin prickle, and she shook her head, wiping the image away like the quick shake of an Etch-a-Sketch. When she looked up, a tall, pale, raven-haired man was standing at the booth looking down at her. She tipped her chin and glanced at the seat across from her, willing him to sit.

He said, sounding almost ashamed of himself, "I shouldn't be here." No "*hi, how's it going*" or anything that came close to sounding like a greeting.

"But you're intrigued," the cinnamon girl stated, skipping the formal greeting and staring him down, really noticing the few freckles that graced his face.

"I am." He studied her too, and slowly his eyes dropped,

skating down her shoulders and finally landing on Matlyn's hands circling a bottle of beer.

"Why?" she asked.

"Maybe it's the color on your skin, maybe the way you walk like you couldn't give a fuck." His eyes shot up and connected with her. "Maybe it's those green fucking pools that I feel like I'm sinking in."

She pressed her thighs together and bit her bottom lip. Being prone to fidgeting, the girl began to slowly turn the bottle in circles on the tabletop.

The Omen paused for just the smallest breath, and admitted, "Maybe I just want, *just once*, to stand next to something beautiful and not feel like I'm the reason it's breaking."

The words threw her, but the tone was so pitiful that she couldn't help reaching out across the table to him. "*Breaking*? I … Who's broken?" she questioned.

He looked around the room, his eyes touching on each person for the briefest second. "Everyone in some small way … a little more every day." The curious man shook his head and looked down at his arm. "But that's my issue."

Something about what he said smacked of secrets to Matlyn, but she wasn't about to go digging into his dirty laundry. Religion, politics, and dark pasts were topics best left for the second date. *Was this a date?* she pondered.

"Are you always this depressing?" She flicked his hand and smiled.

Baker chuckled and shook his head. A crooked smile turned his almost-perfect lips up. "You always get it on in dark alleys?"

A flirty look in place, she sat back with an easy sigh

and ran her tongue over her top lip. "No. That was a first. The alley … not the three-way."

"Exhibitionist?" he purred, his eyes crackling with mischief.

"Sometimes. Voyeur?" she fired back in a coquettish tone and began folding her soggy napkin.

He shook his head slightly. "A first."

"Watching or the three-way?"

"Watching. Unless porn counts. Does it count?"

Amused, the girl laughed and it was a throaty, smooth laugh. Baker reached out and snagged Matlyn's beer, taking a swig. "Not bad," he proclaimed, tipping it toward the waitress, indicating he'd like one, and then placed it back in front of her. "You seemed, and correct me if I'm wrong, *comfortable* with them."

Rosy cheeked, she smiled slyly. She'd known Rumor since high school, meeting in the eleventh grade when Rumor was forced to switch schools mid-year. She was a fighter back then, not a lover—a scrappy, skinny little thing who favored fists over words. Apparently school administrators frowned on that kind of behavior, and Rumor was expelled.

Matlyn took to her immediately, seeing a kind girl buried under issues too heavy for her slim shoulders. Rumor's mother up and left one morning; no note, no explanation, she just walked out the door, bags in hand, and never looked back. The chip on her shoulder was understandable.

"Polite way of asking if we've fucked before." She drummed her fingers on the tabletop and made a sound that could pass for a chuckle. She'd been joining them for years. It was an every-now-and-again kind of thing.

"Scott and Rumor met in college and married about two years ago. They've got their kinks. Other woman … a little breath-play occasionally." She shrugged. She was in no position to judge others and their secret penchants. "I stood in their wedding. Can you picture this in bright blue chiffon?" she said, waving a hand over her body.

* * *

"I'm sure you managed," Baker said, his voice peppered with just a hint of sarcasm.

"Your accent," she said. "You're not from here, at least not originally."

"Castlebar, Ireland. I moved to Chicago when I was fourteen," he told her, omitting the fact that it was the Chicago the world knew in the 1800s. "But I've moved around a lot."

"Army brat?"

"Nah. More like a gypsy. Never in one place too long." Out of necessity, not some wanderlust that pulled at his soul, but he left that out of the narrative. He would have much rather settled down. He wanted the roots, not the wings, but that wasn't his fate, and it surely wasn't his fucking call; someone else was pulling on that string.

Matlyn tipped her head, an inquisitive look on her face as she searched the features of the beautiful stranger across from her. "To see the world? Or to see how much distance you could put between you and your family? It just seems to me that people like you that never stick around, either have an itch inside them that makes them prone to wandering or they're running."

For a moment the ageless Omen was quiet,

contemplating how to best word it. "My family's gone. My parents died a long time ago." Which was the truth. A bullet took his father and Consumption took his mother not long after.

Matlyn's face fell at his words and her fingers laced together, gripping tight. "I was twelve when my parents died. Freak car accident on a rainy night," she explained. "My sister and I were at a slumber party that my mom didn't even want us to go to because we'd been dicks that day. My father won that argument, luckily."

Baker knew luck had zero to do with Matlyn and her sister not being in that car. It wasn't their time. Their Stories had not yet begun, simple as that. Luck was a foolish notion created by humans to explain away things like this. It wasn't luck when a tornado came down on the neighbor's house, but left the next standing. It wasn't luck when someone won the jackpot at the casino. It was all part of a story that was written for them years before they were born. Fate, not luck, kept the Wren girls safe that night. And fate sent that car careening into the guard rail.

* * *

For an hour they lobbed questions back and forth, casual type conversation. His borderline cocky disposition was sexy and the secrets she knew were simmering right under the surface added to the mystery of him. He was the classic brooding male—something that would normally annoy her to no end. A flash of anger or resentment would peek through for just the slightest moment and leave the woman wondering. What happened to build such a dynamic person?

"So the ink?" Baker asked, reaching for her hand and

pulling it across the table. "I've found, and correct me if I'm wrong, that there are three types of tattoo-ees. The follower—the person that does it to follow a trend; the fucking posers of the tattoo world."

Matlyn nodded, watching as his thumb sweep back and forth over the tattoo on her wrist—a small bird in white ink.

"Then there's the artist—the person who sees tattooing as a form of art and their body a canvas. Last, there's the storyteller—the person that uses tattoos as a means of telling their story. The ink kind of represents a moment in their life that they feel needs commemorating. The artist and the storyteller often blend, though."

"That about covers it, yeah." Seafoam eyes remained fixed on her wrist and his warm, rough thumb.

"You're obviously not the trendy sorority house chick with a tiny butterfly on her hip. What about this one?" he asked, his thumb gently tapping her inner wrist, not meeting her eyes.

"That was my first. My namesake." She stared as he traced the thin lines of the white inked wren with its wings spread wide, wrapping around her wrist.

Finally looking up, Baker asked, "No story there, just a name?"

She was watching him, watching the way his thumb moved. A light pink flush had begun to creep over her face, she felt warm.

She took a deep breath and slowly brought her eyes back to his face. "Name aside, I was awkward, long limbs and no grace. Typical wasn't my thing. I never dreamed of being a ballerina. Making it up the porch steps without face-planting was a daily goal. I dreamed of wings that would take me off my feet. Wings that would take me to beautiful places full of color and texture." She shrugged a shoulder in a way that brought that awkward little girl to the surface.

"Past tense. You don't feel that way anymore?"

"No. I grew up and left awkward in the playground. Still have shit for grace, though." She laughed at herself, blushing a little deeper. She decided to move the spotlight. "First time watching, but not the threesome?" His head tilt told her he wasn't following. "Earlier you said the alley was the first time you'd watched anyone have sex." Her voice dropped.

"Yeah …?" He shifted uncomfortably, and Matlyn caught something in his eyes.

"But not the threesome," she said again, grinning like the cat that got the canary.

Baker laughed and Matlyn took notice that his fingers hadn't stopped touching her skin.

* * *

"No. I was younger … there was booze, women, and coke, if I'm remembering correctly." He omitted the part about it being the late 1970s when hair was big, music questionable, and the drug of the moment was cocaine. "I don't remember much," not a lie, "just these big, beautiful boobs bouncing in my face." He held his hands out in front of his chest, as if cupping said boobs.

"A tit man. Figures." Matlyn smirked and shook her head.

"No, no. Really," he defended. "It's not the tits, though, don't get me wrong, lots of love there. Couldn't give a shit if it's an A cup or an F. It's the package as a whole. The smooth skin, the sway and curve of a hip, the underside of a breast, regardless of size or shape. It's just … women."

Polished-metal eyes dropped to her chest; he was openly taking it all in, no shame whatsoever in the way he devoured her colorful skin, the suggestion of cleavage, or the swoop of her long neck.

"You're oh so *very* straight," she said, watching as his eyes moved over her again.

"Guilty. And you're not."

"Nope. Does that bother you?" A hint of self-consciousness seeped into her voice. It sounded old, maybe related to that little girl who wished for wings.

"No. We are who we are. It's when people try to change themselves that things get fucked-up."

That brought a smile to her freckled face.

Noticing the bar had emptied, Baker said, "They're gonna kick us out soon. Walk you to your car?"

"I walked." Matlyn left a generous tip at the table and stood.

Baker rose up from the table. His hand nervously scratched the back of his neck. "I'll drive you home, then."

"It's only a few blocks," she began to protest, shaking her head.

"I wasn't asking, Matlyn. It's three in the fucking morning. I'm driving you." The edge to his voice cut off the I'm-a-big-girl rant that was likely brewing, and she simply nodded and turned toward the door. Baker's hand found the small of her back and led her forward. "Good," he said when she didn't fight him.

"This is yours?" Matlyn asked, her hand gliding along the side of the truck. It looked like a caress.

"Yes, ma'am."

The girl spun on her heels, ginger hair flying about, and leveled him with a glare that would melt a snowball. "Call me that again, dude, and I'll tattoo pink ribbons and fluffy kittens all over your ass. I'm twenty-eight, not eighty-seven, fucker."

Laughing, he held open the truck door. "You got it, Miss Daisy." He shut the door as she faced the window, tongue out and middle finger up.

I shouldn't be here, he thought for the millionth time since he'd entered the bar, pulling open the driver's door. But he'd be a goddamned liar if he denied the pull he felt between them. A pull that had nothing to do with the Witnessing. It wasn't compulsion, it was want. He hated it, wanted it to go away, even so much as resented that beautiful girl for what she was doing to him, but he couldn't, wouldn't deny it. He wanted her.

"Which way?" he asked, fastening his seat belt and looking into the aquamarine-eyes of the girl next to him.

Seven

❖

The four minute ride home had been heavy with tension. Matlyn sat still and silent, listening to the Black Crowes croon. The rumble of the truck's engine sent a comfortable vibration through her body. She sneaked a peek at the driver, side-eying him. His long fingers were wrapped tightly around the vinyl steering wheel and his jaw was clenched, his five o'clock scruff doing little to disguise it. Fleetingly, she wondered what it would feel like to run her tongue along that jaw.

But she quickly recognized the annoyance pluming off him like smoke from a stack, and it made it hard to breathe. If it wasn't for his insistence, she would have thought he didn't want her in his truck. Or anywhere *near* him. His mercurial mood soured her. She brought her eyes back to the road in front of her, pointing to the house on the left side of the street as they approached. Feeling a little put-off, her lips were pursed in a tight line, working hard to keep her mouth shut, rather than ask why he'd even bothered calling.

The old truck pulled into the driveway of the beautiful brick house. Though it was dark and only the headlights lit the exterior, the house was colorfully decorated. Corals mixed with teal details and creams softened the structure. He pushed the gear shift into park and dropped his hands to his lap, jaw ticking, teeth grinding.

Her eyes stayed on him, observing.

"I doubt for a hot fucking minute that a sharp-tongued, sharp-witted lass like yourself, didn't catch that quick the shift in my mood," he speculated, a thick layer of something like guilt brushed over each word. He shifted in his seat, his eyes wandered. "I don't want to leave you feelin' like you're the reason. Everything fades and wilts around me." His voice dropped, and guilt morphed into pain. The raven-haired boy, with the suddenly dark attitude, flexed his hands in his lap and took a deep breath. "I'm sorry. Can we chalk it up to my being an asshole?"

Turning to him fully and watching him force the air from his lungs, Matlyn played with the hem of her T-shirt, something that felt like rejection and annoyance made her jumpy, and her knee bounced. "O-okay," she whispered.

Without a word he slipped out of the truck, walked around to the slender woman, opened her door, and offered his hand to help her from the cab of the truck.

The annoyance that had flared in her lifted and her knee stilled. *Holy fucking whiplash, Batman!* Matlyn thought, taking his hand and sliding out of the open truck door, her Docs landing on the pavement with a light thud. She closed the door behind her and kept her eyes on her feet, taking notice that Baker had yet to release her hand. His thumb swept across her wrist again, prompting her to lift her eyes.

Baker's gorgeous face was set in a smirk that was quickly becoming his trademark look. Slowly, he raised her hand to his mouth and lightly brushed his lips against her knuckles, his eyes steady on her face.

"Goodnight, Matlyn," he said in a deep, but hushed voice. He dropped her hand and slinked back to the driver's seat without another look.

The befuddled woman stepped back and watched as he pulled out of the driveway and then stood and listened to the rumble of the gunmetal truck as it drove off.

* * *

April 17, 2015, 6:20 p.m. ~ GW Fins, New Orleans

"I don't know … she's weird. She's totally distracted. She goes out to meet someone at a fucking spit-hole, comes home at three in the morning, and just stands in the driveway. Weird." Parrish wriggled in her seat, adjusting the skirt bunching under her legs. "There's gotta be a person attached to that dazed 'n' horny look on her face," she deduced, her finger tip-toeing down an expense report, looking for gaps and errors.

"Kettle, meet teapot," Wilson said, tapping her hand with the restaurant's wine list.

Parrish looked up sheepishly and smiled big.

"Maybe she's just in a good mood?" he offered.

She shook her head. "Nope. Good mood Matlyn dances in her underwear to "Walking on Sunshine." Good mood Matlyn eats cherry Pop Tarts and hums "I Wish I

Were an Oscar Mayer Weiner." Good mood Matlyn *does not* wash her whites with her colors or put cheese in the freezer."

"And you assume romantic interference?"

Parrish ordered the wine, closed the file she had open in front of her, and answered, "Three things fuck with my sister's flow: A project—like home renos, a challenging tattoo." She counted off, flicking her finger upward like a jack knife. "Cock." She flicked another finger. "Pus—"

Wilson held up his hand and chuckled.

"Law of probability, sir." She slipped her bright orange stiletto off and let her bare foot wander up Wilson's muscular leg. Lightly, she nuzzled her foot between his legs, applying the gentlest pressure. Her grin grew as he shifted in his seat.

* * *

In the far corner of the restaurant, Ingrid sat watching the couple, feeling their Stories mingle on her skin, one flowing into the other until they were indistinguishable. She smiled sadly, recalling a similar scene.

Once upon a time she sat in a dimly-lit restaurant, flirting with a handsome man, blushing at his acknowledgments. Her life was to take a very different path, but she couldn't help but see a little of her once-upon-a-time self in the beautiful strawberry-blond. The adoration in Wilson's gestures made her smile widen. Small crinkles formed at the corners of her kind hazel eyes. When the warm rush of Witnessing subsided, she finished her white wine spritzer, paid her bill, and escaped without notice.

She slid the keycard into the thin mouth of the electronic keyhole and listened for the disengaging lock. Inside her suite, the Omen tossed her keys to the bedside table, slipped coral shoes off, then her dress. With care, she hung up the gray garment and tucked the shoes into the closet. She dropped onto the king-sized bed with a wistful sigh. After a minute or two, she climbed under the covers and reached for the television remote, surfing for something to ease her out of her memories.

Unlike Baker, Ingrid was well to do. Light Omens tended to fall into luck, and in 2003, Ingrid played the slots at The Excalibur Casino in Las Vegas, winning the casino's largest payout on a progressive machine ever, just shy of forty million. Being an intelligent woman, the woman invested in a couple low-risk portfolios and eleven years later, Ingrid— sometimes Stokes, sometimes Browning—was worth an easy seventy-six million dollars. That money came in handy when travelling for her next *Story*. She knew not all Omens had the carefree-type of life she did, and she pitied those that were forced to roam without shelter, and often food.

Omens, both Light and Dark, existed just outside the world of the living, though they very much lived and breathed like humans. *Like* was the operative word. They appeared human for all intents and purposes, however, Omens required very little to subsist. Food wasn't a necessity, but an indulgence, and sleep was an old human habit that much like breathing, seemed to be involuntary, though not particularly needed.

Lights off, TV quietly humming away, Ingrid slipped off into a dreamless sleep.

* * *

"Four days," Matlyn grumbled, pushing small bottles of

colorful ink into a storage cupboard. "Four days." She gestured wildly in front of her and slammed the cupboard door closed.

Parrish stormed out of her sister's office, hands on her hips and her mouth puckered. "Who pissed in your Wheaties this mornin'? Christ, these doors can't handle much more of your abuse, Matlyn Kharis!"

"I hate Wheaties. An' don't fuckin' middle name me." Her eyes stayed trained to the clipboard in her hand.

With a quick movement, the youngest Wren snatched the clipboard from her sister and promptly swatted her upper arm with it. "Who is it? Who's got your panties all wet 'n' twisted, Little Bird?"

She just shrugged, huffed, and tried to make a grab for the clipboard, but the wily girl dodged her easily, taking a step back and smiling an overly sweet smile.

"Oh, c'mon, Little Bird. Don't go cloudin' over and rainin' all over my parade. I'm right, and I *know* it. Who did you go meet the other night at Redd's?" Her voice pitched high in a sing-song.

Campbell walked over, hearing the conversation. She didn't say anything, she just looked between the two women, a little curious and a little concerned.

Again, the annoyed ink-slinger huffed. "Baker," she finally offered in a small voice.

"Who's that?" Campbell asked, leaning against the wall in the hallway.

"Who's what?" Scott's voice piped in behind Campbell. He stood behind her, his chin rested comfortably on the top of her head.

"Let's call a damned staff meeting, since we're gathered

'round. Christ on a Christmas cookie!" Matlyn groaned, looking at the small crowd that had gathered in the hall. She looked to Campbell. "The missed opportunity outside of Lucy's."

Campbell just grinned knowingly and nodded. Scott and Parrish wore similar well-out-with-it expressions.

"A few weeks ago we were all at Lucy's … the night I introduced Pacey and Adeline," she prompted. "I was drunk, he offered to hail a cab for Campbell and me, and my face was all fucked." Matlyn's hand swept over her face.

"Facial slur," both Scott and Parrish deadpanned, nodding to one another.

"Anyway … I saw him again Saturday. He's the bartender at Lucy's. Gave him my number." She looked to her blue-haired colleague. "He saw us in the alley." Her head tilted just the slightest and a slow smirk worked its way across her face.

"Saw you in the alley, *what?*" Parrish asked, eyebrows hiding in her hairline.

Matlyn cleared her throat and rocked on her heels, but said nothing, just dug her hands into the pockets of her jeans.

Scott stood behind Campbell, silent but smug as fuck.

"Oh. My. God," Parrish whispered, shaking her head.

"Wha—" Campbell stopped mid-word and gasped, holding her hand to her heart. "He saw you … *you two?*" In a childish gesture, she jabbed her index finger through a ring she'd made with her other hand, the universal, if crude, sign for screwing.

"Three," Scott corrected. "And Rumor's still smilin'

about that. Thank you." He rolled his hand away from his head, like tipping a hat, and bowed.

"Holy doodle ... you're all whores. I work with whores," Campbell said, shaking her head and putting her arm around Matlyn's waist. "But I love you all." Campbell's honesty and sweetness were a shining quality that the Parabola crew admired greatly, regardless of how much shit they dished at her, they wouldn't wish her any other way.

Matlyn kissed the mocha-skinned girl's hairline and smiled.

"Want my advice?" Campbell asked, looking to her boss.

"Um advice from *Saint Campbell*, virgin queen of the French Quarters ... mmm ... maybe not," Matlyn hummed the word, shaking her head and wrinkling her nose at her young friend.

Campbell chuckled and pinched her co-worker's side. "Call him. He called you, so you've got his number, silly." She tipped her head in an *obvious-solution* kind of way, then turned and strolled back down the hall toward the front of the store.

"Smart girl," Scott commented, nodding his approval.

Making a shooing gesture, Parrish said, "Go. Call. I'll finish the list. Half of these numbers are probably wrong anyway."

Matlyn made a sound as if to protest, but was quickly cut off.

"I found your toothbrush, by the way ... In the fridge ... next to the jam. Go. Call. Please," Parrish begged, clasping her hands together in prayer.

"Assholes, all of you," she mumbled and turned toward

her office then stopped dead and spun to face Scott and her sister. "Did she call us *whores*?" Her green eyes went saucer wide.

Scott stared for a moment before opening his mouth. "Well pick my peas! I think Baby Campbell just broke her naughty hymen."

Matlyn sat at her desk, wiped her slick hands on her skin-tight jeans—twice—then rooted through her bag for her cell phone. Sliding her finger across the screen, she searched the call log and low and behold, Baker's number. She thought of the way his fingertips caressed the inside skin of her wrist and the way his warm lips grazed her knuckles and then tapped out a quick message and hit send.

Two seconds later the text failed. She tried again. Failed.

"Damn it." She hit call, mumbling something about big girl panties and held her breath. She hated that he made her nervous. Nervousness wasn't a natural part of her repertoire. Her cool, calm (mostly) collectedness she got from her mother, and it was something she prided herself on.

Parrish, on the other hand, was a shoot first ask questions later type of gal, much like their father, Harris. He was sweet, analytical, often a man of few words—not a trait Parrish picked up—curious, and sometimes a little shy.

Veronica, the girls' mother, was bubbly in that infectious, need-to-be-near-you kind of way. She was mellow and not easily shaken. She was honest, sometimes to a fault, but that was the thing Harris had loved most about her. That, and to the best of Matlyn's memory, her killer ass. The sisters would giggle and roll their eyes every time they caught him ogling his wife's backside.

"Um … hello?" Baker's voice was so uncertain and puzzled, she was sure she'd caught him at a bad time.

"Baker, it's Matlyn, did I catch you—"

"Yeah. What?" His tone was clipped, terse.

She pulled the phone away from her ear and gave it a what-the-fuck look before drawing it back to her. *Obviously that was a gentle let down*, she thought of his actions outside the truck, seeing them differently now.

"Okay," she breathed out. "My mistake." She slowly began to lower the phone to her lap, still throwing evil glares at it, finger hovering over the *End Call* button.

"No … wait!" She heard him call.

She brought the phone back to her ear and made a low noise, letting him know she was still there.

"I mean …" he let out a long, defeated sigh "… hold on while I gag that asshole and shove 'em in the closet."

Matlyn chuckled softly, running her finger over the grooves in the wooden desktop.

"Did I get you at a bad time?" she asked.

"No, yeah … no. I … shit."

Again, Matlyn laughed and something inside her relaxed a little more.

"I don't get a lot of calls, what with my *shining personality* and all. I'm an asshole, 'kay?"

"Agreed," she said with a touch of humor.

"So to what do I owe the honor?"

The girl's natural snark and candor spat the words forward before she had the chance to swallow them. "Bored, horny, lonely. Really itchin' for a game of racquetball, actually. Not a euphemism," she clarified, "I haven't played in weeks. Care to join me?"

"Uh … you're asking me out? To play racquetball, not have sex? Just to clarify."

"I don't have sex with assholes."

"Well then, count this asshole in."

* * *

Matlyn walked into the enclosed court in tiny black shorts and a bright green exercise bra.

She's got a thing for that fuck-ugly color.

But the fuck-ugly color took a back seat to the words inked on Matlyn's upper right thigh that Omen couldn't drag his eyes away from.

"It was my favorite book as a child." She interrupted his blatant ogling, bouncing the small rubber ball on the court.

"Can't say I recognize the quote." Gray eyes moved up her body—slowly—to her face.

"*Bridge to Terabithia*. Read it about forty times after my parents died. I kinda felt like its pages were the only thing holding me up sometimes." She turned to Baker. Her eyes were soft and a little lost, and he hated the vulnerability he saw in them. Hated the way it made his chest heavy and full all at the same time.

When he didn't speak, Matlyn looked over to him, giving him a once-over, quirking her brow. "You're gonna sweat balls in long sleeves, Baker. Lose the shirt. I promise I won't stare. Much."

Baker rocked uncomfortably from one foot to the next. It'd been a lifetime since he had anything close to a relationship. Anything that was just his. As his selfish need to connect with another human took over, common sense walked right out the fucking door. He should have said no. He should have hung up the moment he registered her voice. But he didn't.

The Dark Omen was bone tired of being pulled by some invisible pulse. He was tired of watching Death come again and again. He was tired of being alone. For a split second, Baker thought about pulling his shirt over his head and letting it drop to the ground. He thought about laying it all out for Matlyn to see.

How would he explain *her* name on *his* skin? How could he possibly account for the defining moments of her twenty-eight years inked across his upper body? And the way the ink writhed and moved, as if it were a living thing, slithering to a call neither could hear.

No, he would keep his shirt on.

"Lose the green bra-top thing. I promise I won't stare. Much," he challenged, eyes roaming her slender, creamy body, skipping along the subtle cinnamon freckles that dotted her skin, the tattoos popping out here and there making his mouth water.

"A smooth talkin' asshole—unheard of." She shook her head and a sly grin pulled the corner of her mouth up. "C'mere." The pretty Story waved him over and went over the rules, talking about foot placement, faults, service areas, and receiving areas, skips ... and somewhere around balls hitting the wall, he lost his focus on her words and pictured her backed against the court wall, naked; ugly, bright green bra nowhere to be found.

They played for an hour. At first he was lost in the way she moved and grunts that dropped from her mouth every time she swung the racket. The girl's long limbs served her well as she bounced around the court perusing the ball. He watched her muscles tense and contract, watched her soft skin dampen with sweat, watched it follow invisible streams down her neck, between her breasts.

When wanting morphed and was replaced by an old self-hate and anger, he focused it all on that little red ball, relishing the pounding of his feet against the court and the satisfying *smack* of the ball against the front wall. Sweat dripped from him, his breathing was heavy, but his frustration was much less.

"I get it now," the exhausted Omen panted.

"What?" She tossed a towel at him.

"The game. Why you play." He blew out, bending forward and placing his hands on his knees, he looked up at the girl in the ugly bra. "No mercy, no fucks given. Great way to release a little pent up rage."

She nodded, taking a long pull from her water bottle before offering it to Baker.

"So tell me, beautiful ink-slinger, what's got your panties so bunched up that you feel the need to abuse this rubber ball so fucking thoroughly, huh?"

For a moment she said nothing, did nothing, then slowly her face turned toward him.

"You."

Eight

A loud popping sound pushed through the course of voices and music, moving with such force that it displaced the air to the left of Baker's head.

Two fingers of whiskey cupped in beautifully-cut glass slipped from his hand, moving in slow motion, like the world had jerked to a stop. That one glass fought to keep moving, but the strain on it was too much. It clamored to the ground, shattering in a million sharp shards. The amber liquid splattered all around him, dousing his shoes.

Baker reached for his gun, taking aim at the men that had entered the bar. In a hasty action, he flung his arm out in front of him, cocking the hammer and squeezing the trigger. The bullet flew from the chamber, forcing a shudder through his body that worked up his right arm and resonated clear through each muscle and bone, straight to his toes.

The bullet connected with flesh, and Baker watched as a dark stain spread like an inkblot on a light gray jacket. The man dropped his gun and clutched his right shoulder, cursing.

Baker spoke in a loud, harsh voice as he walked toward him, gun still raised and at the ready. "Are you fucking simple? Bringing your men here!" Here was The Lock and Keel—Heeney territory—the bar his uncle, Niall, built (on dirty money). It provided the curtain that hid the Heeney family's dark dealings from the eyes of Chicago's law and had been for eight years.

And now Edgar-fucking-Four-Eyes-Foils was busting up the place, looking to claim the city of Chicago for himself and his pathetic band of merry men.

Baker aimed the gun at Edgar's head. "Fool," he whispered as he pulled the trigger. The smell of gunpowder was strong, and the ringing in his ears nearly drowned out the screams of the women cowering behind tipped tables.

Before he could lower his gun, Baker heard another shot pulse through the room, and just like the whiskey in the glass, he fought against gravity. His knees hit the floor. He blinked and looked down at his chest. The new white shirt he'd bought earlier that day burst into a mix of reds—vibrant and bright at the outer edges of the growing stain, darker and richer in the center.

It looked to him as if it were happening in tiny increments, inching outward at a steady but sluggish pace, but all the while hell roared on around him. The quick and darting movements seemed unreal and out of place to Baker.

Slowly, so slowly, his body slouched to the wooden floor, too heavy to fight anymore.

Gravity wins again, he'd thought.

He turned his head to the side, watching feet scramble about the place; where, he didn't know. Then, through jostling bodies and the chaos, a dark gray image emerged, as if sprung from fog. As it neared, Baker watched the shape shift and within seconds, a man dressed in charcoal was crouched before him.

"A hundred years of service. A hundred years of Witnessing death. You will write their histories. The key to your salvation will be born in pain and written upon your skin."

* * *

Baker stared up at her, tying his shoelace in a kind of rote, mechanical way. He stood and walked slowly toward her, as she shifted uncomfortably. He traced one finger from elbow to wrist, feeling the moisture on her skin.

"Why?" he asked, watching the rise and fall of her chest.

Her breath stuttered on the way in. "A little honesty … I don't know, Baker." She shook her head and dropped her eyes to his hand now clasped around her wrist.

Matlyn had never been the girl that chased down her crushes or obsessed over someone. She'd experienced want. She wanted Kory-Rae, she wanted Cohen, but she never *needed* them. Need would have made walking away impossible. It was much easier to shut the door on want. But what festered inside her was something just outside of want. It was something she couldn't really define and wrap up neatly with a few words. She wanted him, yes, but she didn't know why she felt as though she *needed* to pursue him.

"There's this ribbon …" Matlyn motioned between them and let her hand rest on his chest, feeling him pull at the air slowly, so controlled. "The more I pull away, the tighter it gets. You can't tell me it's not the same for you. You wouldn't be here if it wasn't." She knew it was the truth, and she smiled sadly, her hand dropping away slowly.

"You shouldn't say shit like that."

The warning was in his voice, but she couldn't accept it. "Why? It's honest." She stepped closer to Baker, leaving only the slightest bit of space between them. The air moving around them was warm and carried the smell of sweat.

"It's dangerous." Though his tone was clipped, his face was soft and almost troubled. Matlyn could nearly see the two halves ripping apart, pulling at Baker.

"*You're* dangerous?" she said, incredulous. "Nope. Sorry. I don't believe that for a minute." She crossed her arms over her chest, defiant. Baker's hand never moved. "Do you want to hurt me? Is that what's in it for you?" Staring headlong into his eyes, she watched for a tell, or something that would provide her with a little information. Quiet, patiently, she waited for him to speak, but instead he dropped his head, eying his shoes.

He shook his head.

Was he hiding something? Yes, and she could feel it all around him like a shell, but was he dangerous? No.

Overheating, sweaty, and muscles burning, she reached out again, plucking the soggy shirt way from his chest. She could feel his heart slam against his ribcage. "Your shirt's soaked. Shoulda ditched it."

He lurched forward, walking her body backward, both hands coming around her neck. His thumbs skimmed the undersides of her chin, angling her face upward. She gasped when her warm, exposed skin met the cold wall.

His mouth pressed down on hers, hard and aggressive. Matlyn's fingers spread wide, feeling the small dimples in the concrete behind her. Blood rose to the surface of her skin, heating her from within, and she opened her mouth, letting him in.

He took another step, trapping Matlyn thoroughly. The redhead's chest heaved, her lungs dying for just a little more oxygen, but she refused to give up the kiss.

A tap on the Plexiglass that made up the back wall of the court broke them apart. A girl with a high ponytail and a purple staff shirt stood on the other side, slowly shaking her head and rubbing one index finger over the other. A funny smile flitted across her face, and she turned and walked away.

Shame on us, Matlyn thought, red-faced and panting.

"Fuck," Baker groaned, turning away from the plexiglass and blatantly adjusting himself. Matlyn smirked and quickly slipped past him to the ladies' changing room.

* * *

"Jesus, that's inconvenient!" Baker complained as he closed the car door behind him, Matlyn laughing a full, throaty laugh as she slipped behind the wheel. "You know the average adult male gets eleven erections in a day. Eleven! Fucking inconvenience."

He laughed with her, loving the sound of it.

"Eleven. Christ, that seems … excessive. And what

number was that, dare I ask?" The engine purred and the frame rumbled as the green car came to life.

"Four. That was the fourth, and it's only fucking 6:00 p.m." He shook his head, grimacing. "Morning wood, which though it has its merit, and sometimes serves a purpose, it's mostly useless. Then there was the shower," he continued. "Apparently, a little soap and the right water pressure is all it takes."

He watched from the passenger seat as her tiny frame shook with laughter. She couldn't remember the last time someone pulled a reaction like that from her. Her gut hurt in the best way.

"Oh, and the wicked hard-on I got when you called this morning." His voice wavered just the slightest bit, as if he'd admitted too much. "And, well, you witnessed the last one. Your fault, again."

Her chuckle slowed and she put the car into drive, pulling away from the fitness center toward the old motel where she'd picked Baker up.

Silence filled the car. Awkward silence was something Matlyn hated almost as much as the hum of cicada bugs in the summer. Fuckers kept her up all night sometimes.

"You should come for dinner," she suggested, nervously tapping the wheel. Her eyes darted from the road to Baker and back again.

"You cook?"

"Not even a little, but I have all the best places on speed dial."

He grinned.

"Cooking's a Parrish trait, something she picked up

from Mom. She got all the domestic good-wife skills. Great with finances, food, even finds cleaning relaxing."

"But not you?" Baker tipped his head like a dog trying to decipher his master's words.

"No. No domestic diva here, but I can rebuild the engine of a 1967 Chevy, refinish old furniture, and blend the perfect shade of red for blood." She shrugged and turned the wheel to the right, watching the traffic around them.

"Valid skills," he replied, nodding.

"So is evasion. Come for dinner."

His teeth pinched his bottom lip as he considered her invitation. Suddenly, he winced as if in pain and rubbed his chest. Finally answering, his voice was strained when he said, "Eight o'clock."

"Eight," she repeated.

* * *

Eight o'clock came and went. Matlyn packed up the food and dragged herself up the stairs to her studio-room. The chemical smell of paint filled her nose as she opened the door. With a huff, she stripped out of her clothes and left them in a heap by the door then threw on the white paint-smeared wifebeater sitting on the table top.

The steamy night air poured into the room as she opened the window and pulled a nicely rolled joint from a small Coca-Cola tin sitting on a table covered in art supplies. In her underwear and a slightly oversized, over-worn tank, she held the joint between her lips and tied her hair up in a messy ponytail.

As she lit the end of the joint, she inhaled deeply, pulling smoke into her lungs. After a few good pulls, she went to the canvas she'd begun a few days ago, brush in hand.

Two hours passed and Matlyn had moved on to a blank canvas. Dark colors formed fuzzy shapes. Eyes, delicately patterned feathers, and large, intimidating wings were taking form. Sharp, eye-popping red encased the form. She stepped back, looking at it.

An owl.

She tipped her head, examining its pitch-black eyes that didn't seem quite deep enough. Behind her, the door creaked open, but she didn't turn, she just continued to stare into the bird's dark eyes.

"Sorry, Pare. I'll turn down the music." She moved toward the stereo on the corner of the table to lower the volume when a rough hand reached out and stopped her movement. She jumped and then turned quickly, preparing to fight.

He caught her arm as she swung in blind fear.

"Stop!"

The voice pulled her focus, and standing before her was Baker, a deep sadness in his eyes. He looked defeated and worn down. Exhausted.

"I'm sorry," he whispered, just barely louder than the music still playing. "Your sister let me in. I shouldn't ... I shouldn't be here." His words were strained, as if he were begging her to understand something.

He clutched the hem of her shirt in one hand, his other still gripping her arm firmly.

Matlyn's nostrils flared. Anger and rejection lit her face. She wanted to push him right back out that door and gave him an ineffective shove. "You keep saying that!" She shoved again. "Why do you keep saying that?"

"I'm sorry," he said again.

The desperation in his words, in the way his hands fisted the material and pulled her forward broke, Matlyn's anger and whatever vitriol she was about to spit at him died in her mouth. Her hand reached up and cupped the back of his neck, pulling him down to her.

Inches from her lips, he said, "I won't be able to stop it. I can't stop it. I'm sorry." His hands trembled and his body began to quiver, as though he were stripped bare and left in the cold.

"Don't," Matlyn said in a hushed voice, pushing up on her toes and bringing her mouth to his.

Nine

❦

"Don't," she said again, and Baker didn't miss the edge of anger in her voice. Not anger for being stood up, no. Her anger was hidden in the idea that he might hold back, or worse, walk away altogether.

Her grip on his neck tightened and as her tongue slid against his, he knew the moment his shirt came off he would have 131 years of explaining to do.

Baker pulled her dirty, paint-splattered tank over her head, exposing her small but full and perfectly round breasts. More ink swirled between them, and he bent his body to taste them.

Do I start with the first person I killed?

His tongue swirled around Matlyn's hard, dark pink nipple, and she let out a loud groan.

The first time a gun was placed in my hands?

He dropped to his knees in front of her, his hands

anchored around her waist, head craning upward to reach her heaving tits. He sucked hard on the already sensitive flesh, dark pink becoming a deeper, bruised red. Her hands fisted the Omen's black hair, making him ache all the more.

The first time I saw disappointment in my father's eyes?

His hands shifted down to her hips, fingers digging into her, surely leaving marks. Slowly, Baker lowered his face, letting his hot breath wash over her skin. He breathed in, smelling the excitement on her skin, then delivered a long, firm lick to her panty-clad pussy.

August 27, 1915? The night I died. The night I became an Omen?

"Christ," she panted, her voice wavering. With her hand on the back of his head, she pushed his face into the wet heat between her legs.

He chuckled, grabbing her ass and squeezing. He wanted to give her this, this moment of pleasure, before he destroyed it. He hooked his thumbs into the waistband of her navy blue panties and slipped them down her bare legs, kissing her thighs and her knees as he went.

She stepped out and looked down at him. As he brought his face back up her body, their eyes locked.

"Wider," he demanded, nudging her knee with the backside of his hand.

She obeyed as hard breaths pushed out of her mouth, her head lolling back.

He lost himself in the taste of her; the tang and sweetness washed away his past, his name, and his future.

She came hard, her body curling forward, breathless and spent, but he kept lapping and nibbling until she shook and pushed him away, far too sensitive to tolerate his aggressive mouth another moment.

"Stop. Fuck, Baker." She slumped to the floor, her back pressed to the cold wall behind her.

He stayed where he was, kneeling in front of her, face to face now. Dread started to pool in his stomach, pushing the lust from his veins.

"Why weren't you here?" she asked in a hoarse voice. Her arms wrapped around her knees.

Settling himself, the Omen took a deep breath. He knew he had to tell her, had to let the past destroy this, because *this*—*her*—he knew he couldn't have. Shouldn't have. He reached behind and pulled his shirt over his head. He gripped it in his hands, wringing the material nervously.

* * *

Green eyes raked over his shoulders, his well-built chest, down his arms. There was so much ink, her eyes didn't know where to focus. Then she gasped, not believing what she was seeing. Moving, slinking ink … and her name.

Reaching out, she grabbed his upper arm, twisting it to read her full name on his shoulder. Her mind went in about eight different directions at once. Her name, her parents' names, details of her life all scrolled across his arms and chest. Why? Why did he know these things about her, why had he tattooed them on his body? *Better question,* she thought, *why is that motherfucking ink moving?* She watched it for a moment, hypnotized by the odd, almost snake-like movement of the words penned on his flesh. Then she opened her mouth and spoke the first thing that fell out.

"How … why the *fuck* is my name tattooed on you?"

she demanded, forcing her eyes away from the moving ink. "Why is it moving like that, Baker?"

Suddenly a flash of pain crumpled Baker's face, and he put his hand to his chest, groaning. Matlyn watched in horror as words appeared on his flesh as if penned by an invisible hand. She focused on the words more closely, leaning toward him, fingers tracing letters. His skin burned hot against her fingertips, irritated and slightly red.

"My birthday … my parents' names …" She shook her head, tears welling in her green eyes. Looking for an answer and so very terrified of what he might reveal, she begged, "Baker?" *He can't be human*, she surmised, and her thoughts splintered further.

The rabbit hole grew, plunging Matlyn into a new reality.

"My name is Samuel Baker Heeney. I was born in Ireland in 1883. I died in Chicago in 1915." He hung his head and waited for her to scream, to strike out at him, anything.

She moved closer, surprisingly, and studied the new words that rose to the surface of his skin. "I don't understand," she admitted in a small, scared voice. "Died?"

She aimlessly searched behind her for the discarded tank top, suddenly feeling more naked in that moment than she ever had before. Pulling the tank top down over her head, she stood, her lips pursed, pacing back and forth while Baker sat like a stone.

"Samuel Heeney?" she muttered and looked down at him. "Baker's not even your real name!" She shot an angry, accusatory glare at him. "Didn't even know his fucking name, and I let him eat me out." Now she was just yelling at herself, her pacing accelerating.

"Samuel Heeney died in 1915," Baker said in a small voice, not lifting his eyes off the floor. "And my middle name was Baker, so technically—"

"But how?!" the tiny dynamo screamed, stopping in her tracks, arms pitched into the air. "How in the happy hell are you doing *that*?" She pointed a twirling finger at his torso. She shook her head again then stormed over to the Coke tin, ripped off the lid and headed for the open window, hurling the contents out into the night. "Bad trip … shit's gotta be laced."

Baker almost laughed, watching her chuck her weed out the window, bare-assed and sure a bad high was the logical explanation for this. He choked back the chuckle and pushed to his feet.

"Unfortunately, that's the least fucked thing I've got to tell you." He put his shirt back on and moved to lean against the table.

"Really? 'Cause dead guy with creepy moving tats is a pretty fucked thing, Baker." She stopped and turned toward him. "Wait, what the hell do I call you?"

"Baker. Please. I left Samuel behind a hundred years ago."

Matlyn pulled her navy underwear back on and crossed her arms over her chest in a defensive stance. She stood eyeing the strange being from across the room, watching his face, analyzing his every move.

When someone says they died a hundred years ago, you run, you laugh in their face … you offer them a fucking hard drink! You don't stand there wondering how the hell that *happened.*

Her head spun, addled by confusion, but not an ounce of fear. For a fleeting moment she wondered if she were having some sort of medical emergency, but aside from the residual throbbing between her legs and her slightly raised pulse, physically speaking, she felt fine.

"Vampire?" she mumbled, more to herself than anything.

Baker let out a dark snicker. "No. Dark Omen. Vampires are a fairly modern monster, created by authors and the over-imaginative to tackle issues like mortality, God, good versus evil. All that shit. They live in the pages of fiction, not in reality." He took a deep breath and continued. "Omens have been around *much* longer."

"What the fuck is an *Omen?*" Matlyn pictured black cats, rainbows, broken mirrors, but obviously her knowledge of the subject was a tad … off.

"Get comfortable," he suggested.

She let her body puddle to the floor, sitting crisscross applesauce. She sat like a small child and waited to hear his story and understand him.

Baker gripped the back of his neck and gave his head a slow roll before he spoke. "Right, well … I think the beginning is a fine place to start."

She nodded, not taking her eyes off the creature in front of her. Awe welled up somewhere inside of her, and for a quick moment she considered that maybe that wasn't the sanest response.

"I was eleven years old the first time I felt the weight of a pistol. My father, Finn Heeney, put it there, and it was the first time I saw a genuine look of pride on his face, at least where I was concerned," Baker began. "He dragged me out of bed at first light and brought me out to the field that backed our property. There we stayed, firing off shot after shot until the gloaming set in, and I was so damn tired and sore that my arms shook. He grew frustrated with my lack of skill and sent me back to the house, mumbling about his only son being a waste of 'good seed.'"

Matlyn frowned, picturing a lanky Baker and his cruel father. She took a second to thank the gods that she'd been blessed with wonderful parents, even if their time together had been far too short.

* * *

Baker went on tell the intrigued girl about his father's driven and corrupt ways and about the move that brought him to Chicago when he was fourteen. Finn had quickly and effectively appointed himself the head of a small but growing Irish mob in the heart of Chicago. As his reputation grew in the community, so had his reach. Soon enough, Finn Heeney was shuffling shady deals in nearby cities.

For Baker, following in his father's footsteps was the last fucking thing he wanted for his life, but sadly, it was his only option. Finn would accept nothing less, and so he sent his son to do his dirty work.

In the name of his father, Samuel Baker Heeney had murdered no less than eighteen people by his thirty-second birthday. Each life weighed considerably on his soul, making his body tired and heavy with regret. And hate, so much hate. Hate for his father and the choices he made, for the life he was forced into, but the greater part of the hate and anger he felt was aimed at himself for never leaving.

"His one redeeming quality was his love for women,"

Baker said, looking past Matlyn, so far past her. "He respected the hell out women. Used to say, 'Any creature that can create life deserves the world at her feet, always.' If it weren't for that *one thing*, I'd be inclined to think he was some sort of fuckin' demon sent to make me miserable." Baker shifted his eyes, finally looking at Matlyn. He let the silence span out for a moment before continuing.

"The night I died," he recounted, "a man appeared all in gray. I figured it was Death coming to get me. I was wrong." He told her about the agreement, one hundred years of penance and Witnessing and then, when his soul had been washed clean, he would be allowed to enter paradise and claim the peace he never had in life.

"The sins of the father," angry and riveted, she mumbled, her jaw tense.

Baker leaned back against the wall on the opposite side of the room, head back and his eyes closed. "Yeah ... something like that."

"So now you're all undead and collecting stories on your skin?" Matlyn's knees were pulled up and tucked tightly to her chest, her arms wrapped around them.

An armor of skin and bone, Baker thought.

"Yes."

"It hurts?" she asked.

"Burns like a motherfucker. Lucky fuckin' Lights get a nice rush out of the deal. They get all blissed out and high, while Dark Omens writhe in pain."

"Raw deal." A small smile crept across her face, and Baker noticed the sex-flush had faded. Though her pale pallor was stunning, he rather missed the blush, and he hoped she'd allow him a chance at restoring it. It was a hope that was sure to fuckin' sink, but he wanted for it all the same.

"Why? What's the point?" she asked, pushing her legs straight out in front of her.

God, those legs are amazing. Baker snagged a selfish moment to take in the sight of her naked, creamy legs. His eyes ran up her body and his stormy eyes met her apple green. That question was a loaded question, and the very source of the gnarly chewing, growing pit in his stomach. He hated what was coming next. Baker had no choice but to lay out all the cards.

"Omens have one purpose, record history, take down the stories. History is built from both horrible and beautiful lives and events, some small, others much greater. Omens absorb it all." Swallowing hard, his fists bunched tightly at his sides.

"We're made of two groups. Light Omens and Dark Omens. Light Omens are born of truly good people who've struggled and suffered. They're given the choice to become an Omen when they die, given the chance to see the wonderful side of life. A side they may not have experienced in their prior life. They can opt out at any time. Light Omens collect the stories of life, births, marriages, medical breakthroughs that change the world. Mother Theresa had a Light Omen attached to her from birth to death. Her story was long, powerful, and an important part of human history," he said, hoping the example would put the role into perspective.

Matlyn nodded, but something in her face had changed.

Baker watched the awe seep from her. Something akin to understanding began to surface. "Dark Omens, like myself, are the Witnesses of Death, of loss and grief. We are tragedy. We're made to suffer. That's our penance. I'm not entirely sure, because they weren't exactly handing out the Omens' Survival Guide, but they feel like lessons."

"Baker, why is my name on your arm?" she asked again. Her voice was a murmur, a low hush, but he heard the quiver in it.

"I was sent to Witness your death, Matlyn."

Ten

❦

"I'm going to die?" Matlyn asked, her eyes welling and her voice trembling. In that moment she shrunk, dissolved. The room around her swelled and swallowed her tiny, trembling frame whole.

"Yes," Baker answered truthfully. Beautiful beryl eyes sliced him in two, and he deserved it.

The angry redhead pushed herself off the floor. Shaking her head, she cried out, "No! Get up!" She glared at the Omen, hot and indignant. "Get up and get the fuck out, you fucking *unbelievable* lunatic!" She stabbed her finger at the door as if he'd forgotten where it was.

There it is, Baker thought, *a normal, reasonable response.* He stood and made his way to the bedroom door. "I'm sorry," he whispered, closing the door behind him, leaving a sobbing, furious, confused girl pacing.

He knew it would end like this—another broken, dying

thing he left in his wake. Irrationally disappointed, the Dark Omen took the stairs at a slow pace, fighting the drag he felt in his chest, in his bones, on his skin. It all called to Matlyn.

The pull of a Witnessing came in pulses, something that built with proximity, like a radio signal. The pull he felt toward the angry girl upstairs was nothing like that. Hers was the pull of the tide, the natural and inescapable force of the moon on the ocean. Severing it hurt his heart more than the wicked sting of a new Story branding his skin. He'd take the sear over the heartache any day.

As he rounded the base of the staircase, he heard soft, fast foot falls above him.

"When?" Matlyn called out, looking down at him with her hands on her hips. They looked like weapons, her fists balled and resting on the swell of her hips.

Baker sighed and shook his head. "I don't know." That was the most honest answer he had to offer her.

"How in the happy hell does that work? Uh? You're *Death*!" Her eyes were defiant and her jaw was locked in fury.

Baker looked up at her. "No, Matlyn, Death is another creature entirely. I have no say when, where, or how it comes for you." Though, he figured no more than a few short months. Each Story played out in its own time, at its own pace, and of course, the longer the life, the longer the Witnessing. Death would come when it was due and not a moment before.

A whimper blew through the air, so much louder than her shouting, and her fists opened, hands lying open and wanting at her sides. She folded to the stairs like a single page losing its argument with gravity.

Baker took the steps back to her just as slowly as he had his descent. Two stairs away, he stopped.

"Why?" she sobbed into her hands.

He sat on the stair below and pulled her hands away from her face, just needing—selfishly—to see her.

"I waited for Death once," he began cautiously. "In 1944 … a seven-year-old boy." His mind wheeled backward, and he pictured the small boy he tried so very hard to walk away from. He didn't want such a small life on his skin, such a short Story.

* * *

The boy, James, had been a lively, rambunctious seven-year-old. He was a loving, kind boy and the only child of Claire and Gerard. He'd been their miracle baby.

On a warm fall day, armed with a mason jar, James went out to the field that backed his family's home, looking to capture creatures. A few grasshoppers and a beetle later, the boy had grown bored. He set his sights on a tree.

As he climbed higher, words jotted quickly across Baker's skin, and he knew the moment was approaching. Heat filled his body, an uncomfortable sickening heat. A lump formed at the back of his throat as he watched.

James navigated his way up the tree, little by little.

Blinding pain shot through Baker's body as the moment crept nearer still.

Suddenly, every inch of Baker's tense body was set to burn.

A foot slipped … and the pain increased.

Small hands groped at the air, then Baker's gut twisted, and when James lay at the bottom of the tree, breathing his last breath, the burn receded, the pain disappeared. Baker knew this story had come to an end.

Tears in his eyes, he waited. Death would come to collect him, but not alone. Baker refused to leave the boy in the field alone to face Death. Seconds later, Baker watched the air around the boy's still body shimmer and a sigh breathed through the open field.

It was far from the terrifying scenario Baker had envisioned. It was quiet, simplistic, and even beautiful.

* * *

"I don't know why," he finally answered. "Everything, our birth, our death is written long before we're born. We're all just following a script. Tiny parts in a much bigger picture." He placed his hand on her bare knee and gave it a gentle squeeze.

"Is that supposed to be comforting?" the girl snarked.

"Yeah."

"Fail."

"Sorry," Baker said, facing her. "Can I offer you ridiculously hot sex in lieu of comforting words?" He shot her a devilish grin.

Snot-faced and still looking a little miffed, the girl snickered and wiped the dampness off her face with the back of her hand. "Vodka?" she asked, pushing off the stair and gripping the handrail.

He followed her down the stairs to a formal looking dining room. She switched on the light and padded barefoot across the room to an old cherry wood buffet. Beautifully beaded liquor decanters gathered to one corner of the buffet; an assortment of mismatched glasses sat in front of them.

She poured a glass for each of them, handing one off to Baker as she slipped past him and into the adjoining room. She walked to a large fireplace and bent slightly, pushing a button off to the side.

"As much as I love the look of a natural fireplace, I'm fucking lazy ... and I would probably burn the house down," she added, watching the amber flames dance in the hearth. Half naked, she sat down on a couch facing the fireplace. She tucked her legs up next to her and waved Baker over. He sat and listened as the couch exhaled like an exhausted old man.

For several minutes the two remained quiet, locked in thoughts. Then the inked girl turned to the beautiful creature, glass resting at her mouth. "So you're dead and we ... I ... does ... Did I just get tongue fucked by a dead guy?" she finally spat out.

He burst into laughter, genuine laughter.

"I tell you you're going to die and you're worried about, what? Necrophilia?" He sounded both amused and incredulous.

"Yes." She nodded.

A smirk bloomed on Baker's face, and he answered, "It's not so much that I'm dead, it's that I can't be killed. I eat, though I don't need to. I breathe, sweat. It's just fuckin' impossible to kill me." He shrugged like it was nothing at all.

Curious, she seemed to contemplate that for a moment. "So if I stab you in the face, you're good?"

"Yes, but please don't." He leaned back, feigning fear. "I'd bleed all over your rug."

"But—"

"I bleed, feel pain, don't die." Head bobbing, he pursed

his lips, and gave her a look that said 'Yup, fucked-up. I know.' "Got shot once in 1967. That shit still itches." He pulled up his shirt, exposing an old scar on his left side.

"I suppose if you're standing that close to Death—"

"You get grazed," he finished.

"1915 ..." Matlyn mumbled "A hundred years ..."

Baker sat quiet, letting her put it together.

"What happens when your ..." she searched for the right word "... when your *service* is done?"

"I don't know, doll." And he didn't. He'd been given a directive: collect the histories of humans and when your hundred years is through, the gates will open for you. All sins forgotten. *How* that happened, *when* that happened was a mystery to him. Once Matlyn's story was written, would he simply cease to be? Vanish into nothing and fade into the past? The thought both terrified the Dark Omen and freed him. Being Death's prelude was exhausting.

"You say that a lot."

He shrugged. *Nothing much to say to that.*

"Tell me something you know," the girl with all the colorful skin demanded in a tone that was oddly kind and inquisitive, but left Baker no room to back out.

He smiled, loving the sheer force of will radiating from the woman next to him. Just an hour ago he'd torn her world open, watched as she crumpled, and now he sat there in amazement as she worked out the creases and mended the tear, slowly pulling herself back together. She was strong and smart and seemed to need to understand things on a greater level, not just simply accept them. It was her glue, her tape, the thing that held her together, and if understanding his world just a little more helped her in anyway, he'd gladly spill his guts.

He sipped at the stinging liquid in his glass. "I know my mother was wonderful. I know my father loved her, but only tolerated me for her benefit." His rough hands rubbed the back of his neck, like he was soothing an old wound. "She was kind and soft and had this funny, lilting laugh. She always said the wrong things—wrong words, ya know?—but my father never bothered to correct her."

"What was her name?" Intrigued, she watched his face and the way his features softened at the mention of his mother.

"Iona. Dad sometimes called her *Sunny*; it suited her bubbly personality," he answered with an old, soft smile. "Her mouth made a mess of words, but she had this way with animals, plants … people. She was a natural healer."

"What was your first—"

Baker shook his head. "No, no. Tit for tat, ink-slinger. Tell me something." Witnessing Matlyn's story—anyone's story—didn't mean a free pass into her life. Highlights, significant moments only. That just wasn't enough for him. He wanted to *know* Matlyn, not the Cliff Notes' version of her.

Shifting into a more comfortable position, she ran her tongue over her teeth and quickly finished her drink, setting the glass down on the dark wood coffee table. "I was eleven the first time I heard the word bisexual, but didn't really understand it. I understood my mom and my dad and their relationship. I was thirteen when I kissed a girl and got wet when she kissed me back. Trudy Donaldson. Blond, frizzy hair, braces." A creamy, rose blush lit her cheeks—perhaps the fault of the booze, but more likely the memory.

"I went to a house party with Owen Merlott when I was fifteen," she continued. "He was kinda shy, but had that bad-boy streak in him that called to me. After a rum and Coke, a couple good hits off the cheap fucking pinners being passed around, and Owen's Russian hands and Roman fingers had me panting in the laundry room at the back of the house. That was when I finally understood what bisexual meant."

The Omen leaned forward, drawing closer to her without even knowing it.

"I told Parrish, and she quoted statistics at me—told me to look up Kinsey—but never balked. I was grateful for that, for her acceptance." After a long beat she said, "You're up, sir. Tell me something about Omens. Do we all have one?"

Standing, he took their glasses and sauntered over to the buffet. Refilling each, he looked over his shoulder and simply answered, "No."

"Why? What makes me so special?" she challenged.

"I don't know." There was a mischievous grin set upon his lips. He rolled his shoulders in a lazy shrug and handed her the glass.

She let out a low, sexy growl in warning as she brought the glass to her lips. "Theories?" she mumbled around a half-swallowed mouthful of vodka.

He sat a little closer this time, leaning in and resting an arm across the back of the couch. As the night broke down and dawn started its sleepy ascent, he unloaded his thoughts on the subject. Some things he knew to be true, others fell into the educated guess category. He knew Omens followed family lines and events of historical import. Other things he could only guess at. A favorite theory of his, one that held a special place in his heart—right next to the giant daddy-sized grudge—some stories were just a means of teaching a lesson and the subject was entirely random. It seemed to him that each Dark Omen had something to learn from their past, so why not toss in a lesson or two from time to time?

Each of his theories on the matter held their own weight. Omens following bloodlines would certainly explain why he'd watched the seven-year-old fall to his death, and then some sixty years later Witnessed the twenty-one-year-old descendant of James take her life. And why he was there when a woman miscarried on a city bus—a woman that was the granddaughter of a man he'd Witnessed only two years before. Why those families and those deaths, Baker couldn't figure.

Historical events like the Civil War, the discovery of the atom, the collapse of the Berlin Wall would make their marks in history texts around the world, but who was responsible for the story of the nineteen-year-old farmhand and third-class passenger of the Titanic, Jeremiah Burke?[2] None of these deaths were socially or historically significant, considerable to those that loved them, yes, but not to the world as a whole.

Winston Churchill had said that history was written by the victors, and in many respects Baker believed that to be true. Accounts of happenings written from a safe distance, often from an unbiased perspective, about an event but not about the people that endured it, lived through it, or died because of it. Omens wrote those stories.

Omens took on the life stories of the disobedient farm

boys that shirked their family responsibilities and boarded doomed ocean liners … because history texts certainly wouldn't.

But Baker was certain that some of the stories he'd Witnessed were meant to teach him the error of his ways. Like the fifty-three-year old CEO, Larry Greenwall. Larry was a millionaire, and for all intents and purposes, a dick. He bought friendship, demanded respect, and died in the bed of his mistress, naked with cocaine smeared on his gums and lining his nostrils. Perhaps that was the life Baker would have had, had it not ended that night in 1915. He could have become a bloated, binge-drinking asshole with a penchant for twenty-two-year-old blondes and not a single true friend.

Dawn broke through the windows, pushing a blushed light into the room and reminding them both of the time. Matlyn took the empty glass from Baker, placed it on the table next to hers, and stood up, offering him her hand and a tired smile.

He took it, enjoying the push-pull sensation that ran between them. "You feel that too, right?"

"Yes." It was physical, substantial, and not easily pushed aside. She turned and headed toward the stairs, the raven-haired Omen a step behind her.

Parrish came jogging down the stairs in shorts and a T-shirt, running shoes tightly laced on her feet. She came to a halt and let her eyes run up and down Baker. Baker eyed her right back, smiling a little at the way her mouth twitched.

"Mornin', Little Bird, a tad early for you isn't it?"

"Tell Addy I won't be in. Re-book my 10:00 a.m. and

my 2:00 p.m. Call Lyla and tell her to come in first thing tomorrow for those touch-ups." Matlyn nodded her head once at her sister and continued her way up the stairs.

"Will do. Good morning, Baker." She wagged her fingers at him and shot him a salacious smile then turned and scurried down the stairs and out the front door.

"*Einin*," he whispered as they rounded the top of the staircase.

"Pardon?" She reached out and opened the door to her bedroom.

"Einin," he said again in a thicker accent than she'd heard him use before. "It's an Irish name, means little bird."

"I like it." She dragged her tired body onto the bed and smacked the open space next to her.

"Thought you didn't sleep with assholes." He crawled in next to her, and she readily assumed the position of the little spoon.

"I don't," she said, and he wrapped his arm around her, sighing at the feel of his body pressed to hers. Pink eyelids fluttered and she murmured something about him being her first, a sluggish smile on her face.

He lifted her wrist to his mouth and placed a gentle kiss to the small, white bird. "My Einin." He breathed the words against her skin and watched the goose bumps bloom on her arm. He paced his breathing with hers and drifted off into a dreamless state.

Eleven

❧

Matlyn's dream was full of color and dizzying movement. Bits and pieces of her life sped by in fits of color so bright she felt she had to guard her eyes. She raised a hand to shield her eyes from the overly bright rays as she watched the streams of pictures pass in front of her.

A one-year-old with a birthday hat on and fat tears sliding down her face, watching as the neighbor's dog quickly gobbled up her birthday cake.

Pigtails and freckles, sunscreen and a lifejacket. Her father hoisting her onto the deck of the boat, smiling down at her and tugging on her pigtail.

Parrish holding her hand and soothing her as the doctor stitched the wound closed on her knee.

Far too bright sunlight, two caskets side by side, and flowers sprayed over them. People crying, hands patting her back, rubbing her arm. Her shiny, new, black shoes.

A bright purple dress, layers of color swirling around her. A simple white daisy on her wrist. Music, lights. Owen hovering above her. The weight of him, the smell, the sting, and the pleasure of it. The colorful dress a puddle on the floor.

The cold feel of the keys placed in her hand. Bold letters "SOLD" in the shop window.

* * *

Light slowly bled into the room, inching closer to the foot of the bed and finding Baker's socked feet first. When Matlyn felt the warmth of the sun wash over her face, she rolled to her right and breathed in the smell of the man lying next to her—a man that on a purely logical level should not exist. He smelled of dirt and wind and rain, not at all unpleasant. Running her hands over his stomach, she felt his muscles clench. She knew he was awake.

His eyes remained closed but an easy smile pulled at his lips when her hands slipped under the fabric of his gray T-shirt. Her fingers ran up and down the planes of his chest.

"If you don't need sleep ..." She let the words drop as she pushed the gray fabric up higher, exposing ink.

"I drift and lose myself for a while. It's not as satisfying as sleep, but it beats the hell out of late night talk shows."

Matlyn's curious fingers traced fine lines. Sliding the shirt further up, her eyes inspected the words.

"So all those other stories ... where'd they go?"

"It's kinda like ..." Baker blew out a breath, his bunched gray shirt fluttering around his chin and mouth. "An Etch-A-Sketch. Clean slate for the next Witnessing." He blew out again, making a ridiculous noise.

Matlyn chuckled. "You should just lose that." She

tugged at the gathered material, and Baker graciously complied. Rolling forward to sit, he pulled the T-shirt up over his head.

"Holy shit." Small hands reached out to touch the wings on his back. Matlyn sat up and gently rolled him forward a little more to get a better look at the tattoo that covered the lower half of his back.

A large owl in blacks and grays spread across the span of his back, the tips of its wings just barely curling around his sides to touch his ribs. The talons seemed to clutch at the flesh of his waist, nearly dipping beneath the hem of his jeans.

"Holy shit," she said again.

"Owl's are—"

"Death omens, I know. I've been drawing them for weeks now."

Baker turned his face toward her, his eyes wide and amazed. For a quick moment he wondered how many of his stories before her knew their time was coming to a close. Had they somehow sensed that Death was making its move?

She shuffled behind him, one leg dangling off the side of the bed, the other bent on the mattress next to his hip. Her hands worked over the ink in reverence, caressing the feathers of the owl. The eyes were the only bit of color: a deep, haunting amber.

"It's beautiful."

"I had that done in 1987, in Salt Lake by a lovely, round woman named Beau."

"That's the year I was born," Matlyn observed, looking at the letters that paraded from one shoulder to the next.

"I know, Einin." He turned his head, looking pointedly

at his left shoulder—at her name, her birth date. The hour was even scrolled there: 10:17 a.m. He pushed up on all fours, spun toward her, and pulled her down the bed until she lay under him.

Her laugh was soft and her skin was still sleep warm and slightly flushed.

Fuck, she's beautiful.

Not for the first time, he acknowledged the irony of their situation, but he refused to let the sadness of it swallow him. He leaned in to kiss her and when she exhaled, he suddenly drew back.

"What?" Matlyn asked, her smile as curious as her eyes.

"As much as I want to strip you naked and do bad things to you, I can't." He pushed back onto his heels.

"Why? It's not the dead guy thing, is it? I'm over it." Her hands reached out to draw him back, but he wouldn't budge. She fired a cross look at him.

He chuckled. "Gonna stomp your fuckin' feet too, girl?" He shook his head and pinched her side. "Go brush your teeth. Your mouth smells like a skunk's asshole."

* * *

For a moment she lay there, incredulous and staring up at him. She flung her hand out and it landed with a rather satisfying smack to his chest. "Fucker." She pushed him away, not being able to help the smile that lifted her lips.

"I suppose you've got minty fresh morning breath, Mr. Romance?" She got out of bed and headed to her en suite bathroom, shooting him the finger as he laughed. "Such an asshole," she mumbled to her reflection.

"Nope. Just got up before you. Used your toothbrush, by the way."

Looking down at the toothbrush in her hand, and then at her own reflection, she rolled her eyes. Matlyn brushed her teeth, aware that the gorgeous ink bearer was roaming around her bedroom, picking up this, inspecting that. She spat toothpaste foam. "Would you stop touching my shit," she barked, bringing the brush back to her mouth.

"Afraid I'm gonna find your toys?"

"Top drawer on the left," she shouted with a minty-fresh grin. Matlyn rinsed her mouth and ran a brush through her hair a few times then flipped the light off and stepped back into her bedroom. She watched Baker peek into her drawer and giggled when he reached his hand in and a low vibrating sound emanated from the open drawer.

Turning it off, he closed the drawer and turned to face her with a framed picture in his hand. "Your parents?"

Walking back toward the bed, Matlyn nodded, head down, eyes on her feet.

"Your mother's beautiful. Same hair color," he noted.

She looked so much like her mother, Veronica, that the young woman had no trouble at all imagining where the years would take her. Those years would never come and that thought brought fear and panic.

"Harris's eyes, Veronica's hair and freckles." She sagged onto the messy bed, her eyes blank, vacant. "What do I do now, Baker?"

Loaded with a smart-ass comment about opening her mouth, he looked up from the smiling couple in the picture and the crude words fizzled out right there on his tongue. He put the photo down and sat next to her on the bed.

"Einin," he said softly, tipping her chin toward him, "you do whatever you like, doll. Be it three weeks or three months, that time is yours." He let his fingers dance across the simple letters tattooed on her upper thigh, looking over at the picture of her parents again.

"I'm twenty-eight, I don't have a will set up ... And Parrish ... The shop, I should—" Hysteria inched into her voice and she stood suddenly, fluttering around like a trapped bird.

"Stop," he said, leaning forward, grabbing her wrist and pulling her back toward him. "It's not today, Matlyn. Look." He tapped the words on his chest.

She started reading. "I was nine when I got Kawasaki disease. My feet were so swollen, I couldn't put my new shoes on." She smiled, remembering the high-top sneakers with bright pink laces she'd loved so much.

"You have time." Baker tugged a little more, lying back on the bed and pulling her with him.

The heat of his body seemed to leach the tension from her muscles, and they sank into the mattress. His hands clutched her slim waist and when she slid her body against his, his fingers dug a little deeper.

Creamy, freckled skin flushed with warmth. This was her favorite part: the anticipation. Pre-foreplay, pre-sex, quiet expectancy. She loved the way her body reacted, the rush of heat, the nervous rattling in the pit of her stomach. She loved the intensity of the silence that always seemed to hover in the air just before a searing kiss.

If we could bottle this shit, she thought, letting her eyes roam Baker's handsome, stubbly face.

With a low groan, Baker lifted his head off the bed and

pressed his lips to her warm mouth. The kiss started slow, almost lazy, and built to an all-consuming, panting mash-up of lips and tongues.

An uneasy—and unwelcomed—feeling began to take over, and Matlyn sat up quickly, throwing her shirt over her head and tossing it to the floor before returning to a breathless Baker. His brow furrowed and his lips smoothed into a tight line.

He took her face in his firm, calloused hands and spoke in a low voice, "Slow down, Einin."

Tears welled in her eyes. "I'm sorry."

"Shh," the Omen soothed, pulling her down and locking her in his warm, safe embrace.

Quietly, she sobbed, her body shaking. He held on tight, kissed her hair, and rubbed her back as she broke down again. When she choked out another pathetic apology, he sat them both up, balancing her on his knees.

"That's it, get dressed," he ordered.

"I … uh." She cocked her head and wiped the tears from her face, hating the déjà vu like feeling that took over her.

"Get your ass up, shower, get dressed; we're going out."

"But I want sex. Ridiculous, hot sex," she repeated his words from the night before. Her arms folded over her chest, pushing her boobs up and out, a pout on her lips.

"So do I. Fuck. *Believe* me." He raked his hand over messy, black hair and released a hot breath. "I'm not up for angry, rushed, I'm-gonna-die sex, so get dressed."

Matlyn's eyes widened at his words, her lip curling.

"Too soon?" He shrugged. His tone was unforgiving.

"Pig's ass," she grumbled, pushing up from his lap and

walking toward her bathroom. She plugged the tub, started the water, stepped out of her underwear, and grinned a wicked grin when she heard the lusty groan from the next room. She hadn't bothered to close the door to the bathroom.

Deal, fucker.

Feeling sassy, she put a little extra sway in her movements as she went about gathering her things from her room, more than aware of the stormy eyes that followed her.

"Where are we going?" she inquired as she sunk into the hot water.

"Carousel Gardens. Haven't been there in about fifty years now." Baker lay on her unmade bed, hands laced together on his flat stomach, staring up at the ceiling. the "Last Witnessing that brought me through New Orleans was a ninety-one-year-old snappy little thing named Camilla Bailey. She had a long, eventful life," he commented. "She was what every old woman should be: wits firmly in place, pumped full of piss and vinegar, and a bushel full of wonderful memories. Sad that's rarely the case."

Listening to his story, she sat up a little more, leaning toward the open door. In a light, childish voice, she asked, "Can we go on the bumper cars?"

"Absolutely."

"Can I get ice cream?"

"Shut up, girl. Wash, get dressed," he barked in a playful tone.

* * *

Blue, gold, green, and red bumper cars raced about, randomly colliding and then setting off in another direction. Some got stuck, halting in position until the driver turned the wheel in just the right way. Some dodged around the on-coming cars trying not to get hit; others still took aim on their targets and sought them out, laughing when they finally crashed. Sounds of happiness mingled with the music playing overhead and the sticky heat seemed to simply fade away, forgotten for the moment.

When the cars came a slow stop, Baker popped up out of his shiny blue mini-car and made his way across the smooth floor to the wee redhead, who was still snickering as she undid her belt and stood. Baker extended his hand, and she took it, gracefully climbing over the side of her green car.

"Those things are magical," she declared, her hand in Baker's as they walked down the gated aisle. "Twenty-eight when I buckled my ass in, eight when I climbed out." She smiled widely, her eyes full of youthful memories. "To the ice cream, sir!" She pulled him toward a small, old-fashioned looking stand.

She ordered a vanilla-chocolate swirl cone and turned to Baker, asking him what he'd like.

"And ruin this amazing figure? I think not." Gesturing to his tall, lean body, mock puzzlement wrinkled his face.

"Suit yourself, asshole." She turned to the cashier and handed over a bill. "I mean who passes up ice cream?" she asked the young girl, who looked past her customer to the beautiful creature standing behind her. Her light blue eyes ran the length of his body, and she blushed, handing Matlyn her change with a shrug.

Baker walked quietly by her side as she ate her ice-cream, watching her tongue work over the cold treat. "Heaven," he mumbled to himself.

"Pardon?" Cheeks flushed from the hot sun, the girl looked up at him, ice cream cone hovering by her mouth.

The sun had begun to drop below the horizon, taking with it the glow and shimmer of daylight. Light blues and purples seeped into the sky, making everything inky and new again.

"Heaven," Baker repeated, "I hear it's what you make it and if that's the case ... *this* is my Heaven. Warm air on my skin, sun setting, you and your ice-cream cone. Fucking perfect."

She nodded absently, catching sight of Baker's truck in the parking lot. As they neared the silver relic, her pace quickened, then she spun on her heels, walking backward and watching Baker advance. He moved in long, languid strides.

"How old were you when you lost your virginity?" Matlyn gently banked against the truck's cab, cone still in hand.

"Fifteen." He came to a stop in front of her, unashamedly allowing his eyes to drop to the cleavage her low-cut top afforded. "Luanne. Blond, seventeen, leggy. Not all that chesty. Could suck a penny through a straw." He dipped his finger into her quickly melting ice cream and tasted it.

"And was she your first love?"

"No." His face was serious and his tone tight. "She was the neighbor's youngest daughter." Unlocking the truck, he pulled the door open for her.

Matlyn climbed into the cab of the truck and placed her purse at her feet. Baker gently closed the door behind her.

"So who was she? First big crush? Love of your life?" she fired as he climbed behind the wheel.

"Never been in love." The engine roared to life and the silence that flew between them was nearly as thick as the April air. Baker dropped his hands to his lap and looked out the windshield. "I wanted to please my father and keep a smile on my mother's face, that's all. The idea of loving someone, having someone like that, never entered my mind. The older I got, the more it became abundantly fucking clear that Finn wasn't the pleasing type, and I let the idea of falling in love fade away." He turned to look at Matlyn. "Then I kicked the bucket and well …" A small, but sad smile found his face and he shrugged.

"I think I could have loved Cohen. He just let me be me, and that meant so much to me … but I didn't need him."

He met her eyes and nodded, knowing exactly what she'd meant. Thirty-two years of his human existence wandered past him, and not once had he found something really worth needing. Ninety-nine years mingling among the living, and today was the first he'd truly felt happiness and joy.

His hand shot up and he waved an angry middle finger in the air, looking to the darkening sky. "You think that's funny, don't ya?" His accent flared with the bite of his words. "One hundred and thirty-two God *damned* years, and now ya offer me happiness. Now?" he yipped.

Matlyn broke out into laughter that worked well to distract Baker's little fit.

"You really gonna have it out with the universe, right here in this truck?" Her voice was light and full of amusement. She rolled down the window and chucked the now soggy cone, hearing it hit the ground with a sloppy, wet sound.

"It's as good a place as any."

"Well, if we're throwing out issues, a B-cup woulda been nice. And Alec Fortly? Really? Boy couldn'ta found my clit with a flashlight and a road map."

"Hey…" he pointed a serious finger at her and wagged it "…the A-cups are a non-issue. I quite like them. And I'm sorry about the inept lover. No excuse for that shit."

"Take me home, Omen." A smile lit her face, and she gestured to the road.

* * *

The door closed with a soft click, and Syndal ran from the kitchen to greet them, curling and coiling around Matlyn's legs. She bent to pick up the cat. "Miss Syn, what kind of trouble did you get up to today, hmm?" She pet her furry little head and the cat purred in delight.

She tossed her keys on the table and walked out of her flip-flops leaving them by the door. "Wilson's here," she informed Baker, looking over her shoulder. "Parrish's pretty little man thing. Can't promise they're not fucking. Sorry." She led him up the stairs.

Letting the cat go at the top of the stairs, she watched her paw off to the makeshift studio. She admired the way the cat strode around like she just couldn't give a shit. When her dark-haired Omen followed her into her room and shut the door behind them, she shivered.

Perched on the edge of the bed, eyes crawling up and down Baker's long body, she tipped her head toward the iPod docked on the dresser to the left of the door. "Turn it on."

He did so, not taking his eyes off her. Completely unhurried, he walked to her, music humming around them.

"No crying this time," she assured, looking up at him. "A round of putt-putt, bumper cars, and some mediocre ice cream put it all into perspective for me. Can't change what's comin', can't even slow it down. Tears, what ifs, could have beens … not worth my energy at the moment."

With sure hands, she popped open the first button of his jeans and licked her lips. "Can't hide from it, can't fuck it away." Her hand moved to the next button and she saw the pointed look on his face. "That's not what this is," she defended.

"No?" he asked, cupping her face in his hand, his thumb gently rubbing her temple.

"A hundred and thirty-two years and you've never needed anyone? Tell me you don't need me and I'll stop." Flicking the last button open, she began pulling at his jeans as he lifted his shirt over his head.

Baker gazed down at her, seeing the raw need and lust in her eyes. He watched her work his pants down his legs and said nothing as he stepped out of them.

Want and desire often kept good company, but need … need paired off with love more often than not, and love was a heavy fucking emotion to cop to.

He stood before her bare, completely comfortable, wearing nothing but his inked over skin. Taking him into her mouth, Matlyn hummed softly. She welcomed the slide of his smooth skin against her tongue and the masculine, heady taste of him. She dug her nails into the backs of his thighs and let him fuck her mouth.

She pulled back, his heavy cock falling from her

mouth, and lifted her shirt over her head, letting it flutter to the floor. Reaching behind her, she unhooked her bra and gingerly slipped it off her shoulders.

He eyed her naked, flushed chest and smiled. "Perfect." He cupped a breast, letting his fingers graze her nipple. Leaning down, he captured her mouth in a leisurely kiss. A kiss that couldn't be rushed. It demanded time.

Minutes, maybe hours floated by, and Baker broke away. "Stand up, Einin," he directed.

She stood and Baker dragged the zipper of her shorts down achingly slow. With a quick tug, they dropped to the floor. Arms around her waist, he lifted her, feet no longer touching the floor. Hugging her to his chest, he kissed her again, not so slowly this time. His teeth pulled at her bottom lip, and she let out a yelp.

Lowering her onto the bed, he let his arms slack, and she gently fell to the crumpled sheets.

"You know I can't tell you that. That I don't need you. I can't tell you that, doll," he whispered as he bent her knee and pushed inside her.

Her body tensed for a moment and then relaxed. She rolled her hips, letting him know she was ready to move. Baker braced himself on his forearms, kissed her forehead, and moved in slow, burning thrusts that drove her body back.

One hand gripping his shoulder, and the other reaching around his side and clawing at his skin, she rocked with him. He gritted his teeth and cursed, bowing his back in an almost inhuman way, and once again, Matlyn watched as words bubbled to the surface of his heated flesh. She moved her eyes away from his chest, locking on his steel eyes.

"Are you okay?" she asked, caressing his pained face.

"Yea," he breathed. "Quick way to kill an erection though. Sorry." He sat back on his heels and caught his breath.

Matlyn's eyes dipped to his lap and a wicked glint lit her eye. She spread her legs wider and slipped a finger down into the wetness. Baker watched, devouring the sight before him.

"Fuck, you're either the Devil's best weapon, or God's gift." Moving her hand out of the way, he grasped his now throbbing cock and pushed into her again, loving the primal grunt that dropped from her lips.

Their bodies grinded, pushed and pulled, and wore each other down. Sweat coated their writhing flesh, and when Matlyn came, her nails dug into his flexed ass, leaving small, red, crescent shapes.

With his arms locked around her, he pulled her up onto his lap and let her take over, commanding his body and driving him closer to his own release. She pushed him down, and leaned back, her hands resting on his knees and her perfect tits on display. Matlyn moved her hips in tight circles, loving the friction his body provided her. With a low groan, his hands gripped her waist, stilling her movement.

"Christ," he growled, his hips jerking upward as he came.

She collapsed on his chest, rising and falling with him. "Heaven. You inside me, your sweat on my lips, hands on my body. Fucking heaven."

Twelve

✦

"Move in with me. Live with me," Wilson said, shoving a jar of pickles out of his way.

The knife in Parrish's hand stilled, and she glanced across the kitchen at the back side of Wilson, crouched in front of the fridge. "And leave my sister to fend for herself? Cruel."

"Quit playin' games with my heart, woman." Turning, he slid a small container of fruit dip across the stark white island.

Slipping past him, she opened a cupboard, and pulled out a large plate. "The Backstreet Boys?" she said with a giggle.

With a shrug Wilson said, "Desperate times and all that."

"So now you're desperate?"

With his hands on her waist, he spun the strawberry-blond girl and deftly lifted Parrish up onto the countertop, the pink dress hitching behind her knees. "And you're evasive." His brow arched and his lips pursed.

"We've only been together—"

"Don't go flingin' bullshit in my kitchen, Parrish!"

Her blue eyes widened, caught by his tone.

"We've been throwing passes at each other since the day we met. This…" his hand waved between the two of them "…has been goin' on a long time, puddin'." He let out a shaky sigh. "I get it. Your grandparents, your aunt Marlee … your parents. You loved them and they died. Scary to love someone that might up an' vanish on you one day."

Salty tears pooled in her icy-blue eyes and her lip quivered. She couldn't hold his gaze. In that moment it was too much.

"Scarier still is never getting close, never being open enough to hurt. You can't live like that, baby doll. It's not fucking worth it." His hand cupped her cheek, catching warm tears as they fell.

Slowly, the small woman lifted her face, taking in his handsome, honest features. With a weak smile she said, "Two conditions."

"Anything, doll."

"One: Matlyn guts that sorry fucking man-cave you call a living room." Her head canted and a challenging expression lit her face.

"Done. I was getting tired of that couch. Two?"

"Don't ever quote shitty boy bands again." She wrapped her legs around him and hummed softly at the feel of his body so warm and so close.

† † †

Walking under a colorful umbrella, Ingrid stopped mid-stride and let the exquisite rush of Witnessing fall over her like a dense fog. Words gently surfaced, causing her pulse to push just a little harder and her muscles to relax. A thick buzz hummed through her slender body, and she couldn't help the satisfied sigh that escaped as her skin rippled in pleasure.

* * *

Matlyn slid a bottle of wine across the kitchen island, followed by a corkscrew. Parrish cupped the bottle with ease and began to work off the foil covering the cork.

She reached above her head, stretching up on her toes and grabbed two wine glasses.

"You're okay with this?" Parrish asked, her voice a little sheepish.

Her ginger-haired sister turned to face her, a glass in each hand, and gave her a genuine smile. "That's my job, Pare. To be okay with what you do, with who you are." She watched as Parrish twisted the screw in a little further, chewing on the inside of the cheek.

"I crawled into bed that day, sobbing," Matlyn began. Her voice was far away, tripping backwards through the years. Parrish pulled the cork free with a little grunt. She poured for each of them and settled on the stool next to her.

"You were reading that fucking V.C. Andrews book again."

"*My Sweet Audrina*," Parrish offered. Matlyn wasn't surprised that she remembered such a trivial thing.

Absently, Matlyn nodded. "You put the book down—didn't bother to mark the page—and asked if I was hurt. I remember your hands flutterin' around me, looking for a reason for the tears tumbling down my face."

"Your breath kept hitching. You couldn't look me in the face."

"You'd said 'Matlyn, whatever it is, it's okay. I won't be mad.'" Taking a sip of her wine, Matlyn smiled an old smile, still caught somewhere in that day years ago.

The younger Wren picked up where Matlyn left off. "Then you told me that you'd kissed that girl a couple years ago. How much you liked it. How much you liked kissing Owen too. You'd asked me what was wrong with you." Parrish leaned forward, her elbows on the edge of the counter, and swirled the red liquid in her glass, not really looking anywhere.

"Nothing's *wrong* with you, Matlyn. You are who you are. You just go on and be who you need to be," Matlyn imitated her sister's lilting voice. "You said it so matter-of-factly, like that was that, no room to argue. When I asked if you were okay with *what* I was—"

Parrish interrupted, putting her glass down and fixing her sibling with a serious look. "I said '*Whats* were meant for TVs, cars … *things*. Not people. People weren't *whats*. *Who* you were—*are*—Matlyn, is fine with me. That we were blood, and it was our job to be okay with each other. Always.'"

A tear slipped down Matlyn's cheek and she looked up at her younger sister. "You love him?"

Parrish nodded her head, her lip caught between nervous, biting teeth. "Yes. It's too soon and all too fuckin' much … but he makes me feel … settled. Ya know? Like the storm's just a light drizzle now, an' I can deal with that."

Settled.

Settled was something Matlyn hadn't felt since their parents past away. Sasha, her mother's best friend, had tried so hard to offer stability and a good home—and she had. Wisely investing the money their parents had left behind, cutting the crusts off the PB & Js, and lovingly kissing the scrapes and scratches. But her warm heart and good intentions couldn't ground the ever fluttering, searching, and aching pain in her heart.

The ink slinging sister took a deep, shaky breath, feeling a tiny piece of her soul settle in its own way. Knowing Parrish was happy and loved did wonderful things for the weight that hovered around her.

"So…" Parrish cleared her throat "…in my absence, Little Bird, there will be no all-nighters with coke sprinkled hookers. My bedroom will *not* become Matlyn's Den of Iniquity … or a home gym. Clear?"

"Wouldn't worry about the home gym," Matlyn said with a snort and a wink.

* * *

Ingrid fingered the soft fabric, the color of a perfect summer day. The dress was simple in design, classic even. The beautiful yellow reminded her of a dress she'd once worn, one that proudly displayed the life growing inside her. She pulled the dress from the rack, spun, and held it to her body, admiring her reflection in the tall mirror. Smoothing her hand over her stomach, she remembered her once swollen belly.

"Not your color, I'm afraid."

Behind Ingrid stood a dark-skinned woman with dark chocolate eyes—old eyes that roved over every inch of Ingrid's reflection. She looked to be in her mid-forties and laugh lines had just begun to settle at the edges of those deep eyes.

"No. I think you're right. Not my color at all," Ingrid replied, offering the kind woman a friendly glance. She turned and placed the dress back on the rack.

"With eyes like that, can't see why you'd wear anythin' but blue." The woman's perfect white teeth gleamed as she returned the smile. She plucked a dress from the other side of the rack and moved toward the pretty Omen, ducking and popping like a buoy on the water. The moment she rounded the circular sales rack, Ingrid spotted the cane at her side and understood the awkward movement. Handing over a similar dress in a robin's egg blue, she rested the wooden cane against her leg.

"There," the woman declared proudly, a wide, toothy grin splitting her lips. The blue looked incredible against Ingrid's skin and made her eyes pop. "Now, you'll be needin' a jacket, Omen. Cover those markin's." She patted Ingrid's arm and gave her a knowing look. "White, I think. Got just the thing." The woman hobbled off toward a display of blazers and light jackets.

Ingrid looked over her shoulder at the woman's retreating form and shook her head. The shock of being made like that was momentary, fleeting. It'd happened before and would surely happen again. Omens weren't the only thing walking the supernatural line around here. She shrugged and waited for the woman to return with the jacket.

The woman hobbled back and held the jacket out for the Light Omen to slip into. "Thank you…" she stole a quick glance at the silver nametag perched on the woman's lapel "…Charlene. And right you are, this is perfect."

Charlene rang up the purchase, thanking the Omen-girl for her business, and as Ingrid turned away from the counter Charlene said, "Curious thing, seein' two Omens walkin' 'round my neighborhood."

Dusty-brown hair swept slowly across Ingrid's shoulder as she turned her head to the side, eyeing the sales woman. "Two?"

"Dark Omens are common enough. What with the world in the state it's in, but Light … don't come across you often."

Ingrid's brow lifted. She'd been at this a long time, and she'd only ever come across one other Dark Omen in 1958—a prickly old bugger named Herald. They tended to keep to themselves, hidden away with the shadows.

"The great and the terrible, all comin' together," Charlene mumbled, and Ingrid couldn't help but wonder if her Story was in any way related to the Dark Omen wandering the streets of New Orleans.

Ingrid tipped her head, smiled politely at the clerk and made her way out onto the bustling street. Puddles had begun to dry and the air was damp, thick, and held the heat in a firm grip.

Humans, certain humans, walked through the veil just as easily as slipping through an open door. Psychics, mediums, and other spiritual go-betweens often sensed Omens, somehow knowing that they were something just outside of natural. Some said the Omens' auras gave them away, some claimed to feel "vibrations," and others still had told her of an odd smell that seemed to follow the Omens around.

It would be easy to dismiss it all as snake spit and bullshit, but the fact was that they'd known what she was. Ingrid was inclined to believe that each was true. Much in the way that two different people could look at a painting and offer two very different interpretations; different cultures interpreted the supernatural in varying ways, each adjusting degrees of good and evil, mixing in superstitions handed down over generations, add a pinch of religion and a dash of personal belief, and you have a store clerk who could read auras, or a tarot card reader who 'feels' your unnatural vibes. How they got their information was as unique as the families they grew into.

What was fairly universal, however—and rather amusing to Ingrid—was how each viewed the role of the Omen, Light or Dark. Humans assigned way too much power to things they couldn't understand.

Omens weren't responsible for what happened, or to whom. They were simply there to Witness, to gather an unbiased account. The rainbow Charlene would see on her way home was the work of the rain and the sun—science, but she would undoubtedly attribute it to Ingrid's presence.

The murder of crows lining a neighbor's fence was not the fault of a Dark Omen, nor was the death of that eighty-three-year-old neighbor. Disease was the likely cause, not the Omen bearing his Story's life. Yet that was the common belief; the Light brought the good, and the Dark toted death and disease.

Be them Light or Dark, Omens had no real power. Their immortality was borrowed. The words that formed on their skin did not appear at will, and for the Dark, it came with a great deal of pain. No, there was no power in an Omen. Not the power to bring wealth or fortune or spoil a new carton of cream. Those things just simply happened, but humans being the overly thoughtful creatures they were, often felt the need to point a finger and assign meaning where none truly belonged.

As far as Ingrid was concerned, Omens were glorified scribes with extraordinary shelf lives.

* * *

"So Baker?" Parrish prodded, pulling a cheese covered slice of pizza onto her plate.

"Hot. And very good with his mouth," Matlyn replied, her eyes dancing mischievously.

"Yeah, 'bout that … you've got no damned volume control, you know that, Little Bird?" She stabbed an accusing finger at her sister then unceremoniously ripped into the pizza, sauce collecting in the corner of her mouth.

"I'm well aware." She chose not to mention the fuck-me choir that frequently rolled away from her sister's room, bathroom, Wilson's car … the Parabola staff room. "And he's coming over after his shift tonight, so dig out your earplugs, baby girl." Matlyn's face split into a huge, foxy grin.

"You like ham?" Parrish asked with a mouth full of cheese and pepperoni.

"Ham? You wanted pepperoni."

Parrish rolled her eyes and swallowed the mouthful of food. "*Him*. Do you like *him*?"

"More than I'd like," she replied before biting into her own greasy piece of pizza.

Parrish's brows pulled together and she studied her sister. "What is it? Why do you look so ... *worn*?"

Could her sister see the heaviness about her? The weight of her too-short future? How much peeked through her eyes when Parrish looked at her?

"Ladies and gentlemen, my charming sister, Parrish Lee. Asshat."

"Such a snarky bitch." She chuckled and licked the corners of her mouth, catching the sauce. "You just look like you could use some help carryin' that load is all."

Matlyn suddenly looked like she might burst into tears. Her eyes began to swim in salty unshed tears and her head dropped.

"Hey ... what is it?" Parrish implored, reaching toward her.

Impatiently, Matlyn swiped at her eyes and cleared her throat. "Just be happy, okay? I just need you to be happy. Happy with Wilson, happy with your job. Just fucking happy, it's all I'll need."

* * *

Three slices of pizza and two glasses of wine later, the Wren sisters had changed into ratty sweats and oversized T-shirts. With Parrish's strawberry tresses pulled back in a clean ponytail, Matlyn could see the ghost of their aunt Marlee. She was there in Parrish's cheekbones, the delicate shell of her ears, and in the shape of her eyes. Harris Eugene and

Marlee Rebecca Wren, like the two sisters, had been close in age, if nothing else. Harris was grounded, protective, level, whereas Marlee was like a balloon in the wind.

Grandpa Wren had vied for the name Carrington Patrice Wren, but the matriarch shot that down, claiming one pretentious name was quite enough. Pretension would have never suited Marlee, and sometimes the similarities she saw in her sister and her long-gone loved one amazed Matlyn. Parrish sat crossed-legged and tore off a piece of masking tape using her teeth. She applied it to the seam of the box Matlyn held together for her. "I hate packing," she declared, flipping the box over.

"You hate manual labor."

"My hands are too delicate for this shit."

The cinnamon-haired sibling rolled her eyes.

"Hand me those, would ya?" Parrish pointed to the shelf of books that Matlyn was sitting beside.

With a tiny grunt, she pulled a small stack from the shelf, looked down at the book on top, gave it a face, and passed them off to her sister's waiting hands. When the front door clicked open and a voice wafted down the hall, they both looked up.

"You wouldn't last an hour out there," they heard Baker's voice say.

"In here," Matlyn called out, listening to his approaching footsteps.

Baker walked into the study with Syndal bunched in his arms and a perturbed look on her whiskered face. She squirmed free as he leaned down to kiss Matlyn's temple. "Your pussy tried to make a run for it."

"Shoulda let her go," Parrish mumbled, chucking the books into the cardboard box without a care.

Dropping to the floor next to Matlyn, he asked, "And what are you ladies up to?"

"Packing up Pare's college textbooks."

Baker plucked a book from the line. *Accounting* and another *Economics*. He let the books pile in his lap and reached for one more. His face pinched into a grimace as he read the title. "*Statistical Analysis of* ... Ah, fuck, you graduated with your hymen firmly intact, didn't you?"

Parrish passed him the wine bottle that sat between them and shook her head. "Gave it up to anything with a dick." A statement that wasn't too far from the truth, though she was much more selective than her comment suggested. Parrish went through a handful of boyfriends in college, tossing them aside when things got too intense or too emotional.

Baker chuckled, took a healthy swig, and then refilled Matlyn's nearly empty wine glass.

The three made quick work of Parrish's study, neatly boxing books and taking photos off the walls. Banter flowed, conversation was simple, and Matlyn couldn't help but notice how comfortable and easy this new friendship seemed. Baker just seemed to *fit*. They mingled the way hydrogen clung to oxygen—a perfect working relationship.

Thirteen

✠

Two weeks had flipped by as quickly as pages in a well-read book. Matlyn's brain offered up a new ending for her to contemplate every day. A slip and fall in the shower, mugging gone wrong, or perhaps a ruptured appendix a la Harry Houdini. Every day she forced the train of her thoughts off the tracks and in another direction. She couldn't, *wouldn't* leave without her ducks in a row. It was maybe the one good thing that came of this; the procrastination panties came off and the planning began.

Slipping her hand into Adeline's and gently tugging her toward the office in the back of the shop, Matlyn said, "Come talk with me." Her voice was heavy with secrets.

"But I've got—" Adeline began to protest.

"Nothin' doin', and I got a box of Ferrero Rocher that need some lovin'." Jerking her head, she tightened her grip on her friend's hand.

"Ah, menstruation munchies. Salt and vinegar chips?"

"Of course," Matlyn answered, winking as the curvy blonde followed her into the room. Matlyn settled behind her desk and produced a small, clear box of golden wrapped balls. She pushed them across the table, offering them to Adeline, thinking: *What a meager fucking gift. I'm gonna die ... Chocolate ball?*

Addy got comfortable in the oversized chair, kicking her heels off and hauling her shapely, sun-kissed legs over the arm of the chair. This was Addy, swing skirt carelessly crumbled around her thighs, legs dangling, toes painted electric blue, and her heels forgotten on the floor.

Matlyn popped a chocolate ball into her mouth. Biting down, she steeled herself for the conversation she was about to have. She knew there was a good chance that her friend would call bullshit, but she had to tell someone. Someone in her life needed to know what was coming, needed to prepare.

Matlyn had cried her tears, spat out her frustration, and moved forward. Knowing she was going to die was something of a relief, and it offered her the opportunity few truly had—to stitch up loose ends. It was also a heavy thing, though, and she couldn't handle its weight alone.

Though her sister was brilliant, her world was narrow and not easily adjusted. She would analyze and figure until she came to the only logical conclusion: her big sister had snapped. No, Parrish would remain blissfully unaware.

"Pacey called me last night. Wanted to buy me

dinner … and a pony," Matlyn teased. "Went on and on. Gushes like a girl."

Addy let out a soft chuckle, her cheeks blooming rose at the mention of his name. "Christ, give a guy some decent head …" They both laughed, Adeline swinging her legs like a happy little girl.

"He's happy, Addy. Stupid fucking happy."

"Confession?"

The little redhead sat up straighter and laced her fingers together. "All ears."

"I slept with him," she admitted, flushing a deeper shade.

Matlyn knew this was big for her friend, and a wide, bright smile cracked her face. She leaned forward, letting Addy know she was ready for the details.

The beautiful, inked-up blonde kicked her feet again and sighed. "So good," she confessed in a whisper. "He stripped me bare right there in the living room." Bright red spread across her chest and neck. "Made me stand there in front of him, and he just … stared. I should have been embarrassed, but I felt—"

"Hot?" Matlyn offered.

"*Owned,*" she said at the same time.

Matlyn smiled in understanding.

Addy toyed with the hem of her skirt, her eyes round and lost in a lurid memory. "The way he looked at me … I didn't care that my tummy wasn't flat, or that my thighs are little thick, or about the fucking curve of my backside. Didn't matter, he wanted it. All of it."

"Damn right he did!" She unwrapped another hazelnut

filled ball and watched her friend do the same. "So …
Baker …"

"Tall, broody, fuck-hot. Brought us coffee this morning
Baker?"

"The same." Nodding, her green eyes wandered to the
computer screen on the desk; something akin to guilt, and
a close cousin of fear, began to bleed through her veins. She
cleared her throat. "He's an Omen," she blurted, not knowing
where to start this conversation. *How does one go about telling
someone that they've met a supernatural being?* Matlyn mused,
suddenly feeling lighter for having said it.

Addy's blonde head snapped up and her eyes shot wide.
In the few seconds before Adeline found her voice, the room
fell into a silence. "Light or Dark?"

Startled by her question, Matlyn asked, "You know
what an—"

"What an Omen is? Yeah. Darlin', I grew up with an
aunt that read chicken bones for the neighbors and hung
empty bottles from the tree to snare evil spirits. Light or
Dark?" her friend asked again, sitting up, tension curling
through her bold frame.

"Dark."

"*Shit,*" the curvy girl spat. "You said there were salt and
vinegar chips?" She made an impatient gimmie-gimmie gesture with her hands.

Matlyn reached down beside her desk and pulled up
a bag and tossed it across the desk, giving her pal a soft,
pitying look.

Addy's head beveled and her glossy, blond curls
brushed her shoulders. "How come you ain't itchin' like
you've got sandpaper up your ass?" Furious, terrified, angry,

panicked—hell even upset would do at a time like this, but Matlyn was … resigned, settled.

Matlyn shrugged. "There was tears, yellin'. Even tossed my weed thinkin' I was trippin' balls. Why waste my energy?" She sat back and dropped her hands to her lap. "Train's coming, nothin' I can do to stop it."

Ripping open the bag, the platinum co-worker sat back, and shoved a handful in her mouth. She swallowed hard and tears welled in her eyes. "Greek mythology," she finally said, crumpling the bag and placing it on the desktop. She looked down at her crumb-covered hands and decided that all her shit's had been given today, so she shrugged and gracelessly wiped them on her shirt.

"The Three Fates." For a while the stunned blond just stared at her friend, no more words came, just a calm, expressionless gaze that made Matlyn feel cold and paper thin.

"I remember. The goddesses cloaked in white, a thread running between them. Said to be the weavers of destiny itself," Matlyn recalled. Her voice was flat, as if she were reciting from an old and well-studied text.

"Yeah, them," Addy confirmed. She went on to explain that The Fates were said to be incredibly powerful, each having a hand in the life of every man, woman, and child … and maybe the gods themselves. The thread they held was the design of life itself.

The Spinner, Clotho, began each new thread, passing it to her sister, Lachesis, who measured out the thread and spun whatever pattern she saw fit. When The Measurer was through, she handed the thread to the final and unchangeable Fate, Atropos.

Atropos held her shears not as a weapon, but an

obligation. When she severed a thread, a life ended; its destiny had come to a head and what was done, was truly done.

"Maybe I've been sexed stupid..." she cocked her head like a confused puppy, big green eyes and all "...but what does that have to do with Omens?" Matlyn wondered.

"The Fates, Omens, and Death, not even the gods can shake them. They kinda work together, in the way a group of contractors might all be working on the same house, but doin' different jobs. Ya know?"

Addy's aunt Sophie had been a wise, if slightly off beat woman. She was kind and quick to disperse her wisdom if she thought it might do some good. Her ties to the supernatural world around her were taught through the generations, and she had been correct in assuming there was a relationship between The Fates, Omens, and Death.

Death knew good and well who it answered to. It knew who wielded those shears, who decided how long each human life would be, and when it would begin. The Omens, however, seemed to play more of a monkey in the middle part. They were sent out to take down the history of the humans they'd been 'assigned' to, but that was all. They were workhorses, voluntary or otherwise.

Listening to this, the troubled ginger sighed deeply. Gods, myths, preternatural beings, her world kept expanding and folding open, all the while her time grew shorter and nearer to an end she couldn't see. Pulling on her serious face and her big girl panties, she asked Addy to help her get affairs in order so poor Parrish wouldn't be left to deal with it. She didn't know how much time she had, but it wasn't enough and the last thing she wanted was for someone else to have to deal with the fallout.

Two hours later, financial and legal appointments were made for the following week. A handwritten will was drafted and signed by Matlyn in the event that next week didn't come. She would be leaving the shop to Adeline. Parrish would continue her accounting and bookkeeping position there, if she chose to. Money was moved and shuffled, and in those moments Matlyn was grateful for her guardian Sasha's careful planning and the diligence she took with the girls' money.

"Thank you, sweets," Matlyn whispered, tears stacking, heavy as bricks in her eyes. Her voice was watery and weak.

* * *

Addy stood and rounded the desk, embracing her friend in a long, fierce hug. Adeline Sonnier had never been much for sappy girl moments, but this was Matlyn, her Little Bird, her best friend and her life would soon end. Though she was bold, she had not been crafted in steel, and the thought of losing her beautiful friend pinched her heart and pulled at the very muscles that held it in place, but she had strength enough to lend. Enough to hold her Little Bird up, if she needed it. She could and would do that for her. The girl prayed for a quick, peaceful death for her dear friend. The very thought of a violent end to such a person wasn't something Addy cared to entertain. The idea alone made her stomach revolt and her head ache. Of course the chips and chocolate could have been to blame.

No, my Little Bird will fall with grace, she thought as she held tighter, squeezing the air from the woman's lungs. "Love you," she croaked.

* * *

August 29, 1915, 3:37 a.m. ~ San Jose, California

The smell of dried blood, garbage, and rainwater mixed and joined in a repugnant smell that overwhelmed his nostrils and woke him. Dazed, stinking, and sore, Samuel pushed up off the cold alley floor and sat back on his heels. Looking around, eyes wide and half terrified, he wondered how in the name of the good Father he'd gotten there, and where there was exactly.

In a blink, the days between his death and his awakening came to him.

* * *

The man in the gray suit stood before him, still and waiting like a sentinel. The chaos and storm of bullets that had surrounded him vanished, leaving them both in a quiet space that seemed to exist just outside of everything else. Samuel had never seen such a contradiction before, a space inside of space that was both shimmering with light and utterly dark. He blinked and tried to stitch together his mental facilities long enough to accept what had passed only moments before … his death.

With his pale hands clasped together in front of him, the man in gray cleared his throat, drawing Samuel's attention. He reached out, palms up, and offered Samuel his hands.

Samuel's eyes cut to the stranger's hands and then back to his oblivion-black eyes and made no move at all.

The suit stepped forward, nodded slowly, and gave a

simple, but reassuring smile. Hands still outstretched, he held Samuel's unsure gaze and waited.

With shaky hands still vibrating from the reverberation from the gunshot, Samuel placed his hands in the dark stranger's.

"You are Omen now," the suit spoke, his voice deep and another world away.

And just like the complicated progress of water passing through a membrane, knowledge seeped into Samuel. He knew the kick and rhythm of a Story and felt it grow in his veins stronger than his own pulse. The searing pain of Witnessing lit his body on fire for the first time, and he watched in amazement and horror as the first thirty-two years of his life worked its way under his skin. Black words bubbled to the surface, mapping his life in moments and small stretches of time.

When the pain ceased, he knew what he'd become and what the next one hundred years would bring. Samuel had become Death's siren call, and for a hundred years to come, he would taste Death on his tongue like ash and bitter wine; never again would there be sweetness.

A hundred years of death and pain for the lives he'd taken seeking approval from an impossible man.

When the slim, gray-suited man loosened his grip on Samuel's trembling hands, he took one fluid step backward and watched as Samuel buckled under the weight of the next hundred years.

* * *

As the tiny red-head cuddled in close, Baker let his finger run the delicate lines of her face.

Only two hours before she'd demanded he gather his things and leave the "fucking gross" accommodations. Actually, her preference was that he light a match and walk away, but she'd settle for him simply paying the bill and checking out. She wanted him to stay, wanted him close by.

And as she lay quiet and ruined by exhaustion, a slow, harsh burn crept over his skin. Looking down at his bare chest, Baker watched as ink blacker than the night's sky pooled and gathered, forming words.

Carefully, the Dark Omen separated himself from Matlyn and walked to the mirror. The scroll was hard to decipher, the letters appearing backward. Reading the new words, he recognized that tiny slice of time as the moment Matlyn had come out to Parrish as being bi-sexual.

Fifteen-years old, he'd thought, then quietly counted back the years that remained to be written. *Thirteen years*.

"Not enough time," he whispered into the silent room, gazing back at his Story's sleeping form.

Fourteen

❧

Thick, hungry fog swallowed one house and then the next as it rolled into the Garden district, trapping heat and moisture beneath it. The rising sun gave the fog an eerie glow, and the diffused light spread down through trees and into open windows. Under that curtain of thick mist, a sweat damp, pale body moved over the Omen, like molasses pulling over silk: unhurried, soft, and fluid. Baker gripped her hips, and crescents bloomed on her skin where his fingers bit in.

"Keep up the slow torture an' you'll be late for work," Baker said without a hint of warning or care. He watched the movement of her chest and the slip-slide of sweat that ran between her breasts.

Her hips rolled forward, and she let out a low moan.

"Addy's opening," she whispered and slowly coiled back again, like a snake ready to strike. With soft hands splayed on Baker's chest, she raked her fingertips over his pecs, watching red lines blossom. To Baker it was an absolute blessing and a curse to have a woman that could work his body the way his Einin could. Sliding his hands up her sides, he let his thumbs stroke the undersides of Matlyn's breasts, and with an airy sigh, she let her body drop covering his. She sucked his bottom lip between her teeth and smiled at the groan that rumbled through his chest.

"Turn around," Baker ordered, grabbing handfuls of ass. "Hands and knees."

One body pulled back, the other pushed forward. Flushed and eager, she turned and peeked over her shoulder watching as he rose to his knees.

"Einin, your backside is fucking lovely."

The slender woman winked. "I try."

Hands on her hips, Baker pulled her back to him and let her tease him a little with a wiggle. He slipped back inside her with a growl. Pushing her chest toward the bed, he laid his hand between her shoulder blades and began a quick, deep rhythm that had Matlyn gripping sheets and cursing.

When his body began to shudder and break the rhythm, he slowed himself again, knowing she wasn't ready yet. Baker toyed with her body, moving her this way then that. He sucked, licked, and teased aggressively until Matlyn's breathing was ragged and her demands dropped from her mouth in low growls. Matlyn came, biting down on his shoulder, with three fingers buried inside her.

Lifting one knee, he pushed back inside, not giving the flushed woman a second to spare or moment to relax her coiled muscles. Immediately, Baker's stomach tensed and he laced his hand with hers. Heat ripped up his spine, and he groaned as he fell apart.

* * *

"I've got coffee, creamy pastry stuffs, and a peppermint tea for Miss Campbell," Baker said, sauntering through the front door of Parabola. The bell rang above his head. In his hands he carried two trays and a brown bag piled precariously on top.

Matlyn held the door, taking the opportunity to ogle Baker's back end, loving the almost lazy strut he had. *Man's walk could melt a Popsicle*, she thought. *Pure sticky, slow, sex.*

Baker and Scott settled into an easy conversation about a piece he was preparing while Matlyn set up her tattoo station, filling tiny thimbles with bright fluids.

* * *

Outside The Light Omen stood staring up at the shop's sign. She touched the place where Parrish's name had first appeared, and in that moment she felt the distinct tugging pull of her Story. She ducked into the shop.

* * *

The bell overhead rang out, and Baker swayed on his feet, feeling a wave of dizziness fall over him. And for a few seconds the ever present pulse that flowed between him and Matlyn stuttered and halted like a shorted circuit. He looked up and saw a mousey-brown haired woman framing the entryway, and something tugged at his memory, throwing him back eight years—the last time he'd crossed paths with another Omen.

Across the shop, Addy saw the way Baker's body wavered, and she walked over to him laying a gentle hand on his arm. "You all right?"

"Must be a fucking convention," he mumbled, jerking his chin in the direction of the woman in the light peach dress.

Sharp eyes followed, and she took in the appearance of a twenty-something-year old woman: slender figure, medium brown hair pinned up in a neat bun, and a long-sleeved cardigan. "Omen," she whispered and her charcoal eyes grew wide and worried.

As far as the Dark Omen was concerned, he was no more to blame for Matlyn's impending death than he was for the color of his own eyes. It simply was. It was complicated. Baker knew he was an easy place for Addy to pour her hurt and her rage, but what he was and whom he Witnessed was not of his choosing, and she seemed to accept and understand that. So after Matlyn had confided in her, she'd offered him a shot of cherry whiskey and the rest of her friend's period stash. By the bottle's end, a new friendship was formed.

Now she the buxom blond stood next to him, eyes pinned on the Omen across the room, panic lighting her round face.

Ingrid stared back. Her eyes were clear and bright and seemed to carry a knowledge that only those who've lived more than one life harbor. Baker recognized the look. Slowly, she moved away from the doorway, dropping her gaze. The mousy-woman smoothed her hands over her dress, unconsciously trying to smother her jumping nerves. Stepping to the side, she casually perused the Flash art that hung on the walls.

Addy's grip tightened on his arm. "She can't … why does she have *two*, Baker?" Tears stacked in her eyes, and she struggled to keep them from falling.

"She doesn't. She's here for someone else." Baker tipped his chin, and they both watched as the woman in peach blew out a deep breath and braced herself on the countertop. To the casual observer she looked to be browsing, but Baker saw the way her body almost sighed in pleasure with the rush of a Witnessing. "She's Light."

* * *

Scott stood there quietly confused, listening to the strange conversation between Adeline and Baker until boredom— and that not-so-fun feeling of being on the outside of something private—had him shrugging and wandering into the back room.

He found Matlyn bent over the drawing table, giving some serious stink-eye to an outline she was preparing. Her head snapped up as he shuffled in and dropped to a leather chair. It wheezed and he sighed.

"Think the copier's fucked," she said, sounding none too pleased. "Lines look blown out." She stepped aside so the blue-haired inker could assess the papers pushed out in a messy array in front of her.

He studied the pages and the outline Matlyn had been working on and shook his head. "Nah, Little Bird, these lines are tight. No blur, no bleeding. Looks good."

When he looked back at his friend, her face was puckered in befuddlement.

Her eyes dropped to the pages again and she frowned. Wearing a perplexed expression, she rubbed her forehead and her shoulders sagged.

"You all right?" Scott asked, placing a hand on her shoulder.

"Migraine coming on, maybe." She sounded unsure. "Or maybe I need to have my prescription looked at."

"You good to ink, or do you want to maybe have Campbell do it? This is right up her alley." He eyed the tiny fairies and the weeping willow and though it was just an outline, he could see the color in their wings and the gentle sway of the drooping branches. It'd be a great piece when it was complete.

"I got it." Matlyn laid a blank piece of transfer paper over the sketch and carefully outlined a whimsical looking toadstool. Straightening, she handed the page to Mike.

No breaks in the lines, no warped or uneven lines. The outline looked flawless. "You're good," he said, patting her on the head.

* * *

Wilson walked into Parabola, took his hat off, and chucked it—along with his messenger bag—into his work station as he passed it.

"Mornin', Major," Campbell said, waving to Wilson as he rounded the shop's front desk.

Wilson Kenning of the U.S. Marine Corps had served overseas for nine years as an Imagery Analysis Specialist. He never spoke of his previous job, his rank, or the tags he wore on the chain around his neck. The young tattooist saw Wilson as someone loyal, sharp, and dependable, worthy of the title of General.

The Major bowed, plucked Campbell's hand like a daisy from a garden, and lifted it to his mouth, placing a quick, light kiss on the back of her delicate hand. "Morning, Miss Campbell. Coffee?" He raised his head and dropped her hand.

"Backroom." She jerked her head toward the back room. "Oh, and cream puffs," she gushed, licking her lips.

As Wilson spun toward the backroom his eyes caught a familiar looking woman in peach hovering by the display case. He changed his course and made for the tall, thin woman. "Mornin'. Name's Wilson. Can I help you with somethin'?" He held his hand out for her. When she lifted her face, he immediately remembered a conversation in a small bookstore.

"Not at all. I'm just being nosey. Ya know, I always pictured tattoo parlors as filthy, smoky things, with cracked vinyl chairs and drawings of naked women everywhere. Not the case," she said with notes of pleasure and surprise. Her voice held no accent, and it was as soothing as a caress.

Wilson chuckled. "Some look just like that. Stay outta those ones," he warned, winking. "Sure I can't interest you in somethin' tiny and tasteful? Curb that curiosity."

"Oh no, I'm far too much of a pansy, likely to pass out." She shook her head and pushed away from the display case. Her eyes roamed across the room and landed on Baker again. "Lovely shop, really," she said with sincerity and backed toward the door. Her heels clicked on the black and white tiles.

"Chicken out?" Baker asked as the bell rang out and the door clapped behind the Light Omen.

The Southern charmer hesitated for a moment, and then he shook his head and turned toward Baker. "Nope. Just curious. Art enthusiast." His words dropped slow and unsure. He looked back at the frosted glass door. "Parrish and I ran into her at a bookstore across town. Talked us up 'bout a photographer."

Wilson's thoughts trudged around his head, and he wondered what the odds were of running into the same tourist twice, on different sides of the city no less. At a popular restaurant, maybe, but a local establishment? He shook off the creeping suspicion and set his mind to hot coffee and cream puffs.

* * *

Syndal raced and bounded through the house, her tiny paws barely touching down. She stopped abruptly at the mouth of the hallway, crouching low to the ground and watching the front door. When the key slipped into the lock, her small, furry butt wiggled and her muscles bunched, ready to spring.

Matlyn stepped through the door and the moment her booted foot was over the threshold, Syndal launched herself forward, attacking the cherry Docs with gusto. Matlyn's hand swept out in front of the cat, and Syndal batted a puffy paw, scratching her palm.

"Hey, you tiny demon, you're messin' up the Docs! Unacceptable!" Matlyn gently pushed the combative kitty to the side with her foot and leaned down to give it a stern look. Syndal leaped to the side and swatted at a leather clad ankle again.

Baker bent and scooped up the angry fur ball and brought her to eye level. With warning and more than a bushel of mischief in his voice, he spoke to the wriggling cat. "I hear aunt Adeline has a dog. Big dog, named Titus." Syndal hissed in response and Baker let the cat go, watching as it fled up the stairs. "That cat's an asshole."

Wholeheartedly agreeing, she plopped down on the bottom stair and began to loosen the laces on her boots. "Turkey sandwich?" she offered, looking up at the tall man standing in front of her.

"And egg salad," he added, pulling off the red button-down he'd worn to hide Matlyn's story. He neatly laid it over a kitchen chair and went to work on the egg salad, pulling things out of the fridge. All of it was incredibly domestic, and he found himself smiling at the feeling. *Like roots*, he pondered as the eggs boiled. He'd never felt so grounded and content before. He was perfectly happy chopping onions.

* * *

Baker's eyes opened again, he rolled to his side, and the clock read 2:13 a.m. Slowly he disentangled himself from the naked redhead and quietly dressed. Creeping like a cat in the night, he slipped out of the room. Jamming his feet into his shoes, he grabbed the keys from the table by the door. When Baker started the truck, he sent a quick and silent prayer into the pitch-black sky, hoping that his beautiful girl didn't wake to a cold bed.

The old truck's headlights curved and bent with the road and occasionally caught the glowing eyes of some critter or other. The nearer he came to the swamp, the more like a swamp the truck smelled. Hot, moist, and green. Old, overgrown green, mossy, watery green. On the side of the road he saw a man in beige slacks and a white cotton shirt. The rest of the man faded into the dark night. He held up a hand, indicating Baker should stop the truck there. He killed the engine, locked it, and pocketed the keys.

Without the headlights spreading an eerie white over the landscape, Baker could hardly see his hand in front of his face. He took a few hesitant steps forward and looked over to the middle-aged man standing at the side of the road, his eyes adjusting. As he neared the man, he saw that his white cotton button-down was wrinkled, and he was barefoot. His face was utterly expressionless, but Baker got the feeling that was the man's default setting.

The man in the wrinkled shirt reached out his dark, rough hands and took the Omen's, making him jump. Bringing clammy, white hands to his face, he inspected them. He turned Baker's hands this way and that, and finally dropped them, seemingly satisfied.

"Com'mon din," the man said, turning and motioning for Baker to follow. His accent was heavy—obviously influenced by French—biting off syllables in strange places and rolling sounds together so that 'come on then' became what Baker heard.

As the two men walked in the dead of night, obscured in part by tall grass and other unknown swamp vegetation, a small firelight became visible. Next to the fire, a form was crouched, combing a stick through the fire as if petting it. The water behind him was smooth and black like oil. Trees sprouted from the pitch-like water, reaching upward as if pleading with the sky to pluck them from their watery homes.

"Christ," Baker said under his breath. "This close to the water, aren't you worried about alligators?" Baker's wide, wandering eyes scanned the landscape. He was hyper-alert and veering toward flight. Fight wasn't a fucking option, not when the creatures here had some major home court advantage.

The voice that answered was that of the man stoking the tiny fire. It crackled and spit angry embers skyward. "We have an understandin'." He straightened himself out, and Baker took in his appearance.

He was a short man, no more than five-three, wearing a long, purple linen robe, old beat-up leather sandals, and a straw hat. It was a little dramatic.

Gotta be for show, Baker thought, taking another step toward the fire.

"Whatcha wanna to know, boy?" the man in the hat asked.

Baker was quick to answer. "Can it be stopped?"

"You bring what I asked?"

The Omen was apprehensive, but reached into his pocket and pulled out a necklace, Matlyn's necklace. He held it up and let it unfurl. The heavy locket swung wildly. She'd told him it was a gift from Rumor for standing in her wedding. The locket was a unique flowered wire pattern. Varying shades of blue mingled together.

The Hat reached out and carefully, reverently, tucked the necklace into his palm. "Sit," he ordered, pointing to the ground.

Baker folded to the damp, mossy ground and watched

as the Hat lifted a bottle of whiskey to his lips. He swished it about and then spat into the flames. The fire crackled and flared with delight. He took another healthy pull, this time swallowing the amber liquid and passed it to Baker, tipping his chin, silently telling him to drink—he did.

Taking the bottle back, he used the rest to douse the tiny flames, then reached out an open hand and scooped up the booze-soaked mud and ash mixture. He moved it around in his palm, careful to keep hold of the necklace. He collected a small gob on his index finger and brought it to his forehead, drawing what looked to Baker to be an open eye. Then, quick as a cobra's strike, the Hat reached out and pulled Baker toward him.

"The fuck?" Baker tried to pull away, but the man's grip on his wrist was strong. The old man's fat fingertip moved over Baker's forehead.

"To see," the Hat murmured and then clutched Baker's hands in his. The necklace was warm and seemed to beat like a pulse. "Papa Legba, open da door an' let me see." His plea rang through the night, begging the voodoo god to open the lines of communication between this plane and the other.

For a moment, an eerie silence pushed out in a circle around them. Crickets ceased their night songs, frogs quieted, and Baker held his breath. His heart hammered in his chest, and he instinctively tightened his grip on the locket. It burned like a coal in his palm, but he refused to let go.

The bubble around them burst with a violent gust of wind, ripe with the watery, green smell that had surrounded them. Sound returned in a deafening boom, and Baker raised his shoulders in a feeble attempt to shield his ears.

The man that had led him to the old voodoo priest

suddenly began to sing and dance in a jerky movement that seemed puppet-like. Until that moment, Baker had forgotten that he was even there. When he stopped and dropped to his knees beside Baker, the Hat spoke.

"Omen, what has been spun cannot be undone. Her thread will be cut as it was always meant to be. It's in da design, boy. No doin', no action will change that." His voice was hoarse and sad. The priest pat Baker's arm the way a doctor might a patient that'd been given some terrible news.

Baker hung his head.

* * *

Matlyn sat up, spine as straight as bamboo, sweaty and shaking. Behind her eyelids, dancing in the darkness, she saw the face of a dark-skinned man, eyes pristine and unnaturally white, teeth the same. His features were lost in the darkness; a white, hand-drawn eye sat between his brows, glowing like a beacon.

Shaken, she reached for Baker, finding the bed next to her empty. Abruptly, she became very aware of the stillness, the quiet … and the smell of whiskey.

Fifteen

⚜

With feet like lead, Baker slugged up the stairs. His body felt drained and heavy. He stank of swamp and ashes, and the taste of whiskey still coated his tongue. When he reached the top of the stairs, Syndal sat outside Matlyn's room like a sentinel, licking her puffy little paws. She stopped when she caught sight of the tired man and let loose a nasty hiss. Baker took another step toward the door, and Syndal's back arched high.

"Calm the fuck down, Syn," Baker whispered to the angry cat and shooed her away with his foot.

He pushed the door open and it creaked, breaking the quiet around him into pieces. The lamp next to the bed was on, and Matlyn sat in the middle, bathed in a dim glow, still naked, her knees drawn to her chest. She looked scared and alone and oh so tiny on the oversized bed surrounded by a sea of deep gray. Baker walked to her and slumped down next to her, letting his exhausted body sink down into the gray sheets.

She said nothing, just looked at him, her eyes taking in his defeated posture.

"I went to see a voodoo priest," he admitted.

"Why?" Her voice held neither judgment nor amusement, just mild curiosity.

He looked up, meeting her soft, worried gaze. "I wanted to know ... I needed ..." His words sputtered and faltered, and then his gunmetal eyes dropped. Quiet as a June bug, he said, "All this magic in the world, all this power, and there's nothing—no one—that can stop this." The tired Omen's eyes drew upward again, but his voice remained whisper-soft. "Nothing to *save you*." A solitary tear slid down the planes of a weary face.

Matlyn drew him closer, letting him crumble. He sobbed into her lap and recounted the ritual and what the priest said.

* * *

"No, no. A spell. Something to keep Death at bay," Baker begged, lifting his head and catching the eyes of the old man. His hand clamped around the wrist of the dark priest.

"You want success in your job, I c'n help you, boy. You want revenge on a cheatin' ex, sure. Maybe I give her warts. But, Omen, goin' against The Fates is sometin' I just can't do." The old man gently disentangled his wrist and stepped back calmly. He hadn't feared Baker's advance. It wasn't an act of aggression, just

one desperate man reaching to touch something that might hold a little hope.

"Is it money? I can get you money. Please."

The old voodoo priest laid his wrinkled hand on Baker's shoulder. His voice dropped and pity licked at every syllable. "Picture a thread, fulla color and purpose. Thread witout purpose, witout design, is just a heap. Wasted material. But give that thread a design, a shape ... a reason for bein' an' it becomes sometin' meaningful and beautiful. If ya let that thread run amuck, let it wind outta control, it loses its shape. It's no longer what it shoulda been. Best to cut it off—let it be what it was always meant to be." With that, the dark man in the hat turned and walked into the thick of the forest surrounding the swamp.

* * *

"It hurts," Baker mumbled, pointing to his aching heart.

Matlyn knew it wasn't physical pain that shot through his chest, and it wasn't the sting of Witnessing. She framed his face, her hands as soft and tender as her voice when she spoke. "Nazareth had it right ... love hurts."

Baker snorted and a small smile lifted his face. "Lame, Einin. Fucking lame." He shook his raven head and leaned down to kiss her pouty, pink lips, his weight pressing down on her in a way that soothed them both.

With a chuckle, she parted her legs, allowing him to drop into the space between her bare thighs. "Got ya smilin', though." Her purple painted fingernails raked through his hair, and she pulled his face just a little closer—close enough to see the tiny specks of an icy emerald in his dark gray eyes. "You can't save me, Baker." Matlyn's voice was both weighted and light. A matter-of-fact quality hung on the vowels and understanding clung to the consonants.

"How do I lose you? How do I just *let you* go?" he begged, lifting her hand to his chest. His heart pushed like thunder under her touch.

"You love me until there's nothing left of me. You don't waste time on an out we both know doesn't exist. Be mad, that's fine. Be sad, be afraid, but be *here*, Baker, with me."

At the press of her lips, his mouth opened and his tongue swept gently over hers, drinking her in. She sighed as his body relaxed and seemed to melt around her. His fingertips ran a track up and down her arm, sending a shudder through her body. Baker kissed her until her leg hitched over his hip, until she was flushed and panting. He moved down her body with purpose. His tongue dragged from sternum to belly button. He wasn't teasing, he was tasting.

"I can taste the sweat on you," Baker mumbled against her skin.

It should have disgusted her that her body was coated in dried sweat, but her toes curled and her stomach clenched, and she moaned, her head lolling back as Baker snaked further down her body. When his tongue slid between her wet folds, her heels dug into the mattress and her mouth popped open, and a litany of profanity and half-cooked words spilled out.

Loud, unapologetic moans filled the room as he drove her closer to the edge. He gripped her thighs and pulled her roughly toward him, then hitched her shaky legs over each of his shoulders. Gentle as the flutter of a moth's wing, he kissed her thighs and ran the tip of his finger over her swollen lips before plunging it deep inside her.

"Your cunt is stunning." Baker's voice was rough, like sand caught on fine silk, and the sound of it did stupid things to Matlyn.

"That's a great word," she managed to say between groans.

"Cunt? Yes. Got a bad rep in the '80s."

She giggled, setting off a series of intense spasms that forced her back off the bed, as if possessed. Her body broke down, and Baker growled like a needy animal.

He waited, his finger still inside working the trembling woman down from her high. When her body seemed to relax and she opened her eyes, Baker pushed back onto his knees, opening the zipper of his jeans. He crooked a finger at her, demanding she come to him.

Matlyn crawled over the mess of sheets, licked her lips, and without an ounce of trepidation, she went to work on bringing her Omen to orgasm.

* * *

June 1, 2015, 8:45 a.m. ~ Garden District, New Orleans

"We need a list," the sated girl suggested, raking her fingers through Baker's sweat-damp hair. Muggy June air swirled in through the open window.

"Hmm?" He lifted his eyes to Matlyn's face and squinted at the early-morning sun shining in his eyes.

"Like a bucket list."

"What? You're morbid. I fucking love you."

She chuckled and tugged at his black hair. Rolling to her side, she glanced at the clock next to the bed. It was 8:45 a.m. She needed to shower and wash the layers of sweat off of her. *I need coffee,* Matlyn thought. *In massive fucking quantities.*

Baker's fingertips mindlessly stroked and tickled her knee, occasionally dancing up her thigh as they lay breathing in the smell of summer. "So what do you want to do, then?"

"I can't believe this shit just got all *A Walk to Remember.* Fuckin' drama queen." Baker groaned as if in pain, but his lips twitched with the slightest smile.

She snorted. "You've seen that movie?"

"I *hated* that movie." Twisting his body slightly, he looked at seafoam eyes. "So what's on this list of yours?"

"*Ours,*" she corrected, pushing loose strands of red over away from her face.

Though Baker never mentioned it, never breathed a word of it, she knew the years were pressing down on him. Neither had a clear notion of what was to come for Baker following his one hundred years, but she could feel the period, the exclamation mark, the thing at the end of a sentence.

Baker stopped and put his hand on her hip, facing her full on, an expectant look plastered on his face. He rolled his wrist in *come on, let's have it* gesture.

"All right," she said, sitting up a little straighter cracking her knuckles. "We're fucking in that insanely hot truck of yours."

"I like the list. The list is *good.*" Bushy, dark brows waggled in a lurid way.

"Figured there wouldn't be much in the way of complaints."

Baker laced his fingers through hers and gave her hand

a squeeze, then trailed his palm over the rise and fall of her naked hip. "What else?" he wondered.

"There's a bed and breakfast … my parents used to spend anniversaries there. The Kehoe House, I think it was called. It's in Savannah."

"More sex, good. I like where this is going."

Tongue out, she smacked Baker playfully. Losing herself in the morning's warmth and the smell of his skin, forgetting about the time, she asked. "What about you?"

"What, that's it? Sex in an ancient truck and a B&B?"

"No. There's a few more. I'm just wondering what an asshole like yourself would include."

Rubbing his chin, which was covered in a rough, dark stubble, Baker looked kind of pensive, kind of evil genius. Mischief twisted his smile into something just this side of sinister, and Matlyn's stomach pulled tight. She loved the cocky trouble-maker look on him.

Made from the devil's finest cloth, Matlyn thought.

Face turning red, as if embarrassed to spit it out, the suddenly shy Omen said, "I wanna watch you with another woman." He licked his lips, as if he could taste the sin on them.

"Well damn." Inching closer to him, she could feel the heat flowing back and forth between their bodies. "Wait. This ain't some 'My-girl's-bi-sexual-so-let's-see-what-I-can-get-from-the-deal' type thing, is it?" The very idea made her gut twist in a not so pleasant way.

I'm no side show. Unimpressed lips pressed thin and her eyes narrowed on his face.

"No, Einin." His voice was even, but she easily caught the offense thinly layering the words. "You're not some

curious object for me to show off. I want all of you, doll."
Dipping his head, he captured her lips and mumbled against
them, "I want the parts you hide away. The parts you think
no one wants. I want you, as you are."

A tad stunned, she blinked, and her heart faltered for
just a moment, forgetting its rhythm.

"I look at Scott, and I'm fucking jealous. I have no
right to be, but I am. It's a stupid caveman-kind of thing."
He kissed her fluttering eyelids. "He's had that part of you,
shared that with you. And because I'm nothing but a selfish
troglodyte, I want that too."

Biting her lip, she shimmied away from his heat.
"No big-titted blondes. Not my type." Matlyn wagged her
finger. "We stink. I have to work, and all this talk is a terrible fucking distraction," she declared, walking backward,
blocking the new, bright yellow rays.

"Go. Make coffee," the redhead commanded. "If
you can find an IV drip, let's do that." Stepping over the
threshold onto the cold tile, she shivered. Spinning quickly,
she flipped on the bathroom light, and started the shower.

* * *

Smiling like the cat that swallowed that damned canary
whole, the pleased Omen slipped on his boxers and padded
down the stairs in search of coffee. He moved around
Matlyn's kitchen like he'd been there for years, pulling her
giant-sized travel mug from the dishwasher. Coffee pot in
hand, he headed to the sink. Overtired and mesmerized, the
man watched the stream of water pour into the pot, flooding
it. He breathed out slowly, letting his muscles relax and his
brain shut down.

There's nothing to be done.
Nothing to stop it.
No way to slow it down.

Blinking, he shut the water off, poured the excess from the pot, and turned toward the machine. Staggering pain shot up his spine and across his chest, and just like the whiskey, he watched as the coffeepot fell to the floor, shattering. Water moved over the gray tile like a tiny tidal wave. It washed over his bare feet, splashed the cupboards, and took to the grooves between the tiles, racing away from him.

"Fuck," he spat, reaching out to brace himself. He looked down. New words were forming just above his navel. How many years would that sentence steal from him? How many moments? What was left?

When the burn receded, the Dark Omen bent and began cleaning the tiny shards of glass that littered the floor.

"Needed a new pot." Wearing a concerned look, Matlyn stood, looking down at the watery mess and gave Baker a soft smile.

"Sorry," he said, standing and emptying a handful of rough glass into the garbage.

She took a careful step forward and splayed her hands over his chest, watching the skin quiver at her soft touch. Her fingers gently ran over the still warm words. "My eighteenth birthday. The day I bought the limesicle." She jerked her head toward the front of the house where the lime-colored car sat proudly. "Drove it around all day, music blaring, smilin' like an asshole. Parked it on some dirt back road an' fucked Melissa Armstrong within an inch of her life. I met Cohen a few months later, strollin' around campus, smellin' like a pig's asshole and coming off a frat-boy style bender."

* * *

"So what else is on this list?" Baker casually asked as he climbed into the driver's seat of the sterling truck.

"Ride an elephant."

Baker smiled, picturing it. "Such a girl," he said with a snicker.

"Eat shit, Omen." Sitting back, a wide grin split the girl's face. "So what stupid manly pursuit have you got lined up? Sky diving? Base jumping? Maybe snort a little blow off the backside of a hooker? Hmm?" Matlyn turned away from the window and eyed her Omen, her fucking beautiful, Dark Omen. She studied the lines and sharp curves of his face, watching his jaw flex as he spoke. She reached out and ran the back of her hand along his way-past-five-o'clock shadow, loving the rough feel of it on her soft skin.

Not looking away from the road as he navigated the morning traffic, he said, "Blow is so 1970s. That scene's been done." He peeked at her quick and said, deadpan, "Message in a bottle."

The image made her snort. "Really?" she asked. Her pretty, freckled face scrunched up.

"Get bent, woman! More than a hundred and thirty years, I think I *might* have a little fucking wisdom to impart. Jerk," he snapped at his laughing passenger.

"What would you write?" Now that her laughter had subsided, her voice took on a inquisitive and honest tone.

"Ya know that annoying saying *'it's not about you'*?" he asked, shifting the truck into second and feeling the kick it always gave when the gear shifted. "Bullshit. It's all about you. Always. What you want for your life, how you chose to live it. Each choice you make … it's not about him or her or *them*, it's about you."

"*Ego*centric," she stage-whispered, side-eyeing her driver.

"Who else should you be living your life for, Einin?"

The question hung there for a long moment before Matlyn dared to answer. She thought about how a young Samuel had lived, begging for his father's love and becoming something he never wanted to be in the hopes of pleasing him. She looked back to the man sitting beside her, a man whose choices had been stripped from him. The right to simply fade away and become a part of the past he'd belonged to was stolen. She laid a warm hand on his thigh and squeezed.

"No one, baby." Her voice moved careful and quiet across the cab of the truck.

* * *

"Done." Matlyn scooted her chair back and took in the full picture of the piece she'd just completed. Bold colors seemed to lift the vibrant balloons right off the skin and into the air. The woman stood and looked at the newly tattooed image in the long mirror hanging on the wall.

"It's perfect," she exclaimed, choking on unshed tears. The tattoo was a memorial piece for the younger sister she'd lost to leukemia a year ago. "Thank you." She looked the ink-slinger in the eyes when she spoke.

Matlyn wiped the excess ink and hints of blood from the tiny blonde's arm. "You're welcome." Scooping a glob of Vaseline from the tub on a nearby counter top, she smoothed the goop over the irritated skin. She took her gloves off, washed her hands, and gathered a few supplies from the cabinet. "You can take off the cover in a few hours. Use a non-scented soap to wash for the first little while. No direct water pressure, and don't pick at it." The tattooist gently and carefully covered the blonde's arm, securing the plastic patch with medical tape.

The woman nodded. "It looks amazing," she said.

Matlyn handed her a small plastic container filled with a yellowish paste. "Apply it a few times a day. You can also use vitamin E based products, so long as it's not heavily fragranced."

"Got it," she said, nodding again.

"Great. Take care, Lara, and if you find you need any touch-ups, just give us a call. Adeline at the front desk will help you with the bill."

Lara reached out and hugged Matlyn, thanking her again for the wonderful work she'd done and then left the room beaming from ear to ear.

"Hello, ladies," Matlyn heard the deep, rumbling voice of her Omen say seconds before he ducked into her station. He stood quietly, and she could feel him drinking her in, her copper-haired mess hiding her face.

"Stop staring at me like that."

Baker was silent for a beat. All cool, calm and collected, he asked, "Like what?"

Still rummaging through her supplies, she spoke, "Like you wanna bend me over the cabinet and fuck me 'til I scream."

His keys jingled in his pockets, and she heard his breathy chortle. "You're not even looking at me, Einin." Her name moved across the room like low thunder.

"Don't need to. I can feel it." She pushed a box to the far side and began counting the samples of Tattoo Goop that she had left. Adeline made the stuff from scratch and friend or not it was an amazing product.

Slowly, Baker stalked toward her and as she rose he whispered in her ear, lips caressing the sensitive shell. "In a reputable establishment like this? Never."

Shivers racked her body, and she pulled her shoulders back. She had no trouble imagining the lewd smile he was surely sporting. "Suddenly find that moral compass you've been looking for?" She drifted backwards just the slightest, her body barely grazing his.

He chuckled, soft and low.

Matlyn pushed off him and walked from the station, not looking back at him.

"Unbelievable tease," he accused following a few paces behind Matlyn.

She sauntered down the hall, knowing and *feeling* that Baker was just steps behind her. Her breathing kicked up, and a tiny knot of excitement began to form in her chest. Matlyn walked straight into her office and to her desk. She stood with her back to the door and listened for the soft footfalls of Baker's sneakered feet.

The door closed with a click and the delicious knot in her chest grew a little tighter. Her fingers grazed the wooden desktop, and she anxiously bit her lip. Suddenly, warmth spread across her back. He was close, close enough to feel his heat, but not a single line of Baker's body touched hers.

Infuriating. She breathed in again, smelling that earthy, windy, leather scent that made up the creature standing behind her. She hummed and shifted her feet. She wanted to turn and face him and kiss him. A heavy buzz ran through her as she slowly began to turn.

"Stop. Hands on the desk," he said low in her ear. "Don't move."

She chewed on the inside of her cheek as the nail of his thumb ran a firm line up her outer thigh and over the swell of her ass. The Omen pressed himself closer to her, fitting the planes of her slender body perfectly to his. That taunting thumb of his moved around to tease and torture the delicate skin of her stomach, making her belly quiver. Baker's breath was warm in her hair, so close to her skin.

He licked the spot just below her ear and a sly, cocky grin exploded across his face as Matlyn's body nearly buckled. "Hands. On. The. Desk," he demanded, seeing her left hand slip away from the dark surface. Correcting herself quickly, her hand gripped the edge, fingers splayed wide and knuckles white.

Moving thick stands of hair to one shoulder, he pulled her gray T-shirt, stretching it away from the thrumming vein pulsing in quick rhythm on the side of her neck. He pushed hot breath across her creamy neck, and her body lit up a little more. Maddeningly light, he placed one kiss on her pulse point. It jumped beneath his warm mouth, and she felt a sneaky smile take over his lips.

"Just fucking kiss me, Baker." A little anger bloomed in her, and her voice cracked in desperation.

"No. Not just yet, Einin." He backed up a step, giving her a little space. "Take off those fucking jeans."

Her hand moved to her zipper. "Not even gonna undress me?" Her tone was purely teasing; she wiggled her hips a little.

"You poured yourself into those bastards. Ass looks great ... *but the work*," he whined. When the jeans finally slipped to the floor, he ordered, "Hands back on the desk."

"You're an insufferable asshole," Matlyn mumble-moaned as she pressed her palms to the wooden surface again.

Not bothering to comment on her insult, he stepped forward again, chest nearly pressed to her back. "Close your eyes."

She did.

"Imagine my mouth on your tits."

Her eyes rolled behind pale purple lids.

"My fingers buried inside you, searching, touching."

A small moan danced past her lips and without thought, she rubbed her thighs together.

"My lips leaving a hot, wet trail down your neck ... your back ... right to base of your spine, the curve of your beautiful ass."

Matlyn had no trouble at all picturing this descent. She ached for it.

"Do my fingers feel good inside you?"

"Yes," Matlyn hissed, heat suffusing her face. Excited, wet, and bordering on miserably frustrated, she sucked in a long breath and pulled it deep into her lungs. Behind her the sound of a zipper lowering caught her attention and she began to throb. From the thick vein in her neck to tiny knot of nerves between her legs, her body hummed.

"Spread your legs for me, Einin. Good girl," he praised as she complied, widening her stance. "Tell me what you want right now, Matlyn." Baker's fingers wound through her choppy, coppery mess of hair, stroking the scalp.

"I want you to fuck me," she said plainly.

Baker chuckled. "How, pretty Little Bird? How?"

Taking less than a second to contemplate that, picturing it so vividly she could almost feel it, she answered, "Bend me over ... fuck my ass." *Please, please, please,* she silently begged.

Warm hands pulled her shirt up over her head, and she complied, raising her arms up without another word, eyes still firmly closed and locked on a lurid fantasy he started. Baker pressed himself to her, fitting piece to piece, line to line. His hand came around, pulling her small breast free from the soft pink bra she wore.

Long, able fingers parted her already sticky flesh, and she pushed back into him just a little more. "Bend," he whispered in her ear.

She did.

He took his time, teasing, priming, thoroughly unraveling Matlyn's sanity one caress at a time. "Ready?"

"Yes!" she practically cried. "Either fuck me or *get out.*" Matlyn's voice was loud, demanding, and didn't drop a single hint of give-a-shit. She was well aware her co-workers would hear them and the thought pulled her lips up in a devious grin.

"Relax," Baker said. His voice was tinged with amusement, and Matlyn knew if she turned she'd see that cocky half-grin he wore so well.

* * *

"*Oh fuck!*"

"Wilson ..." Campbell spoke his name in a hush and

looked to him. Her mocha face burned with mortification. "They're um … they're…"

"*Hard. Please!*" they heard Matlyn beg.

"Yes, Baby Campbell, they're fuckin'." Wilson looked up from the sketch he was working on and winked at the young artist.

"Right. I need a boyfriend." Campbell rolled her eyes and walked to her station.

"Or a girlfriend," Wilson called. "Or both."

Sixteen

✣

The door clicked shut, the lock sliding into place. Parrish turned and pressed her back to the cool painted wood of the bathroom door. Her tight green pencil skirt flared just past her knees, and she fingered the material nervously. Her eyes lifted from the slippers on her feet, to the toilet, and then wandered to the box clutched in her perfectly manicured hand.

"Being a grown up sucks," she said to the blue and gray room and took a quick step toward the toilet.

* * *

Perched on the end of her oversized bed, Ingrid's body

buzzed with the exquisite rush of Witnessing. She let her head roll forward as she dropped into a memory.

The mousy woman sat in her bed, legs stretched out, her back against the wrought-iron headboard. Knobs pushed and prodded her shoulders, but she paid no attention. Worrying her bottom lip between her teeth, she rubbed gentle circles across her belly.

The tiniest swell had begun—a swell her instincts told her to protect. The thin, creamy curtains decorating the windows flanking the double bed fluttered as a too-cool-for-late-August breeze carried through the room. A storm was coming. She could smell it in the air, feel the charge of it building outside.

She rose and stood in front of the open window, her pale orange dress clinging to her body, the wind wrapping the material around her like a shroud.

She would leave.

Ingrid closed the window with a sharp bang and moved across the room to secure the other. She looked out at the darkening sky and for a moment watched the warring clouds overhead.

She had to leave.

* * *

Toe tapping out the second, the Wren girl stood, looking down at a tiny stick. Lines began to swim to the surface and her eyes watered. She looked to her reflection in the mirror and watched a faint pink stain spread across her cheeks as a shaky smile threatened to make an appearance.

Her eyes dropped to the white stick, the lines now solid. "Parrish got a bun in the oven," she said to her bleary reflection and scooped the plastic pee test off the sink's ledge. She shoved it in her purse, not caring that that same stick had just been covered in urine only a few moments before. She left the slippers by the bathroom door and jammed her feet into a pair of simple red pumps. Her heels clicked on the laminate floor as she made her way to the front door, snagging her car keys as she went.

"Where's the fire, little lady?" Wilson said, his head poking out from behind the morning news. A single dusty brow quirked over the rim of the reading glasses he had on.

Parrish loved those glasses on him. Yes, they aged him a little, but they highlighted everything good and kind in his face.

She froze for a quick moment, pulling a hasty but plausible explanation from her brain and then turned toward him. She hadn't realized he was awake. "Brunch with my bitch-faced sister," she lied smoothly. Half-lie, really. She was going to see Matlyn and there would likely be food involved at some point in the day, so …

Head cocked in consideration, he finally said, "Well give bitch-face a big, wet kiss for me."

She stepped into the den, kneeled down beside the man she loved, her hands resting on the arm of the couch that Matlyn had picked out, and puckered her pink lips for him to kiss. He laughed at the silly doe-eyed face she gave him and leaned down to touch his lips to hers.

"Movies an' sex tonight?" she offered, standing up. She was sure he could hear the apology in her voice.

She didn't like the tiny deception, and it leaked through the holes between her words. She plastered on a shaky, but sincerely happy smile and bopped his nose with the tip of her finger.

"Yes. On both counts. I'll even let ya pick the movie, sugar." He winked a blue eye at her.

Dramatically, she clutched her hand to her heart. "Be still." Parrish blew him a kiss on her way out and giggled as he caught it and promptly shoved it down his pants.

In the car she pulled out her cell phone and dialed her sister's number.

"Yeah …" a sleepy voice said.

"Good, you're up. Put clothes on. I'm on my way."

There was a pause, and she pictured her older sister gazing down at her naked body like, whatever, deal with it. She started the car, the radio kicking on with the soft sounds of a bluesy love song.

"Clothes, Matlyn Kharis! Answer the door naked again and I'll punch you in the vag. Baker too." She backed out of the driveway.

"I was high," she defended. "You'll punch him in the vag? Wait, how do you know I'm naked?" Her words came out quick and clumsy, sleep still hanging on them.

"You haven't worn pj's since seventh grade, Little Bird."

"Whatever," her sleepy sister huffed. "I'm up. I make no guarantees on the clothing, though." The phone went dead.

Parrish rolled her eyes and made a left turn. Her gaze dropped to the purse in the seat beside her for a quick moment. She wiped a hot tear from her cheek and focused on the road ahead of her.

She never saw herself as a mother. Anytime she was asked the ever-fucking boring and predictable question "tell us about yourself" at a seminar or meeting, she outlined a businesswoman with wit and ambition. She told them about her desire to work solely for human-services type industries, her sister's shop being the exception. She kind of—on the whole—hated people, but she hated the idea of soulless douchebags getting richer. So Parrish Wren went about ensuring the financial security of those that actually gave two shits about the human race. Never had she considered chasing diapered midgets around as part of that plan.

Pulling up next to Matlyn's shiny, jelly bean-looking vehicle, she put the car in park. Nerves rattled and Parrish sucked the air deep down into her lungs. The morning was oddly crisp for this time of year. Her chest rose and fell again, and she reached for her purse. The weight of it seemed disproportionate to its small size.

The front door opened slowly, and the raven-haired man she'd met on the staircase greeted her with coffee, a smile, and thankfully … pants.

"Morning, Parrish," he said, holding out a piping hot cup of coffee. It smelled divine, and she happily reached for it, taking a tiny sip. "Matlyn's in the shower. She figured if clothes were a requirement, showering ought to be too." Death grip on the coffee mug, she sauntered into the kitchen. Heels clacked loudly, and she boosted herself up onto a high kitchen stool. Baker followed.

"What's up with little sister?" he asked, sitting down next to her and pouring a cup for himself.

"New coffee maker?" She artfully dodged the question.

"Hmm." Baker nodded his head in affirmation. "Broke the pot. Had to buy a new machine. I was thinking cheesy omelets and bacon for breakfast. Sound good?" Standing and moving around the island, he looked back at the wee Wren girl.

"Hmm, cheese," she hummed and moved to help him.

Plate stacked with wiggly, not crispy bacon and the most perfect looking cheese omelet Baker had ever seen, he dug in grinning like a fool when the other redhead walked in. Her hair was damp and pulled back in a messy bun, pieces sticking out here and there. She inhaled the smell and smiled. Parrish handed her a plate, equally stacked, and the three sat in silence, mouths full of breakfast goodness.

"Not that I mind, Pare, but to what do I owe the honor?" Matlyn pondered, loading the dishwasher.

Not trusting her mouth, Parrish said nothing. Standing on her red heels, she retrieved her purse. Baker watched as her hands trembled, pulling back the zipper and fishing through the contents. She withdrew a white stick.

Matlyn stared down at the plastic thing, blinking.

Pushing away from his spot, the Omen jerked his head toward the kitchen door. "I'll just … there's laundry.".

"You don't have to go," Parrish said, waving him off.

He kissed Parrish's forehead as he passed her. "Lots of laundry." This was a sister moment.

He gave Matlyn a wink on the way out and left them to it.

Mouth half-unhinged, Matlyn babbled, "That's a … um … you're pregnant." She didn't bother forming a question, and Parrish supposed there wasn't really a need to question the obvious. Salty, heavy tears began stacking and finally spilled over when Parrish smiled, chewing on her fingertip nervously.

Matlyn raced around the granite island that separated them and threw her arms around her sister, crushing her in a powerful hug.

"It wasn't supposed to happen like this," the pregnant

girl half-sobbed. "I was supposed to be the forever hot, completely unattainable business woman." Her voice shook, and she pulled back to see her older sister's face. The beaming grin that lit her features cleared any doubt that this was truly good and what Parrish wanted.

"Now you'll be a *hot momma* business woman. God, how completely unfair," the willowy ink-slinger complained. "Your tits are already huge! Give an A-cup a break, man!"

Wiping tears from her cheeks, the happy girl chuckled. "I'm gonna get all fat," she said, plopping back down on her stool. "And then there's the whole kid plowing through my girl parts thing. Fuck, my vagina will never be the same, Little Bird."

* * *

Matlyn's roaring laugh floated down the halls to the laundry room, and Baker smiled, catching the sound of it before tossing a white load into the washer. That laugh—light and easy enough—had a raw, deep undertone to it that the Omen didn't miss. He knew this news would tear at Matlyn. Her heart would float and sink, float and sink; a little joy, a little misery. But he also knew his beautiful Einin was strong in a way only women seemed capable of. They could open their hearts and feel happiness for another, even when their own world was holding on by a single loose stitch.

* * *

Dragging a stool closer, not caring that the metal legs scraped against the gray tile, the cinnamon sister asked the strawberry sister, "Have you told Wilson yet?"

"No," she admitted softly. "Mom would have been

the first person I told." Her cotton candy lip quivered, and Matlyn knew why she came to her.

Gently, Matlyn reached out and touched the back of her sister's hand. "She would have been so fucking proud of you, Pare. So happy for you both." A sensation, much like vertigo, swelled in her and joy mixed with hurt, regret blended with happiness, and loss stood beside hope.

"There isn't even a ring on this finger." Skeptical words dropped from the young accountant's mouth. Jutting her hand out and wiggling her fingers, she offered up her hand like evidence of some great and terrible crime.

Matlyn shrugged and rolled her big kelly green eyes. "'Cause I'm one for convention, right?" That earned her a giggle. "And, really, Mom and Dad? They used to hide in the basement and smoke up. I caught them having sex in the pool once. I'm pretty sure Mom's hands were tied up with her bikini top. Conventional parents, they were *not*." A goofy grin passed over Matlyn's lips. "Mom would be bouncing around here like a poodle on crack, she'd be so excited." It was nothing but the truth.

Had Veronica and Harris Wren been there to hear the news of the coming of their first grandchild, both would be overjoyed and not a single thought would be left to the state of Parrish and Wilson's relationship. New tears formed, tears filled with memory and the bitter edge of could-have-beens rolled down the rosy cheeks of both sisters.

The two yammered on and on about names and nurseries—which, of course, Matlyn would be painting—and poured over baby pictures. Three hours later, Matlyn sent Parrish home to deal with the father-to-be and a promise to call later.

Closing the door on Parrish's retreating, five-foot nothing form, she slumped against the door. Her head throbbed and her vision blurred in and out like the lens of a camera struggling to focus. Slowly, she dragged herself up the stairs, stripping en route. Her T-shirt landed on the top stair, and she lazily pulled at the button of her jeans as she opened her bedroom door.

A dark-haired Omen lay on the made bed, propped up against the headboard with a basket of folded laundry next to him. A '90s movie was playing on the TV. He turned toward her with a smile that quickly faded when he took in her pale face and her state of undress.

Waving her hand over the bed, she said, "I have a headache, move it."

Baker moved the laundry to the floor, pulled back the sheets, and let a very tired looking ginger crawl in. Eyes closed, she weakly tugged at her jeans, barely moving them past her hips. Baker swatted her hands away.

"Let me," he said with a soft sigh.

She lifted her hips and let him peel her jeans off and then turned onto her side. The Dark Omen pulled the covers over the petite girl. He went to the bathroom and rummaged through her drawer until he found some Advil and filled a glass with cool water. "Sit up, Einin."

She pulled her body upright, and Baker dropped two pills in her palm and offered her the glass of water. Once she knocked back the pills, she snuggled back down into the comfort of her bed and slipped into a sleep full of bursting colors.

Outside, the sun rose higher and moved across the clear blue sky.

* * *

"Get up," Baker said, flinging a red and gray plaid shirt at Matlyn. It landed on her face and a soft moan rumbled from beneath it.

"Why?" the sleepy form grumbled, pulling the shirt away from her face and letting it fall to the floor. She propped herself up on her elbows and glared at the man standing at the end of the bed.

"Because, lovely girl, dinner's ready. Let's go. Haul your hot southern ass outta bed." He tossed a pair of cut off shorts at her and then turned back to her dresser, ignoring the mumbled curse.

Bed-headed and groggy, the girl huffed and rolled to the side, checking out the red glowing display on her alarm clock. It was four-thirty-seven. She'd been asleep for more than four hours. She blinked, clearing her watery eyes, and threw the covers back. A slightly oversized tank top landed on her left shoulder and then slid down the length of her arm. She scooped it up and held it out in front of her. Matlyn nodded in approval and slipped the shirt on over her head. She wiggled into the jean cut-offs and donned the plaid.

At the bottom of the stairs, Baker stood waiting with the front door open.

"I thought you said dinner was ready?" Confused, she looked toward the kitchen.

"I did. You'll need shoes." He rattled the keys in his hands.

"So where are we going?" A little confused, she shoved her feet into a pair of yellow Converse sneakers.

"The truck," he answered, ushering her out the door.

Matlyn watched as he locked the door behind him. "Dinner's in the truck?"

"Yup."

They climbed up into the cab of the truck and the engine rumbled to life. Bon Iver whispered through the speakers. Baker's hand wrapped around the clutch and he shifted into reverse.

"Take out?" Matlyn asked as they moved through rush hour traffic.

"Nope." The deadly smirk on his scruffy face had the girl's brows pinching together.

"One word answers? That's all I get?"

"Yup." The smirk bloomed a little wider.

"Fucker."

She turned her head to watch a woman on a bike weave through the cars and escape onto a residential street. A man walked a Great Dane, the dog wearing a top hat, the human wearing a studded collar. Two men in power suits hustled down the sidewalk—both talking on their cell phones, and a young mother sat with her infant daughter at the bus stop. Her knee bounced as she pulled hard on the cigarette she was smoking.

The sun was still fairly bright, but it hung much lower and the colors in the sky above them began to shift to the richer hues of dusk. They bumped along at a decent pace until they hit a county road.

"Do you know where you're going?" Matlyn asked, side-eying Baker.

"Yeah. Google maps."

Suspicious, hungry, and a little tired of his short

answers and cocky as fuck grin, she reached out and flicked the side of his face.

"Ow. Uncalled for, naughty Little Bird," he chided, rubbing the tiny red mark that appeared. "Ten more minutes. I promise we're almost there."

"Almost *where*, asshole?" hollered the peeved redhead, tossing her arms in the air.

A deep, rumbling chuckle shook Baker's frame. "Easy there. No need to get hostile. Though, I'm not gonna lie, I like you feisty."

She exhaled slowly. "Pig's ass."

"Sticks and stones, Einin." Baker's free hand snaked between Matlyn's thighs, and he yanked with just enough force to easily pry them apart. Her quick, sharp breath put a wicked grin on Baker's lips. His finger went searching upward, slipping under the fray of her worn denim cut offs.

Baker's curious digit caressed her thigh and dared to move a little further. Gently, lighter than the touch of a feather, the tip of his finger grazed her folds.

"Shit," she said in a low, husky voice.

"One little touch and suddenly all your bark is gone." Sounding much too amused, he withdrew his hand and placed it back on the steering wheel.

Matlyn turned to face him. Her willow green eyes could have burned a hole through the side of Baker's skull. "You're a—"

"An insufferable asshole? A pig's ass? A tease?" Baker mocked. "We've established that already, doll."

"You're evil. Pure. Fucking. Evil, Omen."

Turning the wheel, the truck's thick tires kicked up gravel along the bumpy side road that led God knows where.

The feisty, frustrated girl pulled at her bottom lip with her teeth, making them plump and redden.

Baker brought the truck to a stop and put it in park. "We're here," he said, facing his passenger.

"Here where?" She looked out onto an open field.

Baker pushed open the driver's side door. "Absolutely fucking *nowhere*," he answered with a smile so bright and full of mischief it made Matlyn's stomach clench.

"And you needed Google maps to find it?" She pushed the door shut behind her and leaned against the side of the truck.

Baker stalked around the front of the metallic beast and tugged at Matlyn's shirt as he walked by. "The world didn't look like this a hundred years ago. Green, unpopulated space is a pretty fucking hard thing to come by now." Pulling on the latch and lowering the tailgate, Baker climbed into the truck bed. Holding up a red cooler, he said, "Dinner."

A sunny grin lit the girl's face, and she shook her head. The tall grass tickled her bare legs as she moved to the back of the truck. Holding out a rough hand, the Omen pulled her up into the truck bed. A large black duffle bag caught her eye and she pointed to it.

"Ah, provisions." Baker snatched up the bag, unzipped it, and pulled out two blankets, two giant pillar candles, and a dark red, silk tie. The blankets had been absconded from a chest in the guest room, the candles were new—Matlyn thought he must have gotten them while she was sleeping—and the tie ... well that was something she'd never seen before either.

I like where this is heading, she thought, eyeing that damn silk tie. She helped him spread the blankets over the cold steel bed and the two folded themselves down to sit across from each other.

Opening the lid, Baker produced pasta salad, stuffed olives, red wine, and a small but decadent looking cheesecake. He rooted around the front compartment of the duffle bag and handed Matlyn a disposable plate, fork, and a red Solo cup that made her chuckle.

Fork to her mouth, Matlyn announced, "Parrish is pregnant."

Baker nodded. "Pee stick on the counter told me that. I disinfected the shit out of the kitchen island, by the way."

"Many thanks, sir." She pondered her next words, chewing slowly. "I'm not going to see that baby, am I?" Tears stacked.

Baker stopped mid-chew and put his fork down. "You know I can't answer that, doll. I wish I could but …"

"It's not up to you. I know." There was no anger in her words, just sadness.

She'd accepted her death because there was nothing she or Baker could do to stop it. She'd been to her family doctor, and he'd declared her healthy as a horse. She took her vitamins, she exercised, she buckled her seat belt, and never ran with scissors, but none of that mattered because Death was coming for her regardless. The lives of the people around her would go on, *should* go on, but not being a part of that hurt Matlyn all the same.

"Look at me, Einin." He reached out and with two fingers, tipped her chin up. He watched her pretty eyes cloud and swell with moisture. Tears slid over the slope of her cheekbones, and they sat quietly for a few moments. "I love you," Baker whispered so soft it was nearly lost to the gentle breeze flowing around them.

"Not helping, Baker." She smiled a watery smile despite her sadness.

"All right, I fucking hate you. Wanna get high?" His crooked grin grew as he plucked a joint from his shirt pocket and wagged his thick brows. It was a weak diversion.

"Hell yes, Omen!" She swallowed the last few sips of wine, loving the way it coated her tongue and chased away the salt and sting. Wiping her face with the back of her hand, she shook her head in an attempt to rearrange her thoughts.

Sweet baby Jesus, he looks so fucking hot, she mused, her sadness effectively shoved to the back burner as his lips surrounded the blunt.

* * *

He pulled the smoke deep into his lungs and exhaled slowly. He passed it off to Matlyn, not for a second missing the way her eyes went wide at the sight of him. He fucking loved it, loved the smoldering looks she shot him through the heavy smoke, loved the way her pink lips puckered around the joint, and he died a little when her tongue crept out and licked at the delicate bow of her upper lip.

Unhurried, Baker cleared the food away, flung the now empty plates into a small plastic bag, and shoved the cooler back into the corner. He stretched out, leaning his back against the side of the truck bed. Matlyn crawled closer and handed over the joint. Darkness had fully surrounded them, and the flicker of the candles cast dancing shadows all around them. One, two deep inhales, and he held it in his lungs. His come-hither finger called the redhead forward and she kneeled next to him. Two strong hands gripped her waist and lifted her slender form over his lap. His hand travelled up the length of her back until he found the slim line of her long neck. Baker pulled her forward until lips touched lips. She gladly opened her mouth, breathing in the smoke he pushed out.

"Mmm," she hummed, pulling back to see his face. Matlyn snatched the joint from Baker, dragged a few short deep puffs in before handing it back to him. Leaning back, she pushed her hands out behind her, tipped her head back, and blew thick smoke out into the night.

"Stunning," Baker said with a groan. Her body was arched away from him and on perfect display. Tits pushed skyward, head tipped back, and her tank top had creeped up, showing off her pale flawless skin. He laid his hand on her lower stomach and caressed the bare skin and then let it glide up and up and up, exposing more flesh and barely visible freckles.

He reached between her breasts, grabbed the silky material holding them captive, and pulled her forward. The bra stretched away from her, but she followed with a wicked glint in her eyes. Their mouths met between plumes of smoke.

Impatiently, Matlyn shrugged out of the plaid shirt and shoved it away. Her lips nipped and sucked and she grinned like the devil's little play thing when Baker cursed and bucked his hips. Sitting up, she took one last, long drag and snubbed out the joint, flinging it out into the long grass.

A low growl rumbled in Baker's chest as he pulled the cup of her bra down. He wanted the humble weight of her perfect, round breast in his hand. He wanted to feel her skin pebble under his own rough touch.

Making an annoyed sound, she swatted his hands and straightened. "Clothes are such a pain in my ass." Her own fumbling hands worked with the Dark Omen's to peel off the tank top and dispose of the bra.

"Stand." Baker's voice was thick like syrup, and his head jerked as he watched her face.

Flushed and appreciating the subtle breeze, her hands cupped Baker's shoulders and she pushed up off his lap. Tall, and looking a little mighty, Matlyn gazed down at the man. He reached up, popped the buttons one by one on her cut offs, and slid them down her long, creamy legs. His hands made a slow course back the way they came, tickling the backs of her knees and pausing at her hips before pulling the thin material of her underwear down.

She stepped out and pushed them into the corner with the rest of her discarded clothing.

"Just stay right there. Right there." Steel eyes gazed up at the goddess looming over him. Sitting up a little straighter, he inched closer to her.

She chewed at the inside of her cheek, watching him, his hot breath washing over her upper thighs.

"Ugh, *lick me*," she begged, a bossy edge to her voice that Baker appreciated.

Not wanting to be cruel, Baker complied, and in the next second his tongue was flat against her.

"Shit," Matlyn groaned as her knees buckled. She was thankful for Baker's hands guiding her back down to his lap.

He pushed her back, his large hand in the middle of her chest. Matlyn's spine slightly bowed as her shoulders came in contact with the blanket. Closing her eyes, she listened to Baker's breathing and the raw pull of her own.

Charcoal eyes took in every slope and dip, every curve and detail of Matlyn's body before Baker leaned forward, covering her, and reached for the red silk tie. "May I?" he asked, gingerly touching her wrist with the tie.

"Yes." She nodded and crossed her wrists and presented them to him.

He wound the red silk around and pulled gently on the simple knot. "Okay?"

Matlyn's bound hands gripped the fabric of his shirt and pulled him down. "Tighter." Her eyes were lit with dark, deep need, and Baker felt like he might drown in them.

Quickly, he complied and pulled up, kneeling between her legs. His hands drifted over her skin and goose bumps popped up in the wake of his touch. His thumbs caressed her hipbone and she bucked. Baker made a sound of approval in the back of his throat. She reached out to grab at him again, but he caught her hands and pushed them over her head, *tsk*ing. "Hands to yourself, Einin."

"Shut up and take off your clothes. I'm tied up, wet, and getting impatient."

Baker's head tilted to the side for a second, taking in the not so amused expression on her beautiful face. Was she turned on? Yes, no doubt, the roll of her hips told him that. He winked and pulled his shirt over his head and years of Matlyn's life were revealed in ink and skin. Her fingers twitched as if to reach out, but the look on the Omen's face kept her arms pinned above her head.

Stretching forward again, he brought one candle to his

lips. "Safety first," he said and blew it out. The other met the same fate, snuffed out with a forceful breath.

Plunged into darkness and a strange quiet, Matlyn listened as a zipper slid down and then the shift of clothing.

Eyes adjusting to the lack of light, he looked down at the barely visible girl in the moonlight and thanked both the fucking Devil and whatever angel had come together to make her. He licked his fingers, grabbed his cock, and without so much as a warning, Baker pushed forward, sliding into perfect heat.

"Holy fuck!" Matlyn cried out, her legs hitched, tightening around his hips.

The Omen faltered for a moment. "Did I hurt you?"

Matlyn let out a hard pant. "No. Not even." She smiled in the darkness and let him have her body, lapsing into a comfort and calm that only came with trust. There wasn't an ounce of trepidation; she would gladly bend to his will again and again.

Seventeen

❦

June 7, 2015, 8:17am ~ Royal Street, New Orleans

Standing street-side, the air humid and sticky as cars rushed by and people scurried about; trying to dodge the fat raindrops that came down, Ingrid tipped her head back and let the warm morning rain wet her face. Her body shivered with the delicious rush of the Story unfolding on her skin. Details of Parrish's relationship with the scruffy ex-Marine pitched her body into a state of euphoria.

With a sigh, she opened her eyes and slowly lowered her head. Unhurried, she walked around the block and back up to Royal Street. As she approached her hotel, she looked around, umbrellas bobbing, people shuffling—barely paying attention to where they were headed—flags flying overhead, plants hanging from balconies. New Orleans was alive, always humming and moving. She loved the life in this city.

She pulled her top away from her body and gave it a useless shake, as if the rainwater hadn't already soaked the fabric. The doorman held the door open for her, wishing her a good morning. The soggy Omen smiled and tipped her head to him as she moved past the threshold.

The second the door of her room clicked behind her, she stripped off her clothes, leaving them in a sodden heap by the door, and made her way to the bathroom to run a hot shower. Before stepping under the spray, she twisted her body so she could see the new words written on her skin.

"Doesn't matter how we got here, sugar, or how we get where we're goin'. That's a walk I wanna take with you. With this baby."

Bits of a conversation between Parrish and Wilson had surfaced, and she smiled.

* * *

Matlyn sent off one last—surely verging on annoying—text message to Adeline, ensuring she had all the information needed to hold down the shop for the four days that she would be away with Baker.

Addy: Stop harassing me! Feelin' antsy? Ride that beautiful man of yours.

Matlyn laughed and before she could send another message, her personal scribe snatched the phone from her hands and lightly tossed it down onto the bed. "That's not coming with us." He shot the cell phone an evil glare and then shifted his gaze to the girl standing before him. Hair was still damp from her shower, she smelled like honeysuckle and mint. He leaned in, his mouth hovering next to her ear. "Addy will be fine. You, on the other hand, are in for a world of hurt if you don't get your ass in gear and finish packing."

There was more playfulness than warning in his voice, and the deep timber made her skin prickle in a delightful way. "Don't tease, Omen." She glared at him impishly.

Baker turned on his heels, giving the slight woman his back. "I'm no tease, woman." Reaching into the navy blue suitcase sitting on the unmade bed, he shifted a few things, making room for Matlyn's blow-dryer, which according to her was a necessity.

Forty minutes later and several wardrobe swaps, the Omen and the tattooist pulled out of the driveway in the lime green car heading toward Savannah. Amos Lee's bluesy voice piped through the speakers and seemed to drift out the window with the warm air. Ginger trusses danced around the girl's shoulders, barely tickling her collarbone. She adjusted the overhead visor and peeked at her companion.

It was more than a nine hour drive to Savannah, Georgia, and the first true road trip the supernatural gent beside her had ever been on, so Matlyn planned to make the most of it: good music, snacks, stopping at roadside dives, and taking ridiculous pictures along the way.

As dusk descended, with three hours yet to drive, Matlyn asked, "Ya ever wish you had siblings?" She watched him from the passenger seat, having traded off at the last gas station.

"Hell no. Parrish is a pain in the ass," he joked, his eyes on the road.

Tracing a pattern on the window, she snorted. A tiny piece of her agreed with that statement, but a much bigger part knew that Parrish was nothing but a gift. Without her sister, Matlyn's life would have taken on a very different form, one she truly couldn't imagine.

"So who did you talk to about boners and pubes and wet dreams?"

A funny kind of lopsided smile spread across his face. "These are the things you think about, Einin? My junk?"

"*Junk*. If I were your cock, I'd find that shit offensive." She poked a chipped teal-colored fingernail at his ribs. "Seriously, though, first periods, boobs, masturbation, what to do about the fucking station wagon-sized zit ... adolescence would have sucked a lot more without a sister."

Baker shifted gears and rolled his neck. A tiny popping sound could be heard over the babble of the southern preacher tryin' hard to save their souls. "You figure it out. Boys at school talk. Most of it was bullshit wives' tales, and you live in fear of going blind, but yeah, you figure shit out."

* * *

Looking out the window at the darkening sky, Matlyn's hand snaked across the console separating them, landing on Baker's well-muscled thigh. His eyes moved to the warm hand, the road, then to his Story's face. In profile, the lines of her face seemed almost sharp—the jut of her chin, the slope of her nose, the long creamy line of her neck, all of it elegant, but very well defined. She turned away from the window, her fingers raking his jean-clad leg, and she offered up a kittenish grin.

"'Bout forty minutes out," she said, nodding at the GPS positioned between them.

"What are you thinking about?" Baker asked, sure her thoughts were slinking around the gutter.

"The sprinkler," she answered without hesitation.

"Sprinkler?"

"Yeah. You keep those eyes on the road, Baker." Matlyn gestured to the dark lanes stretched out in front of them. "We had a red sprinkler that Momma would put in the front yard. Parrish would run through it, clothes and all, every time."

Baker turned his head toward her, a light sound rumbling somewhere in the back of his throat that sounded like lazy laughter.

A light fog had begun to roll in, leaving cotton-thin wisps here and there. Dexterous fingers drummed out a slow rhythm on Baker's thigh, and he smiled, picturing the smaller of the two Wren sisters jumping through the cold spray.

"I kinda miss being a stupid kid sometimes," Matlyn admitted, shifting in her seat so that she was fully facing him.

"I miss nap time."

"Recess," Matlyn countered with a chuckle.

"Red rover, red rover, send Matlyn on over." Baker's mind wheeled back to the silly games he'd played in a schoolyard as a boy.

"We used to stuff our training bras with socks, wonder how big they'd get. Parrish would tan my hide if she heard me telling you this." There wasn't an ounce of remorse in her voice, just humor and nostalgia. She fiddled with the radio dials while he followed the robotic female voice telling him to merge onto Montgomery Street.

Baker pulled in front of a large, red brick home lit from within by simple soft lights. In the yard, to the left of the main entrance, a sign hung from an iron sign-post declaring the Kehoe House a historical inn. It was also reportedly haunted, but Matlyn was willing to bet that the majority of inns in Savannah had been labeled the same. Butt tingling and half numb, the inked girl got out of the car, stretching her arms high over her head and groaning. A horse drawn carriage pulled up and deposited an older couple. Big smiles deepened their prominent wrinkles.

"Shall we, Miss Wren?" Baker asked, offering her his arm. He led her up the stairs and held the door as she and the carriage couple made their way through the large wooden doors.

Carpeted, creaking stairs led to the second floor of the aged inn. Gleaming wooden doors lined the softly-lit hallway. Baker pushed open the door to room B2, taking in the space before them.

The room was beautiful. Age mingled with the barest hints of a more modern era. The sand-colored walls were decorated with golden framed pictures. The four-post bed was inviting with crisp white linens that offered just enough contrast that both Baker and Matlyn's eyes were drawn to it.

The cinnamon-haired girl tilted her head and gave the bed an odd look. She stepped closer to it and stated, "It occurs to me that there's a not at all remote possibility that either myself or Parrish was conceived in this inn. Maybe that bed." Her head tipped toward the king-sized bed. She reached out and ran her fingertip over the smooth wood, looking up at the top of the tapered post. "I'm not sure if I should be swicked out or …"

"Honored." The Dark Omen's hand reached for her slim hips and drew her back against him. "If *you* were made here, Einin, I'm nothing but honored to share this room with that little piece of history."

Sighing, she turned in his arms. "All the right words." The blushing girl pushed up on her toes and placed her mouth on his. It was a gentle, whisper of a kiss that felt like a thank you.

Drawing back slightly, Baker looked to the clock sitting on the bedside table. "So it is eight-forty-two." His face dropped to meet the eyes of the woman in his arms. "Do I strip you bare and do wicked things to you, or do we leave the room in search of food?" Baker's nose trailed the side of her face, her jaw, her neck. His warm breath drifted across her already heated skin.

"Mmm, I vote for nakedness." As Baker's hand made its way up her delicate spine, Matlyn's stomach made a loud sound. She looked down. "But my tummy has veto power, apparently." She poked her stomach and shrugged.

Planting a soft kiss on her forehead, he agreed.

She quickly changed into dark gray jeans that hugged everything she had and a sheer gray striped blouse. Her bright red bra popped beneath the flimsy fabric. Baker watched as she ran her fingers through her hair a few times, shrugged, and called it good. "Needs a cut," she commented.

"Ready?" he asked, holding out his hand.

The two strolled down the street, following the directions the clerk at the inn had given them. The night air was the perfect blend of Savannah heat and not-quite summer cool. It was comfortable, though the light breeze hinted at humidity that was never far from the surface.

Arm locked with Baker's, she asked, "How'd you rate your first road trip so far?"

Out of control raven locks bobbed as the man put on a thoughtful face. "A solid six," he replied with a nod of his head that looked like punctuation at the end of a sentence.

Her eyes swung up. "Six? That's it? We had breakfast at a gas bar that served *the* best waffles I've ever eaten. I took you to a roadside antique mall that had weird little glass fish heads, and an even weirder old lady that yodelled the lyrics to 'I Will Always Love You'! Six?"

He snickered. He had the urge to pat her on the head, but thought better of it, knowing full well he'd have one less testicle at the end of this trip if he even tried. "Six ... for now." She huffed and he laughed, and then stopped dead.

A terrible burning shot up his side and wrapped around his torso. "Shit," he hissed, trying to keep the pain reined in.

Worry bloomed in her eyes, and she ran her hands over his face, soothing him with her light touch. She remained quiet and focused on his granite eyes, watching the pain slowly seep away.

Taking a deep breath, he mumbled, "I'm good. I'm okay." Baker rearranged his six-foot-three frame, his girl's hand in his, and continued to walk.

Jazz'd lit up the front window in a red neon that seemed to skitter sideways, as if being pulled by the music coming from the bar. Baker held the door open for his beautiful Story, hating the words he couldn't see and the time they stole from him. Inside, a tall, curvy, broad woman sat at a piano tucked in a dimly-lit corner. Her voice was seasoned with smoke and spice and it wrapped around Baker and Matlyn and drew them forward.

A skinny boy, no more than twenty-one, showed them to an open table. A pair of dark-rimmed glasses consumed his face, but Matlyn could see, even in the low light, that his eyes were rich like coffee.

"Evenin'," he greeted. "Whatchaya'll want to drink?" His accent was thick and reminded Matlyn of Adeline's often mashed together words.

Baker ordered two beers while she perused the impressive list of appetizers the lounge offered. When the young man returned, and she still hadn't been able to make a choice, she closed her eyes and blindly pointed to two dishes.

"What's the worst job you've ever had? Not Witnessing," Matlyn qualified, lifting the chilled beer to her mouth.

Baker's eyes toggled around as he raked through the decades of temporary positions. "1976," he answered with a strange look about him—embarrassment or amusement, Matlyn couldn't be sure. "Best job, worst job all in one. I was in California early '76 Witnessing an eighteen-year-old kid. This guy overheard me asking about work at this beat-up night club. Anyway, he hands me a card, says to call him. Two days later I'm at an *interview* in this three-story walk-up with no fucking air, sweatin' balls."

Stopping to take a swig of his beer, he shimmied his chair a little closer to the beautiful girl next to him. "Buddy says he's looking for an assistant. Ya know, someone to run for coffee and shit like that? I figure, what the hell, pay is pay, and tell him I can start the next day. He's all firm handshakes and fake fuckin' grins, like some lousy car salesman.

He scribbles an address on an index card and tells me to report to Huey at nine in the morning."

Baker chuckled, dropping his eyes to the table. "So Huey—nice guy—is a *film* director. He gives me the run-down. Basically I'm the set bitch. Then he shows me around the set. Tits everywhere."

"Ha! Oh shit." Matlyn's eyes went wide and she giggled. "Porno?"

"Yeah." That amused, embarrassed look returned to his face. "*The Bunny Hop.*"

Matlyn almost choked on her drink. "You worked on a seventies' porno? Nice."

Correcting her, he said, "Oh no, darlin' Einin, not just worked *on*." The lingering Irish in his voice was clear and wrapped around the term of endearment. His eyes danced with laughter. Thin lines appeared around them and his lips quirked into a funny half grin.

Amused and intrigued, she set the bottle down a little harder than she'd meant to, pulled a face, and looked back to Baker. "Were you a *fluffer*?" Matlyn leaned in to whisper the last word. "Please tell me you were a fluffer, 'cause that's … I …" Her words sputtered and dropped and a pretty pink bloomed on her cheeks.

Head thrown back, Baker let loose a hearty chuckle. "No, Little Bird, I was no fluffer. Ice Cream Guy," he said, bobbing his head slowly, a crooked grin still planted on his face.

Baker explained that the guy that was meant to play the voyeur cashier at the "ice cream shop" hadn't bothered to show that day, and so the set bitch stepped in to play the role. His direction had been to simply stand behind the crappy cash register, on an even crappier set, and watch "Bunny" and "Mitch" get it on with some sort of perverted interest. Paid voyeurism sounded like a damn good deal to the penniless Omen at the time, so he stepped up to the plate, no questions asked.

"I had these fucking chops …" he motioned to the sides of his face "… that weren't nearly as cool as Hugh Jackman's, but I thought I looked pretty far out."

When the food arrived, Matlyn was still wiping tears away. "Why's it the worst job you ever had? Watchin' people fuck all day?" She shook her head, not able to see a downside.

Baker piled a few calamari rings on his plate and ordered two more beers, noting the way the young waiter's eyes bugged out at Matlyn's last words. When the boy disappeared into the crowd around them, Baker answered, "Beautiful, naked women everywhere, awesome. Free-range cock, not so awesome. When you hear a girl hit a fake O-note six times before noon with a camera shoved up her ass, kinda takes some of the *awe* out of the whole thing, ya know?"

The two crunched and munched on the appetizers and listened to the woman at the piano belt out a tune that carried an old sadness. Between sips and swallows, Baker said, "You're up. Worst job."

It didn't take Matlyn more than a second to answer. "Gift shop at Tulane University Hospital." Putting down her beer, she explained. "There was this smell … floor polish and antiseptic and illness that hung in the air. I never got used to it." The woman on the piano boomed out dramatic notes and held them in the air as Matlyn's brain quickly recalled the scent, making her nose wrinkle.

"Get-well-soon cards for people wasting away in chemo. Twinkies and a soda for the vigilant wife still waiting for her husband to wake up. A stuffed animal for the kid in Peds battling some rare fucking blood disorder." It seemed like the worst piece of irony to Matlyn—fallen faces toting smiling, bobbing balloons.

"You win," Baker conceded, scratching at the thickening, dark scruff on his jaw.

The waiter returned a few moments later, the conversation much more buoyant, and cleared the plates and empties away, offering them both a wide smile before he was swallowed by the bodies shifting this way and that.

"Favorite birthday gift?" Matlyn's feet swung under the high table. Her cheeks were just beginning to blush with the alcohol that trickled into her bloodstream.

A memory crept over the Omen like a heavy fog, and he recalled a multi-colored kite that his mother had made him for his ninth birthday. It took the shape of a bird and its wings were a patchwork of leftover fabrics stitched together with black thread. He remembered the look on his mother's face as he took to the yard to fly his gift. She was proud and happy. So much happiness spilled from her that it'd made little Samuel giddy.

"I must have flown that thing for hours. Racing to catch the wind when it dipped." He chuckled to himself, picturing the kite high above him and the warm, August sunshine that'd poked out from behind gray shifting clouds. Baker leaned forward, clasping his hands on the table in front of him. He waited for Matlyn.

"Wasn't my birthday," Matlyn said, shaking her head slightly. "'Bout a month before Sasha past away, she handed over a stack of letters. She'd gone through my mother's things and found a shoebox stuffed with the letters they wrote each other in high school and college. She paired them with the counterparts Sasha kept in an old suitcase that'd been living under her bed." Matlyn's eyes twinkled and a nostalgic look passed over her face. "My mother was a foul-mouthed, drug smokin' hippie with a fairly serious addiction to Twinkies. She had a tenth-grade crush on her history teacher, fully planned on marrying Rob Hubert in eleventh, and in her freshmen year at Tulane she got piss-faced; lost her keys, her bra, and stole a goldfish, which she later found in her jean pocket."

The Dark Omen chuckled. "Seems mischief comes natural to you."

"Apparently."

Baker's gaze roamed the room, catching on hushed conversations, Roman hands and Russian fingers moving over the generous curves of a rather tall woman. A raucous table of twenty-somethings laughed and slammed shots back. "She's looking at you." His eyes drew a steady line to a woman cast in the soft overhead light. A few strands of bold purple mixed with her black hair.

Matlyn glanced in the direction of the lone woman. "Mmm," she hummed in approval. "She's beautiful." Gray and black ink covered her arms, and Matlyn followed the patterns to the gentle hill of her exposed shoulders.

The woman smiled and stood. Moving like liquid over glass, she slipped easily between the bar patrons. Her high ponytail swayed in time with her hips. She came to a stop, standing between the Omen and the ink-slinger. Her grin was laced with devilment as her big brown eyes scanned the length of Matlyn's body.

"Rebecca," she introduced herself, jutting her hand out. "But no one calls me that."

"Care to join us, Not-Rebecca?" Baker pulled a third chair over to their table and gestured for the curious stranger to sit. He introduced himself and Matlyn, noting the hungry look in Rebecca's eyes. He knew that look well and couldn't blame the girl one iota. He also recognized the odd stop and start of the hum that existed between Matlyn and himself and the sensation of falling that accompanied it.

"You're fucking gorgeous," the stranger cut to the chase, her proper British accent enunciated the words and somehow splashed a new layer of filth on them. Shifting her gaze to address Baker, she said, "And I'm pretty sure you…" her finger reached out and her neon orange nail tapped the tip of Baker's nose "…are an Omen." Rebecca retracted her hand, tipped her head to the side, and cradled it in her hand. "Light or dark meat?"

Eighteen

❖

Frigid air bit at his lungs and nipped his exposed fingers. He sat on a bench across from the frozen playground as cars trudged through the street narrowed by gray-white banks of snow, watching as a thirty-something mother push her young son on a swing. The chains squeaked in protest, possibly just as upset with Mother Nature as Baker was in that moment. He let out a groan of his own, rubbed his chilled hands together, and then shoved them in his jacket pockets.

Baker chuckled as the boy's booted feet lifted into the air and kicked wildly, bits of snow flying. Suddenly, blistering heat tore at his skin and the chill in the air all but forgotten. He grimaced and let out a small whine—it was a pitiful sound easily swallowed by the breeze.

The snow began to fall with a little more gusto, the flakes chunky and soft looking.

Baker knew the time was near. The last notes etched into his flesh only hours before told of a fourth birthday party and a four-legged gift. The boy on the swing was no more than five.

A half-assed, but genuine prayer, floated away from the troubled Omen's lips on a puff of cold air. He prayed the child would remember the mother that braved the cold to take him to the park.

As the burn intensified, Baker's breathing picked up and his blood pushed harder, faster. He watched as the curly-haired woman bent, secured the blue and red scarf around her son's neck, took his tiny, mitten-clad hand and led him from the playground. They rounded the corner and disappeared somewhere in the falling snow.

Baker's heart punched and kicked and his torso throbbed with the burn of a Story winding itself down. Absently, the Dark Omen rubbed his chest in some useless attempt to mollify the ache.

Tires squealed, a woman shouted, and hellfire marched up and down Baker's body. He balled his fists, praying just a little harder that in five years from now the boy would still recall his mother's face with perfect clarity, remember the spring of her tight curls and the affectionate way she gazed at him.

A small, broken cry filled the air and the pain let go like a plug being pulled from a sink. It rushed away leaving Baker with an emptiness. Once again, he was a blank white page waiting to be marred and written upon.

* * *

"Light or dark meat?" The raven-haired girl, who no one called Rebecca, turned her head slightly in response to Matlyn's sharp inhale and gave a soft chuckle as the redhead next to her sucked at the air in shock.

Flicking his gaze to the well-inked girl, he asked, "Omen or psychic?"

"Robbie. Not Rebecca. No one really calls me that," she repeated.

Raising her hand in the air, Robbie called the waiter to the table. A secret grin was pasted to her pale face. "Both." One tattooed, bare shoulder lifted and her head bobbed as if this were the most logical of answers. Something they should have guessed at, perhaps. "Bit it twenty years ago. Lung infection," she said by way of explanation.

The noise in the room seemed to ebb for a quick moment while Matlyn contemplated that bit of information.

Giving up on awe or amazement, Matlyn shrugged and let out a weary sigh. "And the universe just keeps getting bigger," the tattooist mumbled, her words sounding oddly frustrated. *Omens, Fates, Voodoo-swamp men, fucking psychics. Wouldn't be surprised to find a gnome pissin' in the parking lot at this point.* Her brain spat out pictures of winged things, beasts with horns, and other creatures that she thought couldn't possibly exist. Then again, the beings sitting next to her shouldn't, in any right, exist either, but there they were.

Robbie ordered three more beers, grinning and winking at the young waiter whose big brown eyes were traveling up and over every inch of bare skin she offered. He walked away with a little smile of his own. Dropping her hand to the table, she drummed her neon tipped fingers in a rhythm that matched the slow beat filling the room. "So ... light or dark?"

Baker's answer was clipped and sour. "Dark."

"And you're his Story?" Her earthy brown eyes caught on Matlyn's face and stayed there.

Matlyn just nodded, noting the specks of gold that seemed to pop out from under the brown in the girl's eyes.

"Bugger. Well then, this is a fairly fucked-up situation," she said. The strange Omen grinned wide as the waiter returned with their drinks.

Baker watched Robbie pass a chilled bottle to Matlyn, and saw the way Robbie's hand grazed Matlyn's.

"Let's pour some booze on it. Yeah?" She tipped the neck of the amber bottle and let the cool liquid slide down her throat. "Drew the short straw, did ya?" Robbie looked to Baker. "Don't know how you tolerate it, really. All that death." Her voice was still light, but a kind of sympathy wrapped around the words and made them that much heavier.

"Light?" Matlyn asked, head tilted and watching the newcomer next to her pick at the label on the bottle.

"Uh-huh. The gentleman in the gray suit, he's a *trip*. So formal and ... *intense*. I'd been seeing him in my dreams since I was five." The look she gave Baker smacked of shared experience and secret clubs. But Matlyn was a card-carrying member at this point, and she guessed that the couple's new friend had had a very similar experience to Baker's with the otherworldly man following her death.

She nattered on—in rather comedic detail—about the wandering thoughts and odd pictures that infiltrated her mind. "Mum thought I was hooked on PCP. Poor old gal kept bringing home pamphlets, leaving them on my pillow or taped to my cereal box. Then the lights went out, plug pulled, and there he was, hands clasped in front of him, just staring at me with this *odd as balls* look on his pale face." Robbie shook her purple-black locks, and took down another mouthful of liquid.

While Robbie and Baker talked shop, in what was quickly becoming the strangest fucking 'work' conversation Matlyn had ever heard, she pulled her phone from her back pocket and shot Addy a text.

Matlyn: I'm surrounded by fuck-hawt supernatural beings, Adeline. Maddening.

A reply came somewhere between an accidental suicide in Phoenix 1967 and the successful separation of conjoined twins in Kansas 2004. Weird didn't apply to this conversation, *right and fully fucked* seemed more worthy as far as Matlyn was concerned.

Addy: Please tell me you've met the vampire Lastat … and you're playin' monkey in the middle?

A fuzzy, warm grin stretched Matlyn's lips as she read the screen. Her gaze slid over the Light Omen once more, lingering on the shadowed tones decorating her skin. She pictured her fingertips tracing the outlines and a shiver wiggled up her spine. Biting her lip, she felt a blush rise on her cheeks. She could blame the beer, but why bother? She burned a little brighter when she realized that Robbie was watching her and likely caught wind of that hot though.

> **Matlyn: One better. A butter-melting Light Omen. Golden brown eyes, dark hair, great tits, and ink. So much ink. Some seriously wicked thoughts roaming around my head, Addy girl. P.S. Ya burn the shop down yet?**

> **Addy: Nope. Still standing. Pretty sure I rendered Allan incapable of fathering children though. In my defense, the backwater bastard was warned. So if Mr. Wingerbe cries assault, true. No regrets.**

A ridiculous little giggling alien emoji sat on the end of the sentence and brought a smile to Matlyn's face. A second text came quick.

> **Addy: An' why in the happy fuck are ya chattin' me up, Little Bird? Two beautiful creatures with you and you're still clothed. Disappointed.**

Having no trouble at all picturing both Addy's assault on Allan Wingerbe and the shameful way she was surely hanging her head right now, Matlyn snorted, looking at her phone in mock disgust.

"Share with the class?" Baker's voice wafted with the smoke and smell of the bar, and Matlyn looked up from her phone.

Sliding it back into her pocket, she said, "Addy may have assaulted our supplies dealer. Fuckin' Wingerbe. Had it comin' though." She snickered again.

"Not a fan of this Wingerbe, I take it?" Robbie's accent almost made Allan's name sound posh. Almost.

Trying to be smooth and nonchalant, Matlyn shifted closer to the Light Omen.

"The guy's repugnant. Swamp slime. Like jizz drying in your jeans. Makes you *real* uncomfortable. I mean, the guy listens to fucking White Snake!"

Both girls laughed at Baker's analogy. He slouched a little lower in his chair and eyed the two, watching the casual glances, the way they leaned into one another.

Matlyn's eyes made a trail from Robbie's cleavage to her plump lips, and the Light Omen's dark, copper eyes fixed on Matlyn's mouth.

Turning her firm gaze to her Dark counterpart, noticing the roguish grin Baker was sporting, Robbie asked, "That canary taste good?"

Baker sat up straighter. "What are you thinking about, Einin?" The faded Irish accent made the words comfortable, like something to curl up with, but the husk weaving through the tone brought a delicious burn to it, like whiskey warming your veins.

Not being the type to pull punches, she said exactly what was on her mind, just the way Baker knew she would. "Fucking Robbie."

Smug, Baker sat back and leveled Robbie with a wicked stare. "Tastes good."

Without looking at either of the people flanking her, Matlyn slid the half-empty bottle of beer to the center of the table and pushed away. Her Doc's hit the now sticky floor of Jazz'd, and she glided toward the doors. Her hair swayed gently as the overly-warm night breeze hit her. For a quick second, Matlyn looked over her shoulder at the two supernatural beings watching her, delivered a salacious grin, and then stepped out onto the street.

* * *

"Well ..." Robbie said, amusement in her voice. "She's something, isn't she?"

Baker's arm came up and with the flick of his wrist, he called the waiter over to settle the tab. Then he handed the young man a few bills and wished him a good evening. He popped up off his chair and extended his hand for Robbie to take.

As her petite frame rose, he leaned down and spoke low. "Little Omen, you have no fucking idea." With his hand resting lightly on the center of her back, he guided her out of the bar. The door closed behind them and the music became a low murmur.

Standing under a streetlight, encased in a soft yellow-white glow, Matlyn stood looking a lot like foreplay. Robbie took five steady, fluid strides forward, coming to a stop inches from Matlyn's face. Each breathed the other in, pupils blowing out like plumes of smoke as a surge of want passed between them, lips a whisper away from a kiss.

"'Bout three minutes that way." Robbie pointed down the street toward Front River and took Matlyn's hand.

* * *

The heavy door slowly closed behind them with a metallic

click, and Robbie kicked off her black heels. She turned on her bare feet toward Baker and Matlyn. "First time I've had another Omen in my room." Flashing them a crooked smile, she brought her hands to her hair, pulling gently on a black and white checkered ribbon that held it up. Inky hair spilled over her shoulders and down her back. Thin streams of purple ran through the black.

It was a purely feminine gesture that Baker found sexy as hell and something he'd considered a predatory move, one only the fairer sex was capable of. Subtle moves and sway, in Baker's opinion, was the very definition of *woman*. Men didn't do subtle. Men got hard and grunted. Women shook their hair loose, bit lips, and let their fingers roam their collarbone. Soft, seemingly tiny moves that were stupidly effective.

Baker leaned against the door and watched Robbie move further into the room, Matlyn following her. She sat Matlyn on the edge of the bed and worked her way back to Baker. Reaching out, the Light Omen took his hand, leading him to where the pretty Story was unlacing her Docs. He shook his head and backed up, taking a seat on a settee that afforded him a wonderful view of the king-sized bed.

"So this is for you?" Robbie asked, watching Baker get comfortable.

He smiled indolently. "As much as it is for you, Miss Robbie."

The curvy Omen walked backwards, positioning herself between Matlyn's long legs, and really the girl was *all* leg. Matlyn's teal nails raked up Robbie's stockinged thighs and then disappeared around the swell of her hips. Baker heard the slide of a zipper and then Robbie's red pencil skirt shimmied down her legs. It pooled at her feet, and Baker took in the sight of the half-naked girl standing unashamed in soft gray lace. A garter belt secured pinstripe stockings.

Baker sat forward, elbows resting on his knees. He exhaled. "First thing tomorrow, Einin, we're getting you a pair of those fucking things. Christ," he remarked, wiping his hand over his face and running his eyes from toes to hip and back again, taking in the fine lace work.

Matlyn chuckled. "Lovely sight," she said and nipped at Robbie's ass.

Robbie gasped. "Ouch. Didn't tell me she bites," she said, her head turning to look over her shoulder.

"She bites," Baker said darkly, an eyebrow quirking.

The redhead's busy hands traveled over the soft hills of Robbie's hips and danced at the curve of her waist before splaying her fingers wide across her belly. They toyed with the thin band of her panties then disappeared beneath the cover of gray lace. Baker's stomach clenched when Robbie's legs buckled and a soft moan passed her lips. He knew what it felt like to have Matlyn's hands on him, working him.

"Open," he heard Matlyn say, and the young Omen obeyed, widening her stance. The snaps securing the garter on the backs of Robbie's thighs popped easily. "Turn." And Robbie turned. The front snaps unfastened as well, and then Matlyn asked Robbie to rest her foot on the bed and rolled each stocking down, kissing and nipping the skin as she went.

Beautiful, Baker thought. He'd undressed many a woman before and the act, to him, was something like slowly pulling the cover off a priceless work of art, revealing it inch by inch. He saw it now for its sensuality, like an art form all its own. When the last scraps of lace joined the red skirt on the floor, Matlyn stood and pulled Robbie's arms up over her head and let her fingers trail down, down, down until she reached the hem of the beautiful Omen's simple, black tube top. Matlyn worked it up and over Robbie's head and tossed it to the side.

"Fuck," Matlyn said, taking a step back and giving the Light Omen an appraising look. Baker did the same. She was petite, no more than five-three, hints of tone and muscle under soft, near porcelain skin. Her breasts were perfect, pale tear drops. Black and gray tattoos marked her arms, stomach, thighs, and lower back. Flowers, sugar skulls, moths circling a candle. She was beautiful.

Robbie scooted back to the center of the bed and waved a hand at the still-fully-clothed girl, as if to say *off with it*. Baker stood and with slow, gentle hands, he undressed Matlyn, watching Robbie's eyes swallow every line and delicate curve. That was what he wanted to see more than anything. That hungry look. A look, he was sure, mirrored his own every time he looked at his beautiful Little Bird.

He sat back down, adjusting himself as the naked ink-slinger crawled across the bed. Robbie reached for her. Leaning back, she guided Matlyn's warm, wet center to her mouth and practically purred as Matlyn's taste hit her tongue. Baker understood the sensation perfectly well, having devoured the girl many a time.

He watched Little Bird's back arch and her coppery hair sweep back and forth with each roll of her hips. His skin prickled with each moan, each groan, and with every faint whisper. When fingers slipped and slid and moans turned to panting, he couldn't help but stroke his cock. Bodies turned this way and that, tasting, grinding, fucking.

"Do it." Matlyn's voice was breathless, but her eyes were locked on the motion of Baker's hand, absently rubbing his jean-clad hard-on. Not needing any more than that as an invitation, Baker undid his pants and pulled himself free. His fist worked in time with their grinding hips. Baker's grip tightened as Matlyn's teeth carefully closed around Robbie's swollen nipple. And that was all it took; Robbie's breath pushed hard, her chest heaved, and her stomach contracted as she came. Matlyn smiled and worked her down with her fingers.

Once her body relaxed, the young Omen sat with her back against the headboard. She turned Matlyn on her lap so she faced Baker and not so gently lowered the freckled girl down onto her fingers, then reached around with the other and gave her swollen clit the attention it deserved. Matlyn rode her hand, gripping Robbie's calves for balance. A string of colorful expletives flew from Matlyn's mouth, and Baker knew she was close. He saw the way her lips pressed together and the flutter of her eyelids. She was holding on by a thread, drawing the moment out … for him.

He squeezed his cock, pumping it harder, hoping to meet Matlyn and dive off into oblivion together. She watched him, barely able to keep her eyes open, hips moving wildly. "You're fucking perfect, Einin," he murmured, and then groaned loudly as he came. Her body toppled forward and she cried out, fisting the sheets.

Robbie held her waist to keep her steady and then helped her to her side as the spent redhead collapsed to the bed, a fine sheen of sweat visible from where Baker sat.

"Porn is for fucking amateurs. That was brilliant," Matlyn half moaned.

The room was silent, save the harsh breaths and whispered curses. Lust and satisfaction lingered in the air like a slowly fading cloud of perfume. Baker got up and excused himself to clean up, thanking the ladies for a stunning performance. He returned moments later, jeans still open, hanging low on his hips.

He crawled up on the bed and held himself over Matlyn. "Thank you, you splendid fucking creature, you." When he reached her mouth, Baker laid a chaste, thoughtful kiss on her waiting lips.

"Death by swoon," Robbie said, lying in a jelly-like puddle next to them.

"This wasn't a novelty for me. It was something I needed to experience with her," Baker explained in a quiet tone. He pulled back from the two naked wonders and climbed off the bed, zipping his jeans up as he went.

"I know," Robbie said, idly twirling her hair between her fingers. "You did this because you wanted all of her. Not parts of her. I get it."

He nodded and searched the room for the television remote.

"Hey," Matlyn said, sitting up. "Take your shirt off." She motioned to Baker.

"What, ya miss this already?" He grabbed his cock and shot her a crooked grin.

Matlyn shook her head and leveled him with an unimpressed look. "Such an asshole. No, the words. I want to see the new words."

In the haze of the evening he'd completely forgotten

about the pain, the words. Reaching behind him, he pulled his shirt up over his head. Matlyn padded toward him, inspecting his torso.

"Hmm. Here. The day I graduated college. Cohen brought Parrish and me out to dinner. Pare wasn't even twenty-one yet. Flashed her tits to the doorman. He waved the cover charge." Matlyn laughed at the memory. "Did Blue Balls shots all night because Parrish thought it was funny. She'd hold up the shot and holler, 'I've got blue balls!' Drunker than a skunk. She puked blue shit for hours."

Baker remained quiet, trying like hell to hide the agony. He knew this race was approaching the finish line.

Nineteen

❧

Sunlight sneaked in between the curtain seams leaving thin, golden rectangles of light where it fell, like a dashed line. Matlyn groaned and stretched in a cat like way, arms akimbo. She opened her eyes and propped herself up on her elbows. Baker lay on the couch, a blanket draped over most of his body. She watched his chest rise and fall. His face was scruffy—sexy scruffy, the kind that tickles the inner thigh and leaves the skin warm.

"He's pretty fucking gorgeous … as far as men go." Robbie regarded the Dark Omen from across the room, her voice heavy with sleep and a night well spent. She cleared her throat and leaned over planting a quick kiss on Matlyn's shoulder.

"Not much for dick?" Matlyn asked, settling back down on the bed.

"Not at all. Much prefer perky tits and a soft, pink

pussy. I came out to my parents when I was eleven. My dad's reaction when I told him I had a crush on a girl: 'Well, we've got that in common.'"

Matlyn smiled, knowing her own father's response would have been similar.

"Coffee?" Robbie asked, reaching for the phone.

Matlyn quirked an eyebrow and grinned. "Read my mind."

"Girl's hot and has jokes." She ordered a large pot of coffee, juice, and a mix of pastries, then collapsed on the bed without an ounce of grace, the sheet drifting somewhere around her midriff.

"Do you like the work you do?" Matlyn asked, turning her head to look at the dark-haired darling lying in a mess of creamy white linen.

"It's a good thing I died hot. Twenty years can do some *fuck-awful* things to a rack." Robbie chuckled, more to herself, and admired her own chest. "You learn. People are all the same. People are incredibly different. There's a lot of amazing, wonderful things out there, and I get to see it. Brilliant minds that change the way others think, advancements that save lives, babies …"

"What does it feel like?"

Robbie took a moment to pull the words together. "A warm rush that tickles through my veins. It's fucking euphoric. If humans could feel this way … Think of the best high you've ever felt, swirl in a toe-curling orgasm and the sweet burn of a fine cognac, and you're just brushing the surface."

Matlyn looked impressed. "Nice."

"You scared?" Robbie dared to ask, fussing with the edge of the sheet.

Matlyn's chest expanded as she pulled in a deep, thoughtful breath. "Terrified. I'm afraid it'll hurt. And … Parrish." Her voice dropped away and her eyes began to swim. When she spoke again, her words sounded tight, trapped in a fist. "That bullshit about you can't miss what you never had." Her warm eyes slipped shut, and she shook her head. "The list of my nevers is pilin' up every fuckin' day and there's nothing to do but let it roll off my back."

When Matlyn's eyes finally opened, Robbie saw every fear, every instance of regret and loss; the things Matlyn wished she could change and the things she'd never have a chance at. A surge of pain skipped through every beat of Robbie's heart. Matlyn's wounds mirrored her own twenty years ago when her life as a human ceased.

Robbie reached out and pulled the pretty Story close, kissing her cinnamon dusted face. "I know you feel like you're dissolving into nothing, but Miss Wren, you're quite possibly the strongest, most substantial person I've ever met." With a lovely, genuine smile, Robbie asked, "Would you rather not know?"

The answer poured from her, no hesitation. "No. Not knowing would mean not having him." She tipped her head to the Dark Omen, lost somewhere in a useless sleep. Looking down at the palm of her hand and tracing the long lines, she said, "Ya know that list, that list we all made when were young … of things we wanted in another person?"

"Yup. Still haven't found a chick that knows the lyrics to every Spice Girls' song."

Matyln chuckled. "He's that list. I wished for him."

"Should we wake the boy?"

And wake him they did … with soft moans and whispers of ecstasy.

* * *

That adage … it's not about you … Bullshit. Who else would it be about? Who else should you be living your life for? Do the things that bring you peace, make yourself happy, and do them often. Take care of your body, your mind. Be selfish about what you love.

Rolling the scribbled-on piece of paper, Baker slipped it through the mouth of a glass soda bottle. He put the pen down and surveyed the cluster of mismatched bottles. Each contained a piece of advice. A Bakerism. Just like his Story, he knew his life as an Omen would soon be over. Something he'd once looked at as a sentence, a punishment, became a lesson. With each new Story, a sliver of his old life fell away and redefined what life meant.

Sitting on the edge of their own king-sized bed, Matlyn let her feet dangle over the side, swinging to the beat thrumming through her head. She ran a towel through her messy, damp hair, fluffing it, and watched Baker. "We *gotta* do that *Sixth Sense World* ghost tour thing," the newly showered girl said, tapping the pamphlet on her lap.

A crooked grin graced Baker's face. "Not enough otherworldly shenanigans in your life?" He reached for the last of the bottles—an old sea green wine bottle. A small section of the mouth was chipped away and jagged. One side of the bottle was discolored, faded from having lain in the sun. Every flaw drew his eye. Picking the pen back up, he wrote:

I fell in love with a beautiful Little Bird.
A bird with colorful, broken wings.
Broken, but she flew anyway.
Soared.
And she loved me,
loved me,
loved me.

Carefully, he rolled it and dropped it into the bottle.

"Shenanigans is such a great word. Like hoopla or—"

"Cunt?"

"Yes! Like cunt! Still a great word," Matlyn agreed, springing to her feet and moving to stand next to Baker. "Do I get to see these profound writings of yours?"

The Omen turned in the desk chair and looked up at her. "Nope." Gripping her hips playfully, he gave her a light squeeze.

"Then I'll just have to assume you're drawing lewd cartoons."

Baker chuckled. "Stick figures in compromising positions."

"So we're just going to leave these in a park for some poor unsuspecting kid to find?" Matlyn picked up a bottle and swished it back and forth. The little scroll rattled from side to side.

"That's the plan." Sneaky, long, warm fingers creeped under the hem of her shirt and caressed the soft skin of her hip. "Put shoes on those feet, woman. Let's get with the go." He stood and smacked her ass in one quick motion.

"Ouch! Bugger." She glared at him and swatted his bare shoulder. "That's gonna leave a mark."

"Good."

With care, Matlyn collected the bottles and placed them in a shopping bag. Reaching for the last, Baker's hand gently grabbed her wrist, halting her movement. "Not that one. That one stays here." She shrugged and left the bottle on the old oak desk.

Baker and Matlyn left the bed and breakfast, climbed into the green machine, and set out to find the perfect place for each of the bottled messages.

The day had started out dull and hazy, but the murk had cleared and offered bright blue skies. The temperature hovered in the late seventies, not at all uncomfortable. Hand in hand, the Story and the Omen strolled through their first stop: Morrell Park.

"The Waving Girl," Baker said, his chin tipping toward a statue of a girl and a dog. Reading the plaque standing in front of the monument, he informed Matlyn that the girl had been a beacon for incoming ships guiding them to shore with her lanterns in the night, or, as the statue depicted: a handkerchief. Baker decided this was an appropriate place to leave one of his messages. He reached down into the bag and pulled out a clear, tall wine bottle. Placing it at the foot of the Waving Girl, the Omen gave it a long look.

Everything happens for a reason. When I was young it was hard to see reason in the horrible things that happened. What was the reason for

my father's tyrannical behavior? Why do some people struggle and others soar? What reason is there in pain, illness, or death?

I've come to realize that the reason is both incredibly simple and complex. Each of those 'everythings' is a chance to learn. Learn from mistakes, your own and others'. Learn to see others in a different light. Learn to love while you can. Learn to fight harder for what you want. Simple, right? So why do we struggle so much with it? That's the complex part. The stuff that makes us who we are. We don't always pick it up on our first go, so we go through another bad relationship, lose another job, do another stint in rehab. Everything happens for a reason … look for the reasons. Learn the lessons.

* * *

An elderly couple stood bickering over a camera. "I think that's the flash, Jack. It's two in the afternoon. Ya don't need no damn flash," the white-haired wife barked, making a grab for the silver camera.

"It's *not* the flash, it's the anti-glare. Now hush, I got this." The older man swatted his wife's hands away and took aim at the monument once again. "Oh, for the lovea biscuits, the stupid thing's turned off."

Matlyn chuckled, taking a few steps toward the couple. "Would you like some help?" she offered, looking pointedly at the small device.

The white-haired woman smiled widely, snatched the camera from her husband, and gladly handed it to Matlyn. "Kids said it was 'user friendly'. It'd be real friendly if the damn thing just took a picture when I push a button." The woman's cloudy gray eyes rolled. "And so small. Could lose that thing in an empty room."

Tugging his wife by the hand, Jack said, "Stop flappin' your damned gums, Mandy May, and come give an ol' man a kiss." He smiled a soft, happy smile as Mandy May playfully smacked his arm. They stood just off to the side of the Waving Girl, facing each other. As their wrinkled faces drew closer, Matlyn snapped a few photos catching a perfect kiss. The old couple laughed as Matlyn and Baker returned the camera.

Mandy May thanked Matlyn for her help and introduced them to her 'know-it-all' Jack, her husband of forty-five years. "Those are beautiful," Mandy May said, pointing to the winding stems and blood-red poppies that crept around Matlyn's left leg. "Who ya rememberin'?" The woman's voice was soft, and it was clear to Matlyn that Mandy May had seen her share of loss.

"My parents." She averted her eyes for a moment before explaining that both had died in a car accident when she was younger.

The eldery woman offered her a knowing smile that swam with sympathy. "Doesn't get any easier, ya know? Whether they die in their twenties … or slip off to sleep in their eighties, no easier." She paused for a moment, quietly adding, "Hurts all the same," in a voice seeped in some old pain.

Matlyn's heart squeezed tight, and as if reading her

mind, again, Baker slipped his hand into hers, lacing their fingers together and pulling her to his side.

They bid the older couple a good afternoon. Baker quickly explained the camera to Jack before they parted ways. Hand in hand, Omen and Story made their way through the park, enjoying the sun and the simple, comfortable quiet that surrounded them.

Crossing East Bay Street and into Emmet Park, Baker quickly found a home for another of his messages. The Omen snickered like a fifteen-year-old as he placed the bottle at the base of a stone monument and stepped back.

"Of course he picks the phallic looking thing. You're such a twit," Matlyn chided, her eyes rolling. "A hundred plus years … it's true, men never grow up."

"Pft. That shit's overrated. So is sliced bread."

Side-eying the scruffy man, she grabbed his shirt and towed him backward. They took their time walking through the squares, talking about nothing. Talking about everything. Matlyn couldn't get enough of his voice; she thought of it as sea salt and dark chocolate. Smooth and rich, with the hint of a bitter edge. She loved the happy giggle she let out when he got a text from Pacey. It was a picture of Adeline devouring his face, her ruby-red lipstick smeared at the corners of his mouth. Pacey's smile was wide and goofy. The caption said: *Buy her shoes. Trust me.*

The wise Omen had deposited the last of his messages about an hour ago when the sun had begun to creep toward the horizon. Now the sky bloomed with deep pinks, blues, and shades of purple, the last streak of orange washed away and forgotten.

"Come on," Matlyn said, taking a quick step and then

turning to face him. She walked backward for a few paces. "I saw a seafood joint down the river. An oyster po'boy sounds like fucking heaven right now."

"Food. Yes. Good idea. Beer too." For a moment Baker's features screwed into something serious. "You think there's any truth to the oyster thing?" he asked, his tone contemplative.

"Nine hard-ons a day, aphrodisiac or not, pretty sure it's a moot point."

Baker reached out, hooking his finger in her belt loop and pulled her to him. His breath rushed hot in her ear, and she felt his lips and the more-than five o'clock shadow on her neck. "Einin, there's *nothing* moot about this." He made a point of clutching her closer, letting her feel the length of him against her stomach.

The slightest pink colored her face, just barely visible in the dying light. "And what number is that?" Warm fingers tickled her lower back and she shivered.

"Ten," he revealed. "I woke up to you licking a woman senseless. It's been a rough fucking day."

"Dinner to go, then?"

His head dipped, looking down at the girl. The spark in his eyes held a mixture of danger and comfort, and Matlyn would gladly drown herself a thousand times if it meant seeing that look again. He cupped her shoulders and spun her around, swatting her ass as he ordered her toward the restaurant.

* * *

Tubby's Seafood was all hardwood, black iron, and a wide-open deck that looked out over the river. The sun was nearing its death and was nothing more than a blurry ball that seemed to bob on the surface of the water. The air had grown a little cool, but still perfectly comfortable.

Tucked into a booth, Matlyn ordered the po'boy she'd been craving, and Baker decided on lump crab cake sandwich. Toying with the frosty beer in front of him, like a dog with a bone, Baker's mind ground down on a thought he'd been chewing on since they met Robbie.

"Penny for your thoughts, sir." Matlyn watched his hands work at the label, nails picking at the corners and his eyes far away.

Not looking up, Baker asked, "Did you ask her?"

"Ask who what?"

"Robbie. Did you ask her—" Baker's voice drifted off, but his eyes lifted.

She sighed and pursed her lips. "No." As soon as the word left her mouth a war broke out on Baker's face. Curiosity and relief tugged back and forth.

"Why not?" Curiosity won.

"Afraid she'd know. Terrified she wouldn't."

Baker just nodded his head. They both knew she was on a path leading directly to Death's door. Would the specifics really offer either any modicum of comfort or ease? What they both craved was time, and regardless of what Robbie might have seen, she couldn't offer them time. Be it accident or disease, God herself couldn't stop the fate that awaited Matlyn.

The burn on the Omen's skin was an excruciating reminder of that.

Twenty

"Well did you like it? Did it feel good?" Addy's voice was loud, curious, and easily carried over the noise of the bar. Campbell mumbled something that sounded like 'shoulda kept my mouth shut,' and buried her burning face in her hands.

"What's that?" Can't quite hear ya, darlin'." Scott tapped his index finger on the table. His face stretched into a grin that would make the Cheshire Cat proud.

Campbell looked up, her soft features seeming especially young with the blush of embarrassment coloring her cheeks. Her mouth worked to form words.

"You unimaginable whores!"

"Saved by the boss," Campbell hissed in relief, smiling up at Matlyn as she wormed her way into the booth next to her. Baker stood at the end of the table.

"Jerks ate all the nachos," Matlyn complained, lifting her chin toward the empty platter in the middle of the table. She leaned across the table and planted a kiss on Scott's forehead. "Happy birthday."

Shaking hands with each of the men, Baker wished Scott a happy birthday, handing him a fresh beer. "So what'd we miss?" he asked, pulling a chair up to the booth, close to Matlyn.

Pacey cleared his throat. "Well ... Miss Campbell here was about to tell us about her first finger bang." Pacey's grin matched Scott's perfectly.

"Crude!" Campbell spat, tossing a damp napkin Pacey's way.

The ink-slinger gasped dramatically, hand to heart. "I go away for a few days, and ya'll corrupt the girl."

Pushing an empty bottle of Abita away from her, Rumor piped up, "Yeah, we forced her to spread herself for some random. What was his name?" Her snicker was as contagious as a yawn, passing from one person to the next.

"Ugh," Campbell groaned. "Lewis." She drew out his name.

"Oh come on! You've heard endless stories, countless sins. So why not add to the pile? Swallow your embarrassment," Addy encouraged, with a snicker and a salacious grin. "Let's hear about your night with Random Lew."

With her face half hidden by her hands, Campbell spilled the baked beans.

At the prodding of Addy, Baker and Matlyn told the

group about their trip to the B&B and the lovely dark-haired girl—much to Parrish's horror.

"Why do I need to know about your pussy eating escapades? Jesus *fucking* wept!" Parrish grumbled, shaking her head.

Matlyn yammered on at length about the impressive, yet just-as-cheesy-as-she-thought-it would-be Supernatural Savannah tour. Neither mentioned the bottles that now littered the parks of Savannah.

Closing time crawled closer, and Scott and Rumor had said their goodbyes first, quickly followed by Campbell after receiving a mysterious text, possibly—though she refused to confirm from Random Lew. When the group had thinned to Adeline, Pacey, Baker, and Matlyn, Addy leaned to the side resting her head on her friend's shoulder.

"Come home with me, Little Bird," she said, playing with a strand of Matlyn's hair. "Your layers are growing out." She swirled another stand and let it drop back into place.

"Years of trying to flip that switch and all it took was a vacation."

"You wish, buttercup." The busty blond straightened up and looked her friend in the eye. Her face was at odds with her light tone. Matlyn had seen that look before; it was the look of trapped words and secrets. "I just want to talk. You and me."

"What about me?" Pacey whined, batting his thick eyelashes in a ridiculous way that had both the girls chuckling.

Patting his hand, Adeline said, "Well, you and Baker can get some mint chocolate chip and cuddle up with Netflix. Make it a 90210 night."

"New or old?" Baker asked with a silly smile on his face. It was a distinctly slurred face.

* * *

Adeline and Matlyn spilled into the back of a cab, half hysterical, and the only word Addy could muster was leprechaun. The cab driver rolled his eyes and asked the requisite question: where to? With a few dropped consonants and a rolled vowel or two, the bombed blond rattled off her address and adjusted the flowered pencil skirt she wore.

Ten minutes later, the cab pulled up to Adeline's robin's egg blue double gallery townhouse. The pale yellow shutters framing the windows made the house look pleasant and welcoming. A black wrought-iron fence surrounded the structure.

As the key turned over and the lock gave way, a gruff bark sounded from the other side of the door. Adeline pushed the door open and a large brown head nuzzled into the girl's hand. "Titus, we have a guest. Try to keep your nose out of her crotch, yeah?"

Matlyn dropped to the floor, taking Titus's giant-sized head in her hands and rubbing behind his floppy ears. "Hey, big guy. Fuck, what are you feeding him, Addy, small children?"

"Yes. And the occasional goat." Kicking off her purple pumps in the most ungraceful way possible, the platinum blond reached out one hand, splaying it on the wall to keep herself from tipping forward, and spat a colorful curse as her fingers slipped a little.

"I want tea … and chocolate." Tipsy, Addy stumbled to the kitchen on bare feet, a drunken sway to her hips. Matlyn and Titus trailed behind with a little less sway and a lot more drool.

"Cupcakes?" Matlyn was hopeful and her mouth watered at the prospect.

"Reese Pieces!" shouted Addy, louder than need be. Bent over and wiggling her tush to some tune she had stuck in her head, she stood with the fridge door open. When she turned around, she had a plate of chocolate frosted cupcakes and a sloppy grin. The two got comfy at the kitchen table and each made quick work of the two mini cakes.

Matlyn spoke between finger licks. "I saw your face at the bar. Serious and all … serious. You said you wanted to talk. So let's have it, puddin' pop." She reached for a glass of soda, leveled her best you-don't-fool-me look at her, and took a big sip.

"Not in a skirt. I need pj's and ducky slippers." Twenty minutes later Addy and Matlyn were decked out in over-sized sleepshirts, hair pulled back, working on their third cupcake.

Nestled into the navy couch, the redhead curled her feet underneath her. "Okay, blondie, spill."

Adeline grabbed a throw pillow and squeezed it to her midsection, covering the face of a kitten wearing neon glasses. She shifted and fidgeted for a moment then grew silent, staring into the room. Maybe she was hoping to find the words hanging in the air waiting for her to pluck like ripe fruit from the vine. Maybe she didn't know how to start.

The suddenly quiet blond inhaled slowly, no good words seemed to be there. When her voice finally surfaced, it was tiny, thin, and unsure.

"While you guys were gone … I did a little diggin'. The

Fates, curses, death." She let the words float in the air like balloons and waited for them to deflate.

"The Fates?" Matlyn questioned, her gut suddenly tightening.

Addy continued as if she hadn't spoken. "Dug until I found a woman. She's a grand high witch, Hannah Parker, from Paradox, Colorado."

"Addy, we did the voodoo priest thing. He couldn't—"

"There's a spell," Addy interrupted, railroading Matlyn's words. Matlyn's brows pinched together, but she said nothing in response. "I spoke to her for a few hours. She said it can be ... you can trick Death."

Matlyn let go of a lung full of warm breath and pulled a patchwork quilt over her bare legs. She sat quietly and let the words sink down into the wrinkles and crevices of her brain. They wiggled into the gray matter and hope began to build in her chest.

"How?"

"A trade."

"What kind of trade? What does she want? And wait, there's a grand high witch named *Hannah Parker*?" The questions bubbled up in Matlyn's mind, stacking one on the other.

"I know, right? I was expectin', I don't know, Minerva or some such thing. But no, Hannah Parker, who teaches the third grade, by the way."

Matlyn could feel the hope pushing through her veins. Slow and thick, but it was there, working its way to her heart. "So what does Not Minerva want?" She prayed it was something she had to give. Money, an item, blood.

"No, Little Bird. A trade … your *death* for someone's *life*," Adeline qualified.

The redhead cocked her head, confused by what just tumbled from Adeline's mouth. Her death for a life? "I don't understand. My death? I trade my death?"

"A necklace, a ring, something like that is cursed and given to another person. A girl, your age, maybe a runaway, a junkie. You trade her life for yours."

Clarity came sharp and hard and twisted Matlyn's gut. Bile began to march its way up her throat. "She would die, and I would live?"

"Your death becomes hers, yes."

"So if I'm fated to die by gunshot, she'll be shot?" she asked, horror chasing away the hope and washing out her veins with a harsh chemical sting.

"Yes." Addy looked down, fiddling with the tag on the pillow she was still clutching.

"And … and then I would live out her years?"

Matlyn's friend just nodded, lips pursed tight.

"What if she's slated to die in a week? What then? Is there a fucking *return policy*, Addy?" Matlyn half shouted, tears welling in her eyes.

Addy sat silent for a moment before answering. "No. It's a straight trade. No guarantees. If she only has a week, that's all you get."

"Well that sounds fucking peachy." Matlyn stood up and stormed off to the guest room.

"If you find someone that's *healthy* …" Adeline called after her friend.

Matlyn stopped dead. She didn't turn. "You're kidding me, right? So instead of stealing away some poor drug addict's life, I highjack a life that would have been long and well spent?" With her fists balled at her sides, she padded off to the bedroom and closed the door then dropped to the bed with a sigh.

Quiet leaked through the townhouse. It was the kind of silence that made everything loud. Mundane sounds rattled Matlyn's eardrums, but the space between, when it was just her thoughts and nothing more … hurt. Her brain began to run through the conversation again. A life for a death. A trade. A chance for her to live. A chance to be with Baker, to see her sister's baby, to have babies of her own.

It was right there. A future. A life.

And all she had to do was steal it away from someone else.

Twenty-One

❧

The door groaned as it slowly opened. Each inch sounded like hesitance, like caution. The bed shifted and a warm hand reached out swiping hair away from Matlyn's face. The smell of Adeline's lavender soap filled Matlyn's head, along with the mouth-watering scent of eggs and bacon. Addy's eggs were fried in more butter than any human had any right to consume in one sitting. They would kill you, and you'd die smilin'.

Her eyes peeled open, but she didn't turn, didn't make a move. She blinked twice, Matlyn's eyelids felt gritty and dry. The night had been long and pregnant with thought, regret, sadness, and a strange clarity—clarity only gifted to those that knew their fate.

"Please don't be mad with me," begged Addy in a small voice. "I just ... I wanted my friend to *live*. I needed you to live, Little Bird."

Finally, with a sluggish movement, Matlyn rolled over and faced her friend. "I know."

"What can I say, I'm a selfish heffer." The apologetic blond offered a sheepish grin. Fear and a need to keep what was hers close and safe fueled her curiosity and pushed her to seek out answers, answers that Hannah Parker had.

* * *

"Adeline, this is a powerful curse. You're taking years from a person, offering them nothing," Hannah said. Her voice was stern and serious, cut thin by the distance between them.

"Then why tell me about it? Why does it even exist?" Addy huffed, phone pressed to her ear, pacing around her kitchen, wearing a worried path in the tiled floor as if waiting on news from an injured relative.

"Because once upon a time a desperate witch wanted to save someone they loved. Anger and selfishness created this. Last ditch efforts and no hope left. It's what leads people like you to me."

The face Addy pulled was chockfull of shame and a deep hurt that tore new holes into her tired heart. "I'm not angry," she spat, cringing at the petulance she caught in her own voice. She heard a soft sigh on the other side of the phone. "She's worth the world." The tattooed blonde's eyes stung with hot tears.

Hannah gave her the step-by-step breakdown of the spell. She told her how to curse the object, what moon it should be cast under, and the reasoning behind each of those steps.

Addy scribbled furiously, listening carefully to each instruction. "Thank you," Addy said, meaning it from the very center of her soul.

Hannah cleared her throat and when her parting words came out, they dropped thick and heavy like lead. "If you offer this to her, and she accepts, be prepared for the fallout. This is a curse in every sense of the word. She'll not only be cursing another human, stealing away their life …" For a moment the witch was silent. She blew out a long, shaky breath. "She'll be left with grief and guilt. Knowing she took a life, that guilt will never dissipate, never fade away. Good people, truly good … it changes them, rots away a small part of their soul."

* * *

Sitting up, Matlyn reached for the peace offering, wrapping her hand around a large mug of coffee. "I couldn't live with that, Addy. Knowing what my life cost. You couldn't either," she said with absolute certainty.

"No. No, I couldn't." She snagged a piece of bacon and took a bite. "Maybe some child abusin' shit-sucker. Can't say I'd feel too bad `bout that."

Matlyn ripped off the other end of bacon from the strip Addy still held and wagged it at her. "Well if you can dig me up such thing …"

The blonde sighed, shoulders dropping. "Even then."

"Playing God isn't in our job descriptions, Addy girl." With that, the twist in Matlyn's gut released.

* * *

July 1, 2015, 11:11 a.m. ~ Bywater District, New Orleans

A wiry tail wriggled in the air, and Syndal dropped her body down low, stalking the roller that glided up and down the wall. Her furry butt shimmied and as Wilson brought the roller down again, the cat sprang forward, pouncing and leaping sideways.

"Fuck!" Wilson shouted, startled. Pale blue paint tipped and oozed out of the tray onto the drop cloth that was, thankfully, covering the muddy brown carpeting.

With painted paws, Syndal tore through the room and out into the hall before anyone could grab her.

"Syn, I'm cuttin' ya off! No more catnip, crazy fucker!" Matlyn hollered down the hall. Tiny blue paws the color of a clear, early morning sky marked the hardwood outside the bedroom. Parrish would shit a brick when she saw that. The thought lifted the corners of her lips.

"Whose idea was it to bring Hell Cat here?" Wilson asked, cleaning the mess the best he could.

"Guilty," admitted Baker, raising a hand. "Poor bugger was puking last night. Couldn't leave the lass home alone."

"No, 'course not. Bringing the shit-disturbing, vomiting cat here … *superb* idea, Baker." There wasn't an ounce of amusement in Wilson's voice, but they both knew he wasn't mad.

Matlyn smiled and tipped her head to look at the tree she'd begun to paint. Its roots began at the base boards, strong and thick. The trunk wound more than halfway up the wall. Its branches were reedy and pushed up toward the ceiling in an umbrella of brightly colored leaves. Perched on a branch near the center of the tree was a small owl. Its eyes were round and watchful. At the base of the tree, opposite the owl, Matlyn had painted a single red poppy.

She knew there was a sad kind of irony adding two death portends to a child's room, but she saw it as a way of leaving something of herself behind, a little of her own story. She knew, somewhere, hiding in the near future, the day would come when Adeline would begin to tell the tale of the Omen and his Story. She would point out the poppy, the owl.

Today, the boys worked to put the final coat on the three walls surrounding the tree while Matlyn worked on the finer details. She added lighter shades of brown to bring out the texture of the bark, added a knot or two to age the tree.

Wearing a sly grin, Matlyn looked to the puddle of paint, walked over, and pressed her hand down, coating it with blue. Smiling wide at Wilson, who watched the mischief play out, but said nothing, just chuckled as she winked and sneaked up behind her Omen.

Matlyn palmed Baker's khaki-covered ass.

He spun on her. "You wretched little girl, you!" He grabbed her wrist before she had the chance to swipe at him again and pulled her close. "I oughta take you over my knee, Einin," he whispered in her ear, his voice low, a deadly edge riding just under something light and playful.

"Paint now, kinky sex later." Raising up on the tips of her bare feet, she kissed the tip of his nose and winked at him.

Before she could take a full step back, he crushed his body to hers, hugging her tight. She squealed, expecting retaliation, maybe a paint brush to the back, but no, he just held her. Bringing her eyes to his face, she quickly realized that Baker was locked in pain. Jaw tight, teeth grinding in an effort to keep the pain bottled up inside. She kissed his neck and gently ran her hands through his hair and whispered softly in his ear. "Just breath, love. You've got this."

Wilson side-eyed them and turned back to the wall.

"Inappropriate. This is a child's room, you animals." He snickered, unaware of the event being cataloged on Baker's lower back, wrapping itself around his side and etching into his hip bone.

When the pain finally ebbed and Baker could stand alone, he looked down on his Story and murmured a thank-you that sounded more like an apology.

* * *

The sun slipped out of sight, but the stifling heat kept up, as persistent as an Area 51 conspiracy. Baker shut the thick wooden door, slicing through the humidity and trapping it outside. Syndal hissed at him, batting at his chest. Baker rolled his eyes at the puff ball as it leaped to the floor and zoomed down the hall.

Matlyn slumped against the wall, exhaustion clear in her face and her body. She shook out her tired limbs. Colorful spots of paint dotted her arms. She pushed toe against heel and removed her shoes. "Tylenol and a bath. I smell like paint and sweat." Lifting her shirt to her nose, she added, "And Catfish."

Baker pulled her away from the wall and led her up the stairs to the bathroom. "Arms up." He helped her out of her clothes as warm, soapy water filled the bathtub. The paint splattered shirt hit the floor, her shorts were next, until she was bare. Baker held out his hand, helped her into the tub, and then went to retrieve the Tylenol.

"Drugs," he said, presenting two white pills in the palm of his hand.

Matlyn thanked him, swallowing the pills dry. When Baker moved to the door, she sat forward. "Get in."

Slowly shucking his clothes, he stepped toward the tub but stopped when Matlyn's hand reached up and caressed the words breathing and moving on the surface of his hip. They were new: a name and a date. "Marcus," she whispered. Baker sank into the warm water, tucking himself behind her, and sighed as Matlyn let her body relax against his. He was happy to hold her up.

"Marcus was Cohen's older brother. Killed himself. He … he had mental problems. Antidepressants, Lithium. Lots of highs and lows." Absently moving her hand through the bubbles, her green eyes lowered to the water. "The first time Cohen told me he loved me was the day he buried Marcus."

Baker just listened as Matlyn told him about that day, the funeral, the crying mother and detached father. The whiskey that had burned going down, the easy escape of sex, and the honest way Cohen had proclaimed his feelings for Matlyn.

Quietly, the girl filtered through her remaining years, guessing at what might show up next on Baker's body. The day she opened the shop? The night she drove home from a concert at the House of Blues—Band of Horses—and hit that dog. She'd cried for hours. Would that make an appearance?

Kory Rae, she thought, her stomach hollowing out just a little. Kory Rae was the mile-marker she was dreading, the one that told her Death had found its way to her; the one she waited for, ran from.

She stood, milky bubbles dripping from her body. Baker watched as she stepped out and wrapped a towel around her chest, tucking it under her arms. Without a word, she padded off to the bedroom, something cold and heavy moving with her. He heard the bed in the next room squeak with the gentle weight of her body—such an almighty sound.

Baker dried off, dropping the towel on the floor next to the hamper. He pulled open a drawer and scooped a pair of sleep pants out.

"I'd rather you didn't," Matlyn said in a half-dozed voice.

"No pants party?" Seeing a small smile playing on her lips, he walked to the door, turned off the light, and sauntered to the side of the bed. "Scooch, bed hog."

"I don't—"

"Like getting into the ring with a prize fighting octopus," he interrupted. Scooting in, he pulled her close, fitting himself to her. Naked lines melting together.

She snickered, amused by the image running through her head. "Sorry. Feel free to tie me down." She hummed and rearranged the blankets as his body settled in next to her on the bed.

The only desire that tickled her veins was that of comfort, the need to feel his heartbeat softly thump against her back. To feel his warmth and let it wash over her completely. She wanted everything Baker was, the earthen, cold air smell of him to wash away the ache in her head, fill the hollowness in her gut, and steady her own heart.

In a clear whisper, she said goodnight and drifted off, ink swirling through her thoughts.

Twenty-Two

⚜

April 17, 2001, 6:31 a.m. ~ Mariposa, California

Baker stood outside the modest ranch, observing the peeling saffron paint on the siding and the broken latch on the once-upon-a-time white fence. He'd been Witnessing Murphey Brookes for a little over six months. He'd watched the elderly gentleman come and go from a distance. He'd followed the man through the streets of the history-laden town of Mariposa, California and had the ins and outs of the week down pat.

Today was Tuesday, and on Tuesday mornings Murphey would walk to the bank, the post office, and on occasion he would drop by the local library to trade out a paperback or two. Mr. Murphey Brookes would not be making that trek today. Somewhere inside that house, Mr.

Brookes was crumpled over in shock and pain as a massive stroke stole away the last of his vitality.

Baker sucked in a breath as the last jolt of pain slowed, bringing his heart rate back down.

He'd loved fiercely, gave freely, and so Murphey's story was long and full. The wife he'd met when they were only twelve, the defining moments in their relationship. The highest-highs and the lowest-lows of Murphey's life all faded, disappearing from Baker's skin, leaving him ready for the next Story.

* * *

July 6, 2015, 5:53 p.m. ~ Parabola Tattoo & Body Modification

"I'm thinkin' stuffed Portobello mushrooms for dinner. We'll need to swing by Langenstein's," Matlyn shouted down the hall as she tidied up her work station. She flipped the light off in her room and headed toward the back of the tattoo shop, talking as she went. "Oh an' Cafe Beignet, 'cause I need one of the fuckers in my mouth." As she rounded the corner into the staff room, she came to a halt and the naughty little joke she was about say evaporated on her tongue.

Baker was on all fours, muscles pulled tight in agony, the chair he'd been sitting in lying on its side—forgotten. Addy was crouched next to him, her hand hovering over his back, unsure how to comfort the Omen. "He was in mid-sentence, goin' on 'bout fucking messages in a bottle—I thought he meant the movie, ya know, with Kevin whats-his-face—and then this." Addy's face was screwed tight with worry.

Pushing back on his heels, the Dark Omen blew out a hard breath. Sweat beaded his forehead and the lines in his face seemed more pronounced. "Costner," he said, looking down at black and white tiles. "Kevin Costner."

Matlyn stood behind him, running her hand through his perfectly messy, black hair. "That's the second one this week. And they're getting more intense," she noted. Her voice was strangely calm, but her insides raged like a caged animal.

Tipping his head back to look at her, his iron eyes tugged at her willow ones, both round with fear. He said nothing. There was nothing to say. She was right. The story was coming quicker now. Fragments of the conversation that concluded Matlyn's relationship with Cohen as her lover covered Baker's right thigh. Rolling up the left leg of his khaki skate shorts, he revealed an intense argument that ended with Parrish leaving Matlyn standing in front of the Creole Creamery with a melting peach-mint cone and tears running down her face. They hadn't spoken to each other for nine days after that.

Upset, the inked blond let out a strangled sob. "I can't fuckin' hear this." She tossed her arms in the air, spun on her canary heels, and flew out the door. Hot tears trickled down her face.

* * *

Ingrid lay stretched out on a park bench. Dark sunglasses swallowed her eyes. She smiled up at the sky. The daylight had just begun to wane, leaving diffused buttery yellows and creamy oranges to melt above her. She folded her hands over her stomach and smiled to herself as a rich euphoria shimmied up her spine. She was sure she must be glowing.

Words appeared on her skin. She lifted her right arm and removed her glasses to read the eloquent new script.

"Their first ultrasound. How exciting," she murmured.

A soft, pleased smile touched her lips. She stood, straightened her sundress, and fussed with her hair for a quick second before heading back to the hotel. Her stomach rumbled, and she made a quick turn in the other direction, heading toward French Market Place. The Light Omen was in the mood for something smothered in cheese and … maybe olives.

* * *

July 10, 2015, 4:00 a.m. ~ Garden District, New Orleans

Matlyn groaned as her back connected hard with cold plaster. Lemon-colored paint was embedded under her fingernails and smeared along the side of her neck. Baker's eyes never left her face as he guided her legs around his hips and pushed forward. Everything about this was desperate. The sounds they made, the angry, red scratches, and the clipped, demanding words that poured from them like last-ditch prayers.

Give. Take. Push. Pull. Consume. It was never enough, never too much. The need to hide away inside each other, to inhabit the other, pulled them together again and again.

New pieces of Matlyn's life appeared on his skin nearly every day now. Time was wearing thin.

"Hard. *Please!*" she begged.

He knew he was hurting her; he knew she needed it.

She wanted the sting and burn to stay with her, and Baker was more than willing to give her every ounce of pain and pleasure she could handle. Her sounds, her smell, the way she clung to him, the flush of her skin, it all became like a drug. Something he craved and needed, something he wanted almost as much as time. More Matlyn, more time. Always more. Matlyn he could have, here … now. Time, on the other hand, was air … vapor. It moved around him, slipped through his fingers again and again.

Baker's hands flexed, his fingernails digging into her ass as his hips drove forward. Needing more contact, more soft skin, wanting to feel her heart's crazy, strong beat against his skin, he backed away from the wall and lowered them to the floor of the studio. The smell of sex and sweat mixed with the lingering scent of paint.

Digging her heels into the floor, the flushed red-head angled her pelvis for everything he could give her. He stretched out above her, burying his face in the gentle curve between her neck and shoulder, and nipped at her skin. A small, but wicked grin graced his face.

As Matlyn slipped over the edge and dropped into bliss, she exhaled words of benediction and inhaled a shaky breath filled with sacrilege. "Roll," she ordered, pushing at Baker's chest.

He moved to his back and the woman straddled him, sinking down hard and fast. Without an ounce of mercy, she rode him, her hands gripping his biceps with bruising force. His hands skimmed and slipped over every dip and hill, dawdling on the bits he liked best.

When Baker's breathing hitched, Matlyn pulled her body tight, a move Baker seemed to appreciate if the long, drawn-out expletive was any indication. His body relaxed, melting into the floor, as she laid herself over him like a blanket, pressing chest to chest.

"Should run you a tub. Maybe grab a few Advil," Baker mumbled, his hand running a lazy track up and down Matlyn's thigh.

Smiling a small, indolent smile, she lifted her chin to look at her Omen and said, "Roll me a joint and let's go swimming."

"What, in that tiny kidney-shaped thing you call a pool?" He snorted and made no attempt to move, though the cold tile was pressing into his shoulder blades.

"Yup, in the kidney. Roll." Pointing to the tin can on the table covered in brushes and tubes of paint, she eased herself off him and walked out of the room raising her arms over her head, stretching like a cat.

Pushing up on his elbows, Baker watched her leave. He snickered when she hollered "*Joint!*" from somewhere down the hall. Not bothering with his clothes, he did as the woman bid him and made his way to the pool, hearing the water sloshing as she slipped out the backdoor and into the courtyard.

Matlyn's naked body pushed beneath the water like pale ink. He brought the joint to his lips, smelling the sweet, earthy aroma, and lit it.

Breaking the surface, Matlyn watched Baker slip into the pool, joint secure between his lips. She waited, watching him move through the water toward her. The pool's lights cast a soft, green glow, making him seem ethereal.

He stood inches from her, inhaling and releasing thick

smoke. "What are you thinking?" he asked, giving over the joint.

"That you should *always* be in your birthday suit. That 4:00 a.m. fuck looks good on you."

"It's almost five."

"Perfect. My first tat today isn't until eleven. Time enough to mellow and watch the sun come up, maybe some sausages and biscuits."

* * *

July 26, 2015, 1:23 p.m. ~ Central Business District, New Orleans

The ball smacked against the wall, rocketing forward. Baker lunged to his right, swinging … and missed the ball by about two feet. With an annoyed grunt, he straightened.

"Fuck this," he grumbled, eyeing the neon yellow ball with a hatred normally reserved for paper cuts and stubbed toes.

"Hey, it was your idea, Omen," Matlyn reminded him.

And in fact it had been Baker that suggested a game of racquetball. When Matlyn discovered she was out of tooth-paste, the morning went sideways quickly. No creamer for her coffee, a shredded shoelace and a puddle of pee (courtesy of Syndal), and to top it off, her favorite bra died a horrible death at the hands of the dryer. Baker saw her rising frustration and ordered her into gym clothes. He was regretting that decision now.

"I give. I'm tapping out, throwing in the flag," he declared, chest heaving in and out as he tried to catch his breath.

It'd been an aggressive game and his body was spent. He plopped down onto the bench and dropped the racquet on the ground, giving it the same look he offered the ball.

The girl walked over and wedged herself between his knees. "You're sweaty and you smell." When he gazed up, she smiled and winked. "I like it."

His hands spread wide, practically covering the backs of her thighs, and the top of his head rested on her stomach. "I'm not going back to work," he spoke casually, but there was no room for arguments. "I called Huxley this morning, told him I was done and that he could forward my last check to your place."

Matlyn nodded, hearing what he didn't say: they were out of time.

Baker raised his head, pulling his shoulders back. "This showed up this morning, before you woke up." He stood, turned around, pulled up his shirt, closed his gray eyes, and listened to the thick sound of blood pulsing in his ears.

* * *

Dark ink stretched and moved as if inhaling. It mingled in some places with the owl that stretched out across the Dark Omen's back, seeming to give the bird life.

She read the words carefully, slowly. Letter by letter. *K-O-R-Y-R-A-E*. Matlyn closed her eyes, remembering the bold introduction.

* * *

The bar was packed, bodies moved this way and that, music poured down on them in waves, and the heat was just this side of bearable. When Kory-Rae walked in, Matlyn had noticed. She watched as the tall girl pulled her body up onto a high stool with ease, crossed her tanned legs, and began stalking the room.

Matlyn knew that look, and she smiled knowingly. Blondie was on the hunt, prowling.

"This conversation borin' you, Little Bird?" Rumor asked, and when Matlyn looked back to the group of friends she'd come with, she found three sets of identical smirks. "She's hot. I'd do her."

"Goddamnit, it's my birthday! Mine." Parrish jabbed her manicured finger at her own chest. "That's my sex, you ... I ... No, that's not right." She shook her head, looking a tad confused and drunk-flushed.

Matlyn leaned forward, examining her sister's face. "Yup, face is slurred. You should maybe ease up on those, birthday girl." She nodded toward the Abita Parrish was clutching.

Parrish's brows furrowed and she stuck out her tongue.

"Obviously age an' maturity have no relation," Addy said, stealing the beer from Parrish and patting her on the head when she protested.

A gentle tap on the shoulder turned Matlyn around.

"I'm Kory-Rae, and I think we should fuck," the blonde said, holding out her hand.

* * *

August 15, 2015, 7:13 p.m. ~ Parabola Tattoo & Body Modification

Keys dangling from her hand, Matlyn looked up at the sign that hung above the door— Parabola Tattoos and Body Modification—and sighed. It was all she'd ever wanted, a place that was hers. As she walked toward her car, an ache, an odd kind of loss, bloomed in her chest. It wasn't the kind of grief you'd feel when faced with the death of a family member or even the end of a relationship. It was the loss of a personal space, something she worked hard for and earned.

Slipping behind the wheel, the leather seat squeaked. She pulled her hair into a mass and tucked a clip into it. It still needed a cut. The engine rolled over with a comforting purr, and she pulled away from the store. Nine Inch Nails' "Hurt" blaring and sinking into her bones.

The lime-colored car came to stand still outside of Matlyn's home, and she sat for a moment, her mind reeling back to the first few days at Parabola Tattoo. The chaos of it, the excitement. She offered the memories a weak smile, acknowledging them as she would an old acquaintance, and got out of the car.

As she opened the door, mouthwatering scents swirled around her. It smelled like comfort. She followed her nose to the kitchen. A pot of stew sat simmering on the stovetop. Matlyn inhaled deeply and stirred the pot.

"You make this, Omen?"

Baker wasn't much for cooking, so this was a nice surprise.

"Baker?" she called out. Leaving the kitchen, she headed for the stairs. "If you're doin' naughty things to yourself, have the decency to wait for me."

She got to the top of the stairs and saw through the open doorway: Baker on his hands and knees, fingers like claws, digging into the carpet. As Matlyn approached she heard his shallow, uneven breaths and his teeth grinding. She dropped to the floor in front of him, lifting his head in her hands. "I'm here," she whispered.

Those moments, ones that seemed to suspend time, pause it, stretched out before them both and the room folded in on itself.

Matlyn waited, stroking his head, pushing her fingers through his dark, sweat-damp hair. She watched pain rip across his face again and again. She waited, locked in that forever, for him to come back to her.

* * *

Trapped in agony, Baker felt the words of her story searing, letter by letter, into his skin. He worked to draw air into his lungs and winced with the burn of each exhale.

Suddenly—thankfully—the pain receded, pulling away slowly like the tide back to the ocean. When he opened his eyes, deep blue and gold spots swam before him, temporarily blurring the world around him. He breathed deeply, working hard to settle his body. His eyes focused again and found Matlyn's beautiful, worried face floating only inches from his own.

* * *

Matlyn offered her hands and together they stood. She reached behind him, pulling up his navy shirt. There, below his shoulder blades were the words that she'd been fearing and waiting on: The date she and Kory-Rae broke up. The words of the ultimatum she'd handed Matlyn.

Me and only *me, or nothing at all.*

The thin, reedy letters stretched clear across his back, sitting on the wings of an owl. The steady, but slow movement of the new ink gave the giant bird on Baker's back flight. The wings seemed to beat in time with Matlyn's heart.

Blood in.

Beat.

Blood out.

Beat.

Tears filled her eyes and the owl swam. She pulled the shirt back down, tugging at the hem as if hiding it could make it disappear. No story, no problem. When Baker turned to face her, her lips were pressed in a tight line.

"How long?" she asked, her voice like a breeze being carried out an open window.

Baker's eyes slipped shut. "The stew's my mother's recipe. I haven't made it in years."

"Not an answer."

"I don't know, Einin. Days ... hours. I don't *know*."

"That's it? That's all you've got? A fuckin' handful of '*I don't knows*'!?" Matlyn's face burned red with anger, frustration, and panic. Hands spread wide, she shoved the supernatural scribe. He stumbled back a bit, but managed to stay upright.

"Einin, stop! It's a fucking piss-poor answer, I know. Tell me what you want to hear. Tell me, so I know what you need. Do you want me to tell you to pick out your best dress? Is that what you need to hear?" A sharp edge split Baker's words.

On legs a little less than stable, Matlyn walked to the bed and perched on the edge, looking much like a startled bird ready for flight. "Tell me this isn't happening."

* * *

August 27, 2015, 10:03 a.m. ~ Garden District, New Orleans

"My head hurts," Matlyn whined. The backs of her hands covered her eyes as she lay stretched out on the couch in the living room. Sunlight was desperate to get in, and she was desperate to keep it out. The room was bathed in a strange, muted chartreuse—not quite yellow, not quite green.

Baker snorted without much humor. "Well, let that be a lesson. Twister and peach schnapps don't go."

Matlyn let out a pitiful scoff.

"Wilson's got some bold hands. He touched my naughty parts. Left hand blue, not left hand Baker's balls."

A giggle was followed by a moan. "Stop. No laughing. It hurts."

Baker walked over to the couch, folded himself to the floor at Matlyn's head, and dropped his hands into his lap. "Tylenol? Massage? Cold cloth?" he offered, leaning in and peppering light kisses on her elbow.

"No, thanks. Tylenol ain't doin' squat. Probably coulda done without the schnapps … and the Twister," she conceded. "My ankle's still sore." She lifted said ankle a few inches off the cushion and rolled it in a slow, careful circle.

"How about a hot bath, and I'll make something disgustingly greasy?" he offered with a gentle smile.

He'd told Matlyn that he wasn't keen on the idea of having Parrish and Wilson at the house last night, not when … but he understood the need to make some of the last memories sweet and full of laughter, so he kept his trap shut.

"Bacon?" she asked, a grin picking up the corners of her mouth, despite the pain she was in.

"Bacon, sausage, home fries, and coffee, if I can kick some up."

"Perfect." Making a move to stand, the girl quickly gripped her head. "Son of an ugly whore. Worst hangover ever," she groaned, and Baker helped her to her feet.

"Go relax. I'll bring it up when it's ready."

* * *

The Story made her way upstairs, and the Omen headed to the kitchen and began pulling pans out of cupboards. "There's absolutely no order to it. How the fuck does she function?" he asked the empty kitchen.

Next, he riffled through the freezer, tossing meat down on to countertop. Running the tip of a knife between layers of plastic, he opened the bacon first and set it aside, moving on to the sausages.

"Agh!" Baker suddenly doubled over in a pain so deep his bones vibrated. "Matlyn!" he shouted, looking to the ceiling. His lower back burned and his muscles pulled tight in a feeble attempt to guard his body against the pain rolling through him.

Above he heard the clatter of something hitting the bathroom floor. He sucked in a breath and straightened his body. His legs shook with each step he took. His hands were balled into fists at his sides and his teeth bit down on words that never left his mouth.

By the time the Omen made it to the top of the stairs his heart rate had easily doubled and sweat beaded his forehead. His hands clenched and tightened into thick fists.

"Einin?" he called, walking faster now, the need to be with her driving him forward.

On the bathroom floor, Matlyn was on her knees, a bottle of bubble bath lying next to her, its pale blue contents oozing and spreading across the black tiled floor. Matlyn clutched her head in her hands, rocking and mumbling non-sensical words.

Baker dropped down, pulling her to his chest. "Einin, talk to me." But she was talking, babbling, rambling, tears running down her face. Between words with no connection, save the language they were spoken in, she winced and bellowed in pain.

The air in the room shifted, changed, and Baker went perfectly still. His hands stopped reaching, and his charcoal eyes caught on an airy wave that seemed to gently blow through the room.

A man in a gray suit appeared beside the couple, his features unchanged since Baker had last encountered him nearly one hundred years ago. He calmly clasped his hands together in front of him and looked down on them.

With a tone of indifference, he said. "She's dying."

Twenty-Three

⚜

Baker didn't need to look. He knew what words were branding his skin: the night he'd met a drunken girl on Tchoupitoulas Street, outside Lucy's Retired Surfer Bar.

The thought of the words disappearing the moment she ceased to be brought a sob to his lips. Her words, her story, he wanted to keep. He wanted her history to remain with him, marring his skin. It belonged nowhere else, as far as Baker was concerned.

"She's dying. Cerebral arteriovenous malformation. Commonly known as AVM." The suit squatted next to Baker. This close, Baker could smell the immortal, and he carried a strange odor of plastic sandwich bags and pennies.

"You see," the man said, laying a pale finger on the left side of her head. "The blood vessels that connect all those arteries and veins are a tangled mess. Not good for Ms. Wren, I'm afraid."

Baker pushed forward a little, reaching for the cell in his back pocket. His hands shook and his body pulsed with a pain he'd never felt before.

"Call if you must, but she'll have passed before they reach her. There's nothing to be done, Omen. Her story is over." His face looked almost pitied as his empty eyes glanced at the phone in Baker's hand.

"No, *please*," Baker begged, struggling to support Matlyn through his own pain. "Give me another hundred years. Please. Just let her live."

The suit exhaled in a way that told Baker he'd anticipated this kind of response. "I'm in no position to bargain, Omen. That is not how it works."

Matlyn's back suddenly arched and her body began to stiffen and tremble. Her beautiful seafoam eyes stared off into a space Baker couldn't see, blinking again and again.

The man stood again, hands still at his side. "The AVM has ruptured. Blood is pooling and disrupting the circuits in the brain," he explained in a matter-of-fact tone that made Baker's stomach want to empty. "They'll find, when they complete her autopsy, that her particular condition is rather complicated."

"You're not helping!" Baker shouted.

The man only shrugged.

With disturbing quickness, the tremors stopped and Matlyn's eyes focused. "I love you," she whispered.

It sounded like an ending. Like the last note in a love

song. It was goodbye. She offered Baker a weak, soft smile and her eyes fluttered shut. A thin ribbon of bright red blood trickled slowly from her right nostril and the last traces of air in her lungs escaped on a shallow breath.

Baker closed his eyes, the sight of Matlyn burned behind his lids. His brain erased the crimson thread of blood and the tear streaked cheeks. In his mind, she lay peaceful in a perfect state of rest.

"Stand, Omen." The tone of his voice was somehow compelling.

Gently laying her head down on the tile, Baker stood to face the man in gray.

"You've given ninety-nine years of service. I would—"

"For what!?" Baker roared, his hands flying from his sides. Angry tears burned his eyes.

The man in gray stood quietly, unaffected by Baker's outburst. Understandable, all things considered.

He began again. "I may not have the power to bring her back or much to offer in the way of … comfort," he said, the word sounding alien. "In lieu, I offer a gift." Awkwardly, he held his empty hands out.

"A gift? I … I don't understand."

"For you, I give a choice. A privilege." The suit stepped forward. "For ninety-nine years you Witnessed the lives of all walks come to an end. Each Story different, each epilogue a lesson for you, Samuel."

Baker's eyes dragged up and away at the sound of his born name, pulling his gaze from Matlyn's limp hand. The contrast between her too-pale skin and the midnight tile was unnerving.

"I would have been just like him," he murmured, not at

all shocked by the truth of it. "A chip off the ol' block." His voice came out hard and bitter, and every bit of Irish he'd been born into resurfaced right there with all his rage and fear and sadness.

"No, Omen, not like Finn. So much worse. That bullet should not have taken your life, but The Fates, they saw another path. A chance to be greater than the son of a cruel man. You've learned many lessons through the lives of others—a gift all its own. You've moved so far past Samuel Heeney." There was a strange pride in his voice.

Baker just stared blank-faced, the blurry edges of Matlyn's body in his periphery.

With a slight pull of his lips, something that could pass for a smile, the gray man spoke soft and even. "A choice, Omen. Live out the year you owe as a Light Omen. Walk in the sunlight for once. Enjoy the euphoria and leave behind the pain. Or step forward and see what could have been." He held up two fingers and slowly reached toward Baker, pausing only inches from his sweat covered brow.

A look of confusion passed over Baker's features.

"Had Matlyn lived and your meeting not stitched together by the fate of her death," Mr. Gray said by way of explanation, "I can show you the life you could have had … with her." His gaze caught on the motionless ink-slinger for the briefest moment before returning to Baker's face.

Baker's heart beat began to climb again. "Then what?"

The suit shrugged. "You'll have these moments, this … *illusion* I offer and nothing more. Her story is done. You move on collecting Stories as you have been, as a Dark Omen. And you will pass through the final gates when your time comes due, as The Fates had always planned, one year from today."

Baker considered both. A year free of pain and hurt, the opportunity to experience a truly wonderful side of humanity. It was something he'd always envied about the Light Omens. The choices they had, the ease of their Witnessing. But a future with Matlyn, even if it was only a slideshow, a daydream he would never truly experience, was a hard thing to pass up. Another year's worth of Dark Stories was a reasonable price to pay for the façade.

Baker stepped forward, closing the distance. The gray man's cool fingertips tapped the space between Baker's smoky eyes. Sound and color pushed through his mind's eye, inundating him with visions of what could have been. The bathroom fell away tile by tile. A brilliant white-blue light poured in around them. The man in gray disappeared, swallowed by the light. He squeezed his eyes shut and let the dream take him.

* * *

When his vision cleared and his eyes refocused, Baker found he was standing in a doorway, watching a beautiful red-headed girl.

Matlyn was standing in front of a canvas, slinging paint in bright colors. She wore a red racerback tank that was covered in smears the shape of fingers. Her hips swayed back and forth to a summer song.

"What are you working on?" Baker asked, coming to stand behind her. Pain picked at his heart, knowing full well she was nothing more than a lucid dream. He shoved the sting away and lost himself completely in the illusion.

"For the baby's room." She nodded her head toward the painting. It was a city view of the Crescent City bridge, painted in primary colors. She spun and faced Baker, beaming ear to ear.

In this world, one that only existed because the suit allowed it, Baker had moved into a new stage of his immortal hereafter. One hundred years of service as a Dark Omen had taught him a great many things, and though he witnessed more pain in that life, he was grateful for lessons each offered. When the man in gray had appeared on his one hundredth anniversary, he'd offered Baker a choice to leave this world in peace and walk to the gates with his head held high, or take on the life of a Light Omen and continue his service.

Baker's choice was easy. His life was with this girl. He would live and march beside her to the end of her days.

"Baby's room?" His eyes dropped to the flat belly she was poking with the end of her paint brush.

"Three weeks," she announced with an excitement he'd never heard creeping into her voice as she bounced on her heels.

* * *

"Dad, stop," whined a small dark-haired boy as Baker tucked in his shirt for the third time.

"Listen, little man, that shirt stays tucked until the reception. Got me?" He wagged his finger and winked.

"Go hassle your momma," Pacey said, ruffling the boy's hair. "I think Auntie Adeline's got gummy worms."

The child ran from the room, singing a cat food jingle. He had a thing for jingles, odd but undeniably endearing.

"Nervous?" Pacey asked, fussing with his tie for the millionth time.

"Not even a little." He had everything he ever wanted folding out before him, family and a reason to be.

"So is this, like, against the Omen rules? Are there rules?" Pacey pondered, his lip curled in question.

Baker chuckled, pushing silver cufflinks into place. "Outing myself as a preternatural being, letting her whole family in on the supernatural secret … yeah, crushed a few there. Marrying a mortal chick, nah. Don't know that it's ever been done, but what the hell's so great about convention?" he answered with a wide smile.

"It's time." Parrish poked her head through the door and grinned. Her face had grown round over the last three months, just as it had with her first child four years ago.

Soft, acoustic guitar floated down the hall; Baker's cue to take his position.

* * *

"I'm serious, Baker!" Matlyn whisper-yelled, flinging fluffy bubbles at the man standing next to her. Her words and tone contradicted one another. "He was humping the sofa this morning. He's nine. Is that even normal? Do nine-year-olds get hard-ons?"

Baker laughed a full, deep laugh, taking the dish from her. "And so it begins. Poor bastard."

"Not funny," she chided, the words bouncing on a giggle, and looked over her shoulder to ensure their conversation was not being heard by little ears. "Last night Wilson caught him rubbing his tiny boner on the bookshelf. The fucking *bookshelf*, right next to *The Hungry Caterpillar*! You

need to talk to that boy before you leave, Baker Heeney."
She jabbed at his chest a few times before dipping her hands
back into the soapy water.

The Heeney family had become accustomed to Baker's
comings and goings. Days, weeks, months. Sometimes
they traveled together, particularly in the summer months.
Sometimes Parrish and Wilson would stay at the house to
keep her company. Baker would often email Matlyn and
their son, telling them about the Story he was Witnessing,
filling them in on the wonderful events and people he
encountered.

In the morning he'd be leaving, his body pulling him
to the west. Another Story to unfold.

* * *

A "Sold" sign sat on the lawn of the home on 1st Street. The
home that saw Parrish and Matlyn grow into women, the
home they'd brought their newborn son to. They both knew
this time would come. Baker could only disguise his youth
for so long.

"That's the last of it," Pacey said, clapping Baker's
shoulder. "Off to Savannah with ya."

Addy held Matlyn close, tears running down her
cheeks. "You'll call when you get there." It wasn't a question.
"Stop if you get tired. Oh and don't hang your purse on the
hooks on the back of the bathroom stalls; people take 'em.
Just reach on over and snatch it."

Matlyn rolled her eyes at her friend. "I'm sure we'll be
fine," she assured her, smoothing her platinum blond hair
and cupping her face. Pushing up on her tiptoes, she kissed

the tip of Adeline's nose. "Shop's all yours, beautiful. Do good."

* * *

"Keys, keys, keys! Why can I never find my fucking keys?" Matlyn groaned and headed back to the kitchen.

"Go find the graduate. Dollars to donuts the boychild has them. Thinks he's driving today." Baker stood with the fridge open, a carton of orange juice in his hand.

"Tell me you didn't just drink from that carton, you asshole."

He screwed the yellow cap back on. "I may have." Sliding it back onto the shelf, he turned fully to inspect his wife. "Beautiful. So beautiful." Matlyn had aged with a grace most would envy. Fine silver strands had mixed with her copper waves, creating a look of pure delicacy. Her tattoos were showcased by a simple, close-fitting white dress with a keyhole back. Edge meeting elegance. She wore bright purple heels that made her long legs amazingly longer. Everything about her, Baker thought, was perfection.

"Not so bad yourself, Omen." She swatted at his ass as they made their way to the living room in search of the key thief.

* * *

Baker looked down at the woman he'd loved enough to take on eternity and smiled.

The man in gray appeared between breaths and the pain in Matlyn's head gave way just enough for her to know, to understand that he was there for her.

"You've lead quite the life, Matlyn. An amazing journey,

but it's time to come home." He reached out to the frail woman on the bed. Her son standing to one side, watching a one-sided conversation take place. The lovely wife he chose for himself stood next to him, gripping his hand, sobbing quietly.

"Goodbye, Einin." Baker dipped his head and kissed her lips one last time.

* * *

August 27, 2015, 11:03 a.m.

Baker lived every second of that dream. Every birthday, every goodbye, every cloudy day and every touch as if he were there, feeling, seeing everything firsthand. When the walls around him began to splinter and blinding white light forced its way in, Baker was violently snapped back to the bathroom. Matlyn still on the floor, twenty-eight and lifeless.

Tears ran down his face. He looked down at his arms. The words began to sink deeper into the surface of his skin, like a boat losing its battle to the dark sea. Soon there was nothing. His skin was clean, save the patch on his right arm that simply said:

Matlyn Wren.

Where his own Story truly began.

Epilogue

Baker stared down a long hallway. The over-polished peach floors created the illusion of fiery glass. The occasional nurse skittered by, face buried in a patient chart. He sipped his coffee and waited. The smell of industrial cleaners and illness circled him again and again.

He startled when the normally quiet cell phone in his back pocket rang. Placing the cup on the window ledge he'd been leaning against, he retrieved the phone and smiled at the name appearing on the screen.

"It's a girl!" Addy shouted into the phone, no care at all for Baker's earholes. He brought the phone away and gave it a pipe-down look, but the smile never left his face.

"Bet she's beautiful," Baker said, picking up his cup again, hating the way the warm Styrofoam smelled.

"Perfect," Addy replied with a wistful sigh. "Where are you?"

"Ellisville, Mississippi. 'Bout two hours away. How's the little momma doin'?"

"She's already sworn off sex. Never doin' it again, she claims. Right." Her voice was flat, and he could picture the eye roll that surely accompanied her statement.

Baker chuckled.

There was a beat of silence before Addy asked what she always did when she called. "When are you coming home?" Though Matlyn had gifted the house to Baker in her will, he'd spent no more than three or four days there since her death. Like a hollow shell, it sat empty and waiting to be filled with sound and life once again.

"Soon. Won't be long now." Baker winced, breathing out as his heart kicked up a few paces.

Months ago Baker had wandered into Ellisville, following the beat of a new Story. A Story that he found standing on a park bench, talking very animatedly, gesturing and stretching his limbs in exaggerated movements. Baker stood back, sipping an orange Crush, and watched the teen tell a tale of monsters sailing the seas to two enraptured blond-haired children. The Dark Omen smiled when the small girl, quite obviously the twin of the fidgeting boy to her left, gasped and put her hand to her mouth.

He decided then that he needed to know this boy. And so, three days later, at a not-so-chance run in at a local skate shop, Baker introduced himself to his Story.

Now, down the hall, in room 407, Jonathan Cole was

taking his last breath, fighting a mighty fight. The nine-teen-year-old had lived a life most ninety-year old people would be envious of. Each day he woke with a smile and a plan to make himself and the people around him happy.

Ewing's Sarcoma was not part of that plan. He'd responded well to chemo and the surgery had barely slowed him down. The radiation, however, left Jonathan weak and unable to fight the massive infection ravaging his body from the inside.

Closing his eyes and leaning back into the window ledge, Baker tucked the phone back into his pocket, and let a tear fall for the boy that lost the battle.

Four hours later, dusk had settled on New Orleans, bringing with it the slightest breeze that was just this side of cool. Parking the gunmetal beast in the hospital's parking lot, Baker pulled the keys from the ignition and let them drop to his lap. His gaze shifted to the yellow sunflowers next to him. He took a deep breath, grabbed the flowers, and slid out of the truck.

At the front doors, he paused, seeing a familiar face floating among the visitors and hospital employees. The Light Omen attached to Parrish. The one he and Addy had seen wandering Parabola.

"Omen," he said by way of greeting, nodding at her.

The woman swept her mousy-brown hair over her shoulder and stood from the bench she'd been perched on. "Ingrid," she offered, extending her hand and adjusting a pale pink shawl. With the grace only a woman could execute, she stepped to the right and dropped back down to the bench, crossing her legs in what seemed to be one easy movement.

Baker introduced himself and sat down next to her.

"It's curious," she began. "The baby was born hours ago, yet her story … it hasn't gone." She let the shawl slip off her arm long enough for Baker to see the black script moving in gentle waves on her shoulder. "This Story will be a long one. This child has a tale to tell. Something magnificent. I can feel it in my veins. So much death in this family, and for so long, balance is due. Time for the tides to change."

Ingrid smiled at the Dark Omen, and he was struck by how comforted and at ease he felt sitting next to her this time. No vertigo, no odd skip in his pulse.

He offered up a small smile in return and stood.

"Take care of each word, Ingrid." Turning, he entered a hospital for the second time today. Birth and death in the span of a day; it was both exhausting and humbling.

Tentatively, he knocked on the door, not wanting to interrupt a private moment. A squeak of a voice came through, telling him to come in. He looked down at the pale puce floors—*horrid fucking color*, he thought—once more and pushed the door open wide.

Wilson sat at the foot of the bed, his camera clicking away as Parrish held a naked, pink bundle to her chest. She looked tired, ecstatic, worn and pale, but easily happier than she'd ever been. Overwhelmed, but in the best possible way.

"Baker. Come say hello to Miss Lorelei." Parrish shifted the tiny human in her arms and smiled a brilliant, beautiful smile. In that moment, she looked so much like Matlyn, and no doubt like their mother, Veronica.

"Lorelei," Baker repeated as he closed the distance. He clapped Wilson on the back. "You done good, Major Kenning. She's stunning."

"The *major*, over there, nearly fainted. I *told* ya to stay up here, but *no*…" Her eyes flipped over to Wilson, and she gave a tiny shake of her head before returning her gaze to Baker "…he had to have a peek." She huffed and rolled her eyes, but Baker could see the amusement twinkling there.

"It was a bloody battlefield down there," Wilson said, still looking horrified. "It used to be a magical place … it was all angry and … so angry." Wilson stood and tried to shake the vision from his head. "Sorry, sugar, but that was some scary business."

Baker chuckled and gave his shoulder a good squeeze. "For you, Momma." He presented the flowers to Parrish and sat down in the chair next to the bed. "May I?" he asked, tipping his chin to Lorelei, soundly sleeping.

Wilson moved between them, passing his daughter off to the Omen. "Lorelei Einin, this is Baker. You can call him Baker." His grin was wide as he placed the tiny girl in Baker's waiting arms.

Taken aback by the gesture, Baker just stared at the new parents for a moment before he found his voice. Looking down at the baby, he said softly, "Little Bird…" tears filled his eyes "…I'm sorry I left." Baker's fingertip gently caressed Lorelei's miniature hand.

"It was a shit thing to do, Baker," Parrish said. There was no bite in her voice. It was a simple statement full of truth. "Coulda stayed for the funeral. You should have been there." Again, fact. He should have been there.

"It hurt so much," he admitted, still looking down at the girl in his arms.

"I miss her every day. She left me that fucker of a green bean, you know that?" Parrish admitted, her own eyes welling and spilling over. She swiped at the warm tears falling. "Fuck, I hate crying. I'm not built for all this emotional crap."

Both Baker and Wilson grinned and laughed in a half-assed way. "Well, it was the car or Syndal," Baker said, still smiling, though it had died a little. Talking about Matlyn, holding the niece she'd never know, never love the way she wanted to was ripping him apart.

"Addy told us," Wilson blurted out, earning him a heavy dose of stink eye.

Baker didn't need to ask what he'd meant. He knew. He took a quick breath and told them about the Light Omen, Ingrid, that was sitting outside, soaking up the words of their daughter's story. "This girl, this Little Bird, has something very important to share with the world. Ingrid will see that it's written. Share your life with her, for as long as she's here to Witness."

* * *

August 27, 2016, 12:11 a.m. ~ St. Patrick's Cemetery No.2

Baker stood at the doors of a mausoleum, the name WREN carved into the gray stone above the narrow archway, two birds, wings outstretched, flanked the family name. Flowers sat inside the small building, some withering, petals crumpled on the hard ground, others new and bright.

Baker found Matlyn's name etched below her parents'. His fingers slipped over each letter. The space was small, but there was enough room for Baker to sit on the dusty floor, back to the names of those passed. He let his eyes close for a brief second, his memory catching on his Einin, paint covered, angry, and stunning. An old smile lit his face for a moment.

Breathing in, Baker opened his eyes when he felt the air around him shift, grow thinner, as if making space for something. It seemed to shimmer for a quick second. The smell of pennies and plastic surrounded him. A voice, a drone, familiar yet new sound that was not unlike the man in gray poured in all around him, like music from a loudspeaker.

"Come with me, Omen. Your time has come. Paradise and rest await you now."

Acknowledgements

These pages began some time ago. They were born in the land of fanfiction. Yup, fanfiction. For those of you not in the know, or not incredibly dorky (read awesome), fanfiction is a community, or fandom, of writers and readers. They are some of the most kick-ass people I've ever met. They are my clan, my tribe. And they are the reason I decided to take this leap. Thank you for letting me play in your sandbox. You're all amazing and lovely!

People don't wander into our lives by chance; each is a blessing or a much needed lesson. Lynsey and Max, in your own ways, you taught me to trust myself with my words and helped me grow. Each time you talked me around a block I thought was too big to move, or offered up your time and talent, I counted myself lucky. Blessings. Without a doubt.

Special thanks to Andrea Michel. The cover is perfect

and wonderful and I'm so glad I sucked you into my dorky little world.

Jill, the formatting queen that cleaned it all up and made my pages look pretty, it's truly been a pleasure working with you. Here's to keeping it in the fandom!

Christina, woman! Good pizza, questionable booze, and maybe a flock of seagulls is all we've ever needed. Your support … No words. I love you.

Kate, I can't believe how lucky I got. Friends that are truly happy for you and see you up every hill, no matter the size, amazing. I'm so proud to call you a friend. Thank you for everything.

And finally … To my family, my friends: The "easy way" has always been something of a mythical creature to me. A unicorn; the thing others talked about and maybe even glimpsed. And as many times as I tried to ride that damned unicorn, it never quite worked out that way. But you, my family, my beautiful friends, never doubted that I'd get where I was going, whatever it was I was doing. Thanks for dusting me off each time I fell on my ass. I love you all in ways I can't even give words to.

[1] The events described in chapter three are based on actual events that took place in Baker County, 1907 and can be found in any online search.

[2] Jeremiah Burke was a passenger on the Titanic as mentioned in chapter ten.